DEATH
OF A
JESTER

A BRANIGAN POWERS MYSTERY

DEB RICHARDSON-MOORE

LION FICTION

Published by Lion Fiction
an imprint of
Lion Hudson Limited
Wilkinson House, Jordan Hill Business Park
Banbury Road, Oxford OX2 8DR, England
www.lionhudson.com/fiction

ISBN 978 1 78264 264 0
e-ISBN 978 1 78264 265 7

First edition 2018

A catalogue record for this book is available from the British Library

Printed and bound in the UK, April 2018, LH26

"Deb Richardson-Moore *knows well the worlds she writes about: Upstate South Carolina, the newsroom, and the world inhabited by our homeless population. In this third novel in her series she once again weaves a suspenseful tale where these worlds intersect.*

As we get to know the main characters in greater depth, our understanding of the human condition also deepens. Death of a Jester *is not just a good mystery; it's a wonderful story that leaves you sad to say goodbye to these 'flesh and blood' characters, but hopeful that book four in the series is just around the corner."*

Sally Handley, president of the Upstate SC Chapter of Sisters in Crime and author of the *Holly and Ivy Mystery* series.

"Deb Richardson-Moore *pulls off what the best mystery novelists do, and manages way more than most ever could. Her seamless, energetic writing rings with verisimilitude and sings with compassion.*

From the first page she pulls you into her story, introduces you to a raft of characters you absolutely have to know more about, makes you care about crucial issues like homelessness and the state of journalism, and propels *you into a mystery you want to solve alongside her lovable people. This is Southern storytelling at its best, without the shopworn goofiness of Southern caricature. Those feats alone are the stuff of a bestselling mystery-writer rock star.*

Beyond all that, Deb serves as pastor of a ministry that would sap even the most superhuman of writers. Together, these are the rare ingredients Richardson-Moore magically blends into her hearty Branigan Powers stews of delightful, delicious, and, yes, nutritious entertainment."

John Jeter, author of *Rockin' A Hard Place* and *The Plunder Room*

"Deb Richardson-Moore *has done it again — given us a thrilling page-turner that will pull at your heartstrings. Not only did* Death of a Jester *make me bite off all my fingernails and feed my family cereal for dinner just so I could finish a couple more chapters, it also made me think about the homeless folks I sometimes encounter and consider the stories behind their stories. Thank you, Deb, for another mystery that lifts our hearts!"*

Rebecca S. Ramsey, author of *The Holy Éclair: Signs and Wonders from an Accidental Pilgrimage*

Deb Richardson-Moore is a former journalist and the current pastor of the Triune Mercy Center in Greenville, South Carolina. Her first book, *The Weight of Mercy*, is a memoir about her work as a minister among homeless people.

She and her husband Vince are the parents of three grown children. To find out more about Deb, go to her website: www.debrichardsonmoore.com.

Online reviews are always appreciated.

Also by Deb Richardson-Moore

The Weight of Mercy: A Novice Pastor on the City Streets

Branigan Powers Mysteries:
The Cantaloupe Thief
The Cover Story

To Sippio,
who showed me what kindness looks like on the street

Acknowledgments

There comes a point when you are reluctant to ask your friends to read another draft. Thanks to the following for jumping in and offering before I had to ask: Elaine Nocks, Madison Moore, Lynne Lucas, Lynn Cusick, Mary Jane Gorman, Michelle McClendon and Debbie Dawes.

Thanks to my writers' group: Susan Clary Simmons, Wanda Owings, Allison Greene and Jeanne Brooks. I boast about their brutality, but could just as easily praise their thoughtfulness.

A special thank you to Lynne Lucas, Lynn Cusick, Wanda Meade and Carol Mueller for an unexpectedly generous launch party. And to Lori and Robert Bradley, Dustin Moore, Mary Beth McFadden, and Doris, Rick, Candace and Maggie Richardson for braving the heat to serve at another launch party.

I appreciate the people at Fiction Addiction, Mr. K's, The Café at Williams Hardware and Joe's Place, who've gone above and beyond to promote my books.

A big thank you to all the book clubs in Upstate South Carolina who have included my books on their reading lists. Who knew there were so many of you? It's always a pleasure to visit your meetings.

I am humbled that the worldwide United Methodist Women rekindled interest in *The Weight of Mercy* by placing it on their list of recommended reading. Thank you for that.

Thanks to the board and staff of Triune Mercy Center for a sabbatical to finish this book. I wouldn't be writing today without your gifts of time.

Thanks to my editor, Jessica Tinker, at Lion Hudson.

Thanks to my mom, Doris Richardson, for her unfailing support.

And as always, thanks to Vince, Dustin, Taylor and Madison. Let's try to keep the ending a secret this time.

CHAPTER ONE

Malachi Ezekiel Martin didn't know where he was. The dream placed him in the desert in Kuwait or Iraq – he had never known where he was over there either.

He tasted grit in his mouth and saw the canvas roof of a tent overhead. Yeah, that would be the desert.

The boy, he thought, looking around wildly. *Where is the boy?*

He groped for the tent flap, fully expecting to look onto a barren, forsaken landscape, where everything, everything, was the color of sand – the tents, the uniforms, the rations always liberally sanded, impossible to keep out of your teeth. His head pounded, whether from the dream or from the crumpled empties of King Cobra, it was hard to say. He counted five of the forty-ounce malt liquor cans beside his sleeping bag.

He peered outside now, squinting, anticipating rows of tents and buzz-cut men headed for chow; he braced for the impaling of the desert sun. Instead, he saw cool shadow and a single man, gray hair pulled into a ponytail, hunched over a fire pit with a teetering grill rack on top, coaxing a battered coffeepot to boil. Malachi shook his head, clearing the cobwebs, involuntarily looking around the campsite for the boy, though his brain was catching up, telling him there was no boy.

Slick turned. "Coffee?" he offered.

"Soon's I pee." Malachi stumbled from his tent, past the picnic table that held two-liter Cokes and cereal bars, cans of ravioli and chicken noodle soup, all the sugars and starches those church do-gooders thought homeless people wanted to eat. He shuffled past the river birch, its lime-green leaves newly sprouted to provide lacy shade over the entrance to Tent City. It reminded him of his granny's doilies.

By the time he rezipped his camo pants – dark green and darker green, not the sand and khaki of his Desert Storm uniform – he was back to himself, back home in northeast Georgia where the red clay beneath his feet was as familiar as the honeysuckled air. He shook a clean Styrofoam cup from a package on the picnic table, and let Slick fill it with his thick bitter brew. He dragged a rusting lawn chair to sit across the fire pit from his neighbor.

"Where Elise?"

"Aw, she in jail again."

Malachi knew better than to ask why. It could be drunk and disorderly or possession of crack or even assault, but most likely a prostitution charge was in there somewhere. He didn't want to rub Slick's nose in it.

"Sixty days?"

Slick shrugged. "Dunno. Guess we see her when we see her."

Malachi changed the subject. "Today Friday, right?" He didn't wait for an answer. "Farmers' Market should be open soon. I'm ready for me some 'maters and cantaloupes."

Slick grunted. "Nah, too early. But Jericho Road be giving out that stuff, too. Pastor Liam said last Sunday."

Malachi thought of his grandparents' farm, of the okra and beans and squash and tomatoes and corn and cantaloupes and watermelons and pecans and peaches it had produced so plentifully they'd sold the bulk of it at a vegetable stand. That was his job, sitting on a stool at the end of the driveway, welcoming visitors, talking up the produce, collecting money, counting change. Between customers, he got to read, which was fine with his granny. She was quite a reader herself and they'd swapped library books back and forth.

That's a job he'd like, sitting on a stool at the Grambling Farmers' Market, ringing up produce. But he guessed those folks were all family members of the farms they sold from. They looked it, anyway, those farm-fed ladies with their tight perms and sleeveless flowered-y blouses from the Walmart. Not much call for outside help.

He took a swallow of coffee and felt a grain of something on his tongue. He spit it out. "Slick, you got grounds in there. Or dirt." He spit again. The dream of the desert resurfaced. There was always sand in his mouth in those days. That was probably why his mind had gone there.

He looked around, wondering what he wanted to do today. It was chilly here under the bridge but it was warming up out in the sun. He heard a rustle in the tangle of brush at the edge of camp and watched as a bird shot up.

Slick spoke again but his voice was lower, and Malachi had to lean into the fire to hear him.

"Family moved in last night." He nodded at the railroad tracks atop the hill that divided their section of Tent City from the unimaginatively named Tent City 2. A towering bridge spanned acres of these woods, and small encampments could be found wherever it crossed flat ground. It wasn't much, but the bridge did provide shelter from spring rains and summer's brutal sun.

"A family?" echoed Malachi. "You mean, with kids?" He hadn't ever seen kids living out here. These inner-city woods hid tents for the lucky ones, cardboard and blankets for the not-so-lucky. But they didn't hide kids.

Slick nodded. "Look like a mom and dad and teenage boy and a passel of littl'uns. I think they been staying in a old VW bus and it broke down. Somebody give 'em a big tent."

"How you know they had a bus?"

"Just what I heard."

"Aw, man."

Slick shook his head. "I know."

Malachi settled back in his rickety chair, taking another sip of coffee and getting another piece of grit. He put a finger in his mouth to snare it. It'd be worth a walk to Jericho Road to get a decent cup of coffee.

As he rose, his eye fell on the bursting undergrowth crowding the far side of the camp, where the shade from the bridge gave way to the morning sun. Deeper in the woods, he saw a flash of white, billowing white. It looked for all the world like a flowing Kuwaiti robe, but surely that was one more remnant of his dream.

CHAPTER TWO

Harley Barnett took the first call, and in the days to come, when everything had gone so wrong, he would remember how it'd been on this day in late April. How warm and sunny the day had looked outside the newsroom windows, how filled with promise. How nothing more pressing than a softball game had loomed for his weekend.

He'd come in before lunchtime to write a story on a local rock band that was opening the Main Street Sundown Series. Harley was a drummer himself and writing a music story didn't feel a bit like work.

He was reading over his copy one last time, his lips moving, testing for cadence as Marjorie had taught him. Marjorie was old enough to be his grandmother and more crotchety than anyone in the newsroom, including publisher Tanenbaum Grambling IV. But the woman could write.

Harley reached for his telephone, answering it with his mind still on a quote from the lead singer.

"Can I speak to a reporter?"

"You got one," Harley answered.

It was a woman's voice, young from the sound of it. "We already called the police, but I thought you ought to know, too."

"Okay." Harley grabbed a pen and notebook.

The voice on the other end hesitated. "You know the woods behind Oliver Creek Apartments?"

Harley did. The apartments were older two-story brick units, low-income since snazzier complexes with pools had sprung up on the Eastside. "Yes."

"Well…" The voice hesitated again. "This is going to sound crazy. But there was a clown back there trying to lure a kid into the woods."

"A clown? Like Bozo? Like Ronald McDonald? Like, um, what's his name? Pennywise?" Harley's knowledge of clown personalities was now exhausted.

"Exactly."

"Did the kid go with him?"

"No. He was scared."

Harley laughed. He could identify. He'd found the Ringling Bros and Barnum & Bailey clowns terrifying when his parents took him to the circus as a pre-schooler. And that was before he was old enough for Stephen King's take on the subject.

"It's not funny," the caller snapped. "Can you imagine what coulda happened? I want to make sure all the moms know to look out."

Harley was chastised. "But you've called the police, right?"

"Yeah. They're here but the clown's gone."

Harley took the woman's name and address. "Okay, we'll be right out," he told her. "Thank you for calling, ma'am."

Harley spun around in his chair to face city editor Bert Feldspar and signaled for cops reporter Jody Manson to join them. "You're not going to believe this," he said, grinning. "Caller says a clown behind Oliver Creek Apartments tried to lure a kid into the woods. A real clown. Police are already there."

Bert snorted. "Well then, we'll send in our clowns."

Branigan Powers heard the exchange and smiled to herself. *Bring on the clown jokes*, she thought.

She wondered if Chester Scovoy had been called to the scene. Probably not. He was a detective and would be called in only if a child had been snatched. This half-baked attempt sounded like a job for uniformed officers. The jokes would be as bad down at the Law Enforcement Center as in the newsroom.

She sighed and returned to her story on community gardens. She had it and a home story for the *Living!* section due before she could leave.

But *Style* editor Julie Ames was headed her way. That was never good.

Jody was back in the newsroom within the hour, unsure if he had a story or not. The three-year-old boy was too shy to speak, he told Bert, and his teenage sister was the only one who claimed to have seen the clown, holding out candy to her little brother. She got off her cell phone – fast, she reiterated in front of her mother – and yelled for the boy to come back. The clown spun around and disappeared into the woods. Police searched and came up with nothing.

They wondered if the teen was merely seeking attention, but she hadn't backed off her story or her description – orange wig, red nose, floppy red shoes, and huge white pants with red stripes.

"Write it for online," Bert directed. "We'll play it short and inside for tomorrow. No sense creating hysteria if it's a hoax."

Jody nodded and sat down at his desk. Within twenty minutes the first clown sighting story was posted online. It was April 28.

Darkness had fallen by the time Branigan pulled into her driveway, a deep, velvety dark, the kind that could be found only far from city lights. She wished she'd left her stoop light on, which at least would have provided a circle of orange-yellow against the inky sky. She hadn't realized she'd be so late. At the last minute, Julie had switched her story on community gardens to the Sunday *Style* front, so she'd had to stay until the editing was finished.

Now she was tired and hungry and cranky. It was just as well Chester was working late and wouldn't be coming out to the farm.

She opened the door of her Honda Civic, expecting her German shepherd Cleo to bound out of the cotton patch. But all was quiet – well, as quiet as the Georgia countryside got when its crickets, cicadas and tree frogs were warming up. The lofty pecan trees beside the driveway were quivering with sound; their chirping, whirring, croaking symphony provided the backdrop for every warm-weather memory Branigan held.

She stepped into an evening still balmy. "Cleo!" she called. "Where are you, girl?"

When she saw and heard no sign of the dog, she became more aware of the darkness that enfolded her. She remembered seeing bad homemade videos of "creepy clown" sightings in other areas of the country a few years back. Clowns on rural bridges, lonely highways, empty parks. She'd assumed they were staged as the videographer breathed heavily and yelled at the figure in the distance. But what if they weren't?

She looked around uneasily, but the crescent moon provided next to no light, and her Honda's headlights clicked off. *Oh, for goodness' sakes,* she told herself. *Get a grip.* She raised her voice and made a megaphone of her hands to project past the barn and chicken houses, down to the pasture and lake. "CLEO! WHERE ARE YOU?"

She thought she heard a bark, way off in the pasture. She couldn't be sure. She waited a moment longer, listening hard and hearing nothing beyond the cacophony of tree critters. But there, finally, came the tell-tale rustle of cotton husks. And then the big dog sprang from the gloom, tail wagging, whining happily.

"Where were you, goofball?" Branigan hugged the shepherd but hurriedly drew back; the dog's coat was wet and muddy. "You went in the lake?"

Cleo licked Branigan's hands excitedly and tried to leap on her.

"No, no, you'll ruin my slacks," she said. She pulled her briefcase and purse from the car and started up the brick steps, closing the screen door to keep Cleo out. "Let me get a towel first."

She flicked the porch light on, disarmed the alarm, then pulled her rattiest towel from the linen closet in the hallway. She returned to the side porch and in its circle of light worked to dry the dog's feet and fur. "That's about as good as we're going to do," she said, opening the door for Cleo to enter. The dog rushed to her water bowl and slurped noisily. Branigan watched her. "I swear I don't know what you've been up to, but I hope you don't make it a habit."

Branigan walked to her bedroom at the far end of the ranch-style house, wearily wrenching off her watch and rings and earrings. She peeled off her clothes and pulled on soft pajama pants and an oversized, long-sleeved T-shirt from the Grambling Police Department's softball team, tugging her sleek blonde hair from where it caught. It wouldn't do for her publisher Tan-4 to see it. He'd yanked her off Grambling PD stories once she'd started dating Detective Chester Scovoy. She'd never wear the shirt in public, but here in the privacy of her farmhouse, it was a comfortable and welcome reminder of the man she was growing increasingly fond of.

She whipped up a late supper of a ham and cheese omelet, and popped two slices of wheat bread in the toaster. She found a jar of her Aunt Jeanie's fig preserves in the refrigerator and perched on a stool at the kitchen island, reading parts of the day's newspaper she hadn't gotten to earlier. She felt herself relax from the long week. She'd worked on stories for the front page, the *Style* section and the *Living!* section, grumbling with her colleagues that they'd be writing sports before long. Downsizing was a fact of life for newspapers, but knowing it was a worldwide phenomenon didn't make it easier for those left to fill the news hole.

After she'd fed Cleo and washed the dishes, she settled on the couch in the den, which looked more like a sunroom with its tile floor, painted armoire and vivid canvases purchased from local artists. Branigan sipped from a cup of hot chocolate and felt her neck and shoulder muscles release some of their pent-up tension.

She was halfway through a digitally saved *Father Brown* on PBS when she realized she'd been nodding off and transposing the cleric into the *Grambling Rambler* newsroom, the suspect into one of Pa's empty chicken houses. Definitely time to give up. She hit the remote and clicked off the lamp next to the sofa, stretching out to rest her eyes for a moment before going to bed.

She couldn't tell whether it was a click or a scratch, but a small noise broke through her sleep. She sat up to listen, neck tensing, eyes straining in the pitch black. The TV clock told her it was 3:11 a.m. At her feet, Cleo raised her head, listening.

The sound had come from the opposite end of the house. "Did you hear something?" Branigan wanted to hear a human voice, even if it was her own. Suddenly Cleo took off, racing through the dark kitchen and Branigan's office, howling with a high-pitched fervor that sent Branigan's heart racing. Then there was a loud thump and Cleo's barking stopped abruptly.

Branigan froze. Was Cleo hurt? Why wasn't the alarm going off? She glanced at the console, realizing almost instantly that she'd fallen asleep without resetting it.

Now she heard Cleo whimpering. She slipped into the living room to grab a poker from the fireplace, then as quietly as possible tiptoed through the unused room. Groping the walls until she located a light switch, she hesitated before turning it on: she had the advantage in the dark house she knew so well.

She crossed the hallway and reached the doorjamb of the guest bedroom, running her hands over the wood frame and open door; she could hear Cleo whining inside. She raised the poker and reached in to flip the light switch. Blinded by the sudden brightness, she and the person on the floor screamed simultaneously.

"Brani G! Stop!"

Before she could even register the voice, Branigan noticed Cleo's tail thumping the floor as she gently nosed the woman at her feet.

"Jimmie Jean Rickman! You scared me to death!"

"You scared *me* to death! Why are you threatening me with a poker?"

"Because you broke into my house at three in the morning!"

"Actually, Gran and Pa's house. And as you well know, this was my favorite way in."

Branigan glanced at the open window. The screen, she knew, would be on the ground underneath, flipped open by a trick Jimmie Jean had perfected in her teenage years when she lived a quarter mile down the road.

Branigan put down the poker and hauled her cousin to her feet. "What are you doing here?" She pulled her into a bear hug. "Good to see you, by the way."

She held Jimmie Jean at arm's length, noted the auburn hair pulled into a messy bun, the brown eyes tired and bloodshot, the crow's feet accentuated by weariness.

Jimmie Jean grinned at her, and some of the old sparkle returned. "I haven't seen you in forever, Cuz."

"I know. I saw Izzy B, Summer and Robert Jr at Christmas. We missed you and Beau."

"Well, I'm home now."

"Well, no, you're not. You missed it by a quarter mile."

"Close enough. I didn't want to crash in on Mom and Dad in the middle of the night."

"So you thought you'd crash in on me instead."

"That's exactly what I thought. The one thing I didn't count on was how twenty extra years impacted my landing. I think I bruised my hip."

"Serves you right. Can I get you pajamas or hot cocoa or decaf or anything? Have you eaten? Have you been driving all night?"

"I've been driving since early afternoon. I've got lots to tell you. But then maybe you've heard?"

"Heard what?"

"About Mom."

Branigan looked at her cousin with a sinking heart. "No. What?"

"Mom's got breast cancer."

"Oh, Jimmie Jean, no." Branigan sank onto the bed, and Cleo came over and put her head on her lap. She adored her Aunt Jeanie, the funny, sassy wife of her Uncle Bobby. She absently petted the dog. "How bad?"

"Bad enough that she's going through radiation *and* chemo. That's why I'm home. We ended our run of *Little Shop of Horrors* last weekend."

Branigan scarcely heard her. "Do my mom and dad know? I can't believe no one told me."

"I imagine it took everything Dad had to tell us. I'm sure he'll be calling your folks this weekend."

"Jimmie Jean, I am so sorry. You know I love your mama."

"I know."

"Are you the only one coming home?"

"No, Isabella's coming, too. The other three are waiting to see if Mom and Dad will need more help later on. Plus they've all got kids in school for a few more weeks."

Branigan hesitated, then plunged ahead. "And Jackson?" Even now, even after all these years, she felt a twinge at saying the name.

Jimmie Jean paused at the mention of her husband, lowered her eyes from Branigan's gaze. "The official story is he can't take time off work. Which is true, I suppose. Construction is booming in West Palm Beach. The unofficial story..." She stopped. Branigan remained silent. "The unofficial story will require a bottle of wine. Let's just say the chance to be apart came at an opportune time."

Branigan didn't know what to say. The history of the three of them ran long and deep. But blood was blood. "Come on," she said. "Let's find you something to sleep in."

Jimmie Jean accepted a worn camisole and flannel pajama pants, but the women didn't go to bed. Instead, they sat on opposite sides of the den sofa, drinking hot chocolate, Cleo asleep at their feet. They spoke quietly out of habit, as if Gran and Pa were sleeping in the back bedroom.

Jimmie Jean was the second child of Branigan's Uncle Bobby and Aunt Jeanie, and had grown up with her four brothers and sisters in the antebellum house "next door". Their two-story, white-columned house would've looked more at home on the Georgia coast, down near Savannah, where Aunt Jeanie was raised. But Jeanie saw nothing wrong with transplanting that coastal grandeur to the pastures and farmland of the state's upcountry. And Uncle Bobby saw nothing wrong with giving his beauty queen bride whatever it took to make her happy as a farm wife.

Branigan had spent many nights with Jimmie Jean and her younger sister Isabella, both here at Gran's and in the girls' home. Sometimes their little sister Summer had insisted on coming, but she was five years behind them, and Aunt Jeanie could usually convince her and little brother Beau they'd have a special night with all the big kids out of the way.

Branigan and Isabella were born within three months of each other, a year behind Jimmie Jean. Branigan could still hear her Uncle Bobby, spying them in the branches of an oak in the Rickman back yard.

> Who's that sitting in my tree?
> Izzy B and Brani G!

"What about me, Daddy?" Jimmie Jean called from her higher branch. "Say me, Daddy!"

> Someone else in my tree today?
> Must be a girl named Jimmie J.

The three of them had squealed with delight.

Jimmie Jean broke through Branigan's reverie. "I tried to write you about Davison. Several times. But I never got it how I wanted it."

"That's all right." It'd been nearly a year since Branigan's twin brother Davison showed up in Grambling. It had been a devastating time for Branigan and her parents, and she wouldn't pretend they'd recovered yet. Jimmie Jean's eyes actually looked sympathetic. "You look like your mama right now," Branigan told her.

"I take that as a compliment."

"As you should."

"I gotta say, Brani G, you look fantastic," said her cousin, tilting her head to one side and appraising Branigan's tousled blonde hair, emerald eyes and lean frame. "Even in PJs in the middle of the night. You must still run to be as skinny as you are."

"Yeah, some. I have to keep Cleo in shape." She was uncomfortable under Jimmie Jean's scrutiny and changed the subject. "You say Izzy B is on her way?"

"Yep. Have you talked to Liam Delaney lately?"

"Not really."

"She's going to be working for him at Jericho Road."

"What?"

"Yeah, apparently his social worker is going on maternity leave. Izzy B offered to step in for six or eight or ten weeks, whatever he needs, and he jumped on it. He told her they were planning to limp along without a social worker, but summer is a busy time and he was dreading it. So *voila!*"

"Wow. And that's pretty much what she does at her school, right?" Isabella was a counselor in a Title I school in Atlanta, which meant dealing with children and families in poverty.

"Yeah. She has three more weeks but is going to be coming up on weekends until then."

"Like today?" Branigan looked at her watch.

Jimmie Jean yawned and nodded. "We're supposed to meet at noon."

"Don't you want to take a nap before then?"

"Yes, I do, but I want to catch up with you first. Oh, and to tell you what I heard on the radio coming in."

"Do tell."

"There was a story on a station around Daytona about a clown trying to snatch a little kid in Grambling."

Daytona, Florida, had that story? "Boy, that was fast."

"You mean it's true?"

"Yes. Or maybe no. We don't know yet. There was a report at an apartment complex this afternoon, or rather yesterday afternoon. But our reporter thought it might be a hoax."

"How creepy."

"Yeah," Branigan allowed. "If it's true."

"Pretty creepy if someone made it up, too." Jimmie Jean yawned again. "I guess I am ready to crash. You want me in the guest room?"

"Have at it. And you can use the big bathroom in the hall."

"Still got Gran's pink and turquoise color scheme? I love what you've done with the kitchen, by the way."

"Thanks. And yes, I haven't gotten to the bathroom yet so it's still got the Pepto-Bismol thing going on. Mom and I may attack that some day."

The women walked through the familiar house, flipping off lights. They had an hour and a half before daylight.

CHAPTER THREE

B ranigan and Chester were supposed to meet at Bea's Bakery downtown at noon. He called at 11:30. "I wanted to catch you before you left," he said. "I'm running an hour late."

"What's up?"

"We got a report of a clown behind J.T. Rogers Elementary this morning."

Branigan glanced out of the window over her kitchen sink. In the light of the sunny day, the cotton patch and pastures and lake were familiar, comforting, and she wondered at her unease of the night before.

"On a Saturday?"

"Yeah, kids use its ball field on weekends, and anyone can use the track. A teen from the high school track team reported it. Same as yesterday, a clown trying to lure a girl playing outfield to come to a gate that opens into the woods. I'm at the school now."

"I'm surprised they have you on it."

"My choice. I'll fill you in when I see you."

"Okay. Bea's at one o'clock then."

"Right."

Branigan could hear him talking to a colleague before his phone clicked off.

She was already dressed, so she poured herself another cup of coffee. Jimmie Jean padded into the kitchen in her borrowed PJs, her hair a mass of brown tangles. "Coffee," she croaked. "My fortune for coffee."

Branigan laughed and poured her a cup. "I know you're supposed to be at your mom's at noon, but I thought you needed to sleep."

"You were right," said Jimmie Jean, helping herself to milk from Branigan's refrigerator. "They'll understand. Whew, I'm still whipped."

"That was a monster drive all at once."

"You're telling me."

"So you starred in *Little Shop of Horrors* this spring? I love that show."

"In a blonde wig as the squeaky Audrey. Surprised I have a voice left."

"Your mama and I saw that at Theater on the Square. It saved Uncle Bobby from going, and they always do a good job."

"I hope so. The director of the West Palm Players emailed them that I'll be in town this summer, so I may do a show if they have a part for me."

"Really? That is so cool. Aunt Jeanie and Mom and Izzy B and I will cheer you on. Oh, and I almost forgot. I got a call about a second clown sighting today. At an elementary school."

Jimmie Jean plopped onto an island stool. "Why'd he be at a school on a weekend?"

"I wondered that too. Apparently, kids use it for ball games. A teenager running the track reported it."

"But he didn't grab anyone?"

"No. He's rather inept, it would seem."

"Well, he *is* a clown. Whaddaya expect?"

Branigan passed her cousin the morning *Rambler.* "The first story is on page 6A," she said. "Not much to it. It'll get bigger now."

Jimmie Jean got up and rummaged through Branigan's cupboard until she found a blueberry Pop-Tart. Then she looked around blankly. "You have hidden the toaster so cleverly I can't find it," she said.

Branigan opened a cabinet that sported a waist-high shelf that held toaster, electric can opener and blender. Below were pull-out drawers for coffee and cereal. "Ah, you and Aunt Eileen went all fancy, I see," Jimmie Jean said. "In south Florida, we're still using the lowly appliance garage."

25

"Fortunately, Mom had renovated the kitchen in their beach house, so she was still in full kitchen efficiency mode. She picked out most of this and I followed behind, nodding."

"Very nice. If I get divorced, I'll move in with you."

Branigan looked up in alarm.

Jimmie Jean laughed. "Just kidding, Brani G. Calm down."

Jimmie Jean rifled through the paper while munching her Pop-Tart, then took her coffee with her to get showered.

Branigan let Cleo outside and spent several minutes throwing a tennis ball for her to fetch. She wondered if Jimmie Jean was serious about a divorce. Jackson Solesbee single again: out of all the thoughts she'd had of him over the years, that one had never crossed her mind.

She hugged Cleo's neck. "Stay out of the lake," she warned as she hopped into her Civic, carefully pulling past Jimmie Jean's bulky white Range Rover.

Branigan didn't have any trouble finding a parking place on Main Street on a Saturday. She pulled in front of a vintage dress shop three doors down from Bea's, and walked in the mid-day sunshine to her favorite lunch spot. Chester Scovoy was already seated in a booth with a wall that sported black and white photos of Grambling from the 1930s and 40s. The courthouse lawn dedication of the Confederate statue fondly known as Johnny Reb. The old Randall Mill in its prime. The first version of the stately Nicholas Inn before its decline and comeback.

Chester wore khaki pants and a white golf shirt, his arm muscles bulging beneath the short sleeves. His hazel eyes took her in, and he stood and hugged her, brushing his lips across her forehead.

Her stomach fluttering, she slid onto the red vinyl bench across from him.

"So why did you go on a call today?" she asked. "I thought you wanted to look at houses."

"I did. I do," he said, spreading his hands out on the table. "But

I started worrying about this clown business. Most of the guys think it's a hoax and are trotting out the clown jokes. But I'd be the one called in if anything bad happened. So I started thinking, 'Do I want to wait for that?' Didn't seem smart."

"I see what you mean."

"Not that it did any good. But I did talk to the teenager who says he saw a clown in the woods."

"And?"

Chester wagged his head sideways to indicate indecision. "Seemed credible. But why did no one else see anything?"

"What about the girl?"

"A six-year-old picking daisies in the outfield. The coach's attention was on the infield. The little girl *said* she saw a clown. too, but by the time we got there, the teenager had repeated it so many times she could've been parroting him." Chester shrugged. "So there you have it."

"My cousin drove up from south Florida last night and said it was on a radio station in Daytona."

"Yeah, I heard from the dispatcher as I was driving over. We've had phone calls from New York, Philly, and New Orleans."

"At least they're not sending news crews."

"Yup, wouldn't want to deal with *those* clowns."

Branigan kicked him lightly under the table.

Bea Boswell, her silver hair escaping its bun, hurried over to take their order. "What can I get for Grambling's finest?"

"Getting waited on by the owner is pretty good for starters," Chester said. "What's got you working the front?"

"I let Tommy *and* Virgil go fishing. Need to have my head examined."

"Well, we are honored," Branigan said. She ordered a turkey sandwich on Bea's freshly made pumpernickel bagel, and Chester asked for a Black Forest ham on plain.

Bea lingered after writing it down. "Detective, what do you know about this clown at the school yard?"

"How in the world did you hear that? I only left thirty minutes ago."

"The boy who reported it is Virgil's nephew, and Virgil's sister called here looking for him. When she couldn't get him, she told Allison." Bea nodded toward the young woman behind the counter.

Chester shook his head. "I forget what a small town Grambling can be."

Bea stood waiting for an answer.

"Yes, we did get another report," he said.

"Was it the same description as the one behind the apartments? Dressed the same?"

Chester sighed. He was uncomfortable talking to the public about cases, but there had been a *Rambler* reporter and a TV crew at the elementary school. It wasn't as if any of this was going to remain quiet.

"Pretty much," he said. "This kid talked more about the white face and big red lips. But yeah, sounded like the same description basically."

"Hmm."

"Miz Boswell, do you know something?"

"No," she said, tucking a piece of errant hair into her bun while trying to hold onto her pad and pencil. "It's just that Theater on the Square held that clowning workshop last year – you all wrote about it, Branigan. Let's see, it was before their Christmas show, I believe. I imagine they had all kinds of costumes and make-up on hand."

Branigan nodded. "I *do* remember that story."

Chester pulled a notebook from his hip pocket and jotted something down. "Thank you, Miz Boswell. That may be helpful."

When she left, he turned to Branigan. "If something over there is missing, it'd be a place to start." He put the notebook away. "So how does it feel being sidelined if this turns into a story?"

"Honestly? Kind of good. I like being able to hear and read about a story like a normal person rather than worrying what I'm missing and what TV's got."

"Good." He grinned. "I can't help but worry how I'll stack up if a really good story comes along."

"Well, all I'm shut out of is the Grambling PD. If it became a big story, I'd still be free to talk to victims, witnesses and everybody else."

"Good deal."

"So tell me what kind of places you're looking at today."

They spent the rest of their lunch talking real estate and kitchen arrangements and square footage. It was April 29.

On Sunday morning, Branigan met her parents outside the First Baptist church of Grambling. "Have you talked to Uncle Bobby?" she asked immediately.

Her dad hugged her, then moved aside to let her mother in.

"Yes," her mom whispered in her ear. "Poor Jeanie. I'm so glad the girls are home."

Branigan's father was greeted by another couple and he turned to speak to them.

Eileen Powers raised an eyebrow at her daughter. "I understand Jimmie Jean stayed with you Friday night. I hope there wasn't too much drama."

Branigan and her mom spoke in shorthand when it came to certain family members. "She threatened to move in with me."

"Yikes."

"Right."

Branigan's father looked back at his wife and daughter. "What are you two talking about?"

"'Say me, Daddy,'" said Branigan, straight-faced. Her mother laughed at Jimmie Jean's old attention-demanding catchphrase. Her father looked bewildered, and Branigan took pity on him. "We're being silly. And uncharitable. Shall we go in?"

First Baptist Grambling boasted the city's largest sanctuary and arguably its most influential congregation. As was the case with many Southern cities, the First Church was also relatively moderate in its theology. It was no Jericho Road, where Branigan's friend Liam Delaney ministered and which she visited every month or so. But it wasn't the fundamentalist stronghold of so many Southern churches either.

The choir sang two choral anthems, and the first-class organist played a lovely offertory. Branigan would've said it was her favorite kind of church service – until, that is, she'd attended Liam's services with their raucous, clapping gospel and musical styles that spanned the Staple Singers, Bob Dylan and Bach.

Reverend Mann was halfway through a sermon on loving the unlovable neighbor – *Liam could've preached this one*, Branigan thought – when out of the corner of her eye she saw Cornel Arnett stand. He signaled his fellow Cannon County deputy Mark Wiseman, and the two slipped quietly through the narthex, leaving their unsurprised wives and children.

Branigan stayed through the rest of the service, wondering what had drawn the sheriff's deputies out of worship. She declined her parents' invitation to lunch and called the newsroom.

Business writer Art Whittaker, acting as weekend city editor, was the only one on duty. A clown, he said, had been spotted behind Glenden Arms Apartments, a low-income complex on the western outskirts of town, inhabited by many of the county's black and Hispanic residents.

"I'm handling it," he said, "and I've already called Tan-4 and Bert. They want all of us here at nine on Monday to plan our coverage."

"I'll be there," she said. "But tell me what else you have."

"Not much. Officers are out there now." He stopped for a moment. "Hey, Branigan, I just realized. It's in the county, not the city. Do you want to drop by?"

"Actually, I do. I'm at church. I'll stop on my way home."

She headed west, passing the massive parking lot of Jericho Road which easily identified it as a former grocery store. The lot was half filled with the cars of middle-class people the mission church had attracted. Inside there'd be another eighty or so people who'd arrived on foot.

"You go, Liam!" she said aloud, saluting the church and sending up a prayer as she'd promised she would every time she drove past.

Once she had traversed the Michael Garner Memorial Bridge, the roof of various tent cities, there was little traffic. She arrived at Glenden Arms, a tired-looking collection of three-story apartment buildings set among parking lots and weed patches. She could see the distinctive navy and yellow cars of the Cannon County Sheriff's Office, and looked for her church mates Cornel and Mark.

Knots of Hispanic men and women kept a close eye on their children as deputies walked among them. It looked as though everyone in the entire complex was out, and Branigan wondered how the deputies were going to get coherent statements. Finally, she spotted Cornel; he was talking to two black women and one white one, who were gesturing wildly. She inched closer.

"You need to do something with all these crazy clowns runnin' round, scaring these babies half to death!" one woman screeched. "You need to keep a car out here, keep they crazy asses away."

"Ya'll ain't never here when we need ya; just when you be hassling us," accused another.

"That's right!"

The black deputy tried to steer the women back to the issue at hand. "Okay, ma'am, but can you tell me what you saw?"

"I didn't see nothing," the first woman said. "I didn't have to. Kenisha saw him."

"Kenisha?" Cornel asked, looking around.

"I'm Kenisha," said a fourth woman standing outside the circle, distancing herself from her complaining neighbors. "I saw him."

Cornel positioned himself so that his back was to the other three, offering Kenisha a measure of privacy. Branigan wished the trio would stop jabbering. They were making it hard to hear.

Kenisha was much calmer than her neighbors. Branigan could see the relief on Cornel's face as he bent to take her statement. She pointed to the woods behind an aging swing set. There was no fence at this complex, only dense woods running right up against the play area. She could barely make out Kenisha's words, but she caught "orange wig" and saw the woman hold her hands away from both ears to show the size of the bushy hair.

Holding back, waiting her turn to talk to the deputy and witness, Branigan looked into the dark interior of the woods, where even the strong noon sun didn't penetrate. She turned and saw a boy, maybe five years old, sitting on the apartment steps behind Kenisha. The woman had positioned her body to pen him there while she spoke to the deputy. Branigan looked at him sitting still, seemingly engrossed in the deputy's uniform and gun. If you really wanted to lure a child, would you dress as an outlandish clown? Did kids like clowns better than, say, superheroes or cops or firemen?

She tried to remember going to the circus at five years old. Because her dad's bank had sponsored it, she got to ride on an elephant's back, her arms locked in a death grip around her brother's waist. Now *that* was scary. But the blond clown with the huge blue shoes had been gentle as he handed Branigan a balloon dachshund. So, okay, she thought, gazing at the small boy, maybe clowns could be alluring.

She stood patiently until Cornel finished with Kenisha, then she moved in to talk to the young mother.

It was April 30.

CHAPTER FOUR

Malachi crossed the train tracks on the hill above Tent City, and sat on the other side. His dreadlocks hung nearly to his shoulders beneath a nylon do-rag, and he wore sunglasses someone had left on a table at Jericho Road. From this vantage, he could see Tent City 2.

Like his own camp, there was a picnic table, a plastic rolling trash can provided by the city, and a few tents. Unlike his side, there was an actual plywood structure at the far end that hid a latrine. That part *wasn't* sanctioned by the city. From what Malachi read in *The Rambler*, city officials didn't know what to do about it. Bring in DHEC? Add portable potties? For now, they opted to sit on their hands.

Tent City 2 was also missing the concrete incline that was on Malachi's side, where a ledge under the fifty-foot-high bridge provided space for multiple "apartments" separated by hanging blankets. The plywood structure that had anchored one end last summer had toppled off this winter. The wood went into the fire pit.

Malachi saw the tent Slick had mentioned. It was hard to miss, a new tent, and big – big enough for the six people Slick said were living in it. As he watched, a woman stepped through the unzipped opening, a black woman, nearly as ebony as Malachi himself. Her hair was caught in a red kerchief, and she wore a matching dress and flat sandals. Three kids tumbled out after her, and from their light complexions, Malachi figured the husband must be white. Or maybe Hispanic.

The woman glanced up to where Malachi sat but appeared not to see him. He watched as the children ran to the picnic table and rummaged through cardboard boxes. Church folks were always bringing stuff in. He could see that she limited the kids to one breakfast bar and juice box apiece, then the four set off through the woods that led to Jericho Road. At least, he hoped that was where they were headed. Pastor Liam would be their best bet for getting out from under this bridge.

Malachi took a shortcut and arrived at Jericho Road before the woman and children. He got a kick, as he always did, out of the folk art painting on the plate glass that showed multi-racial diners sharing a meal, with the words "Where the elite eat – with Jesus" scripted across the bottom. Tiffany Lynn did that one. He'd had to spell "elite" for her.

Pastor Liam, tall, slim and red-headed, stood inside the sliding electric door that identified the mission as a former grocery store. He greeted visitors and pointed them to a battered coffee urn outside the kitchen. He seemed delighted to see Malachi, grabbing the shorter man in a bear hug.

"Pastor, a family with kids may be on they way here."

"They'll certainly be welcome."

"Yeah, but…" Malachi hesitated. He didn't relish getting involved in lives out here.

"But?" Pastor Liam was looking at him quizzically.

Malachi lowered his voice. "They got kids living in Tent City. I ain't never seen that before."

Liam's smile faded. "Neither have I. Well, I'll be on the lookout for them."

It didn't take long. The woman arrived, ushering a girl who looked about ten and two younger boys. The children looked clean, and Malachi, standing next to the coffee urn, wondered how the mom managed it. Liam made it a point to greet the family, asking if this was their first time at Jericho Road. When the woman said yes, Liam handed her a brochure listing the hot meals, food pantry and other services the church offered. *Transformational services*, Malachi had heard him say on many occasions.

"I know it's too much to keep in your head at once," Liam said, "but we'd be pleased to have you stay for lunch, then come back later for anything we offer. We also have an art room this afternoon that your children might enjoy."

The family found seats near the back of the dining hall, and Malachi slipped into the row behind them. He didn't like this, didn't like it one bit. He wondered if the children were in school. He wondered where the dad and teenage son were this morning. He wondered what had gone so terribly wrong that the family had moved to Tent City 2.

The young girl saw one of Liam's volunteers with crayons and coloring books and rose to get a set for each brother. She sat between them, handing them crayons, murmuring encouragement, as their mother stared ahead. One little boy looked to be about seven, Malachi estimated; the other maybe four. For a moment, the youngest reminded him of the boy in Kuwait, the smooth mocha skin not unlike the Middle Eastern boy's, and Malachi grew dizzy with the memory. The clattery Jericho Road dining hall faded away, and Malachi was once again nineteen years old, going door to door as the smell of burning oil filled the air.

A sandstorm had blown up suddenly, turning the afternoon to brown dusk and separating Malachi from his unit. He staggered into what he'd later learned was a Bedouin village, into the doorway of a small home made of concrete and aluminum, seeking a reprieve from the stinging sand that filled his mouth and nose and eyes with painful grit. He tripped and fell into a front room where a group of people huddled. Malachi couldn't open his eyes completely, so all he could see was movement against one wall. He tried to pry his eyes open, but the sand scratched painfully. Malachi knelt and stared, half blind, toward the occupants. An elderly man, apparently realizing the American was alone and unable to see, grew brave. He stood and hurled a stream of angry words at Malachi. Malachi didn't understand a single one, but he sure got the message: the foreign soldier was unwelcome in this home.

Malachi stood for a moment under the torrent of curses, wavering as he struggled to blink his eyes clear of sand. He thought of his grandparents and how they'd react if a soldier slammed into their home uninvited. He was embarrassed and reluctantly stepped through the doorway and into the raging windstorm again. Immediately, his face felt as if it had been stung by a thousand bees, and he lurched to the next house, the sand punishing him at every step. This time he knocked. Then he pounded. When there was no answer, he pushed the door open and stumbled inside. The relief was instant.

Malachi sensed no one in the front room and felt his way to the back wall, where he made out a basin and pitcher. He plunged his hand inside the pitcher and was grateful to find water. Pouring it into the basin, he brought handfuls to his face, letting the water flush out his eyes. When it was done, his eyes felt sore, but he could see again.

Belatedly holding his rifle at alert, he walked into the only other room, calling out as he went so as not to startle anyone. It seemed to be a room for sleeping, with mats and rugs covering the floor, empty like the other. Malachi was relieved to have the vacant house, barely more than a hut, to wait out the storm. He'd turned to leave the sleeping room when he heard a rustle and saw a rumpled blanket on the farthest mat move. He stopped, wrestling with himself, with his training. Should he point the rifle at the blanket, or at the ceiling? After all, he was here to free the Kuwaitis, not terrorize them. Remembering his grandparents again on their farm in Hartwell, Georgia, he pointed the gun at the ceiling, and called, "It's okay. Come out," hoping his tone would convey his message even if his words were not understood.

Little sun-browned arms wriggled out of the blanket first, then a striped T-shirt that could've been worn by Opie Taylor. The child stood, huge black eyes staring at Malachi without fear. Malachi grinned in spite of himself. "Well, hello, little man," he said softly, using the nickname his grandpa had called him. "Where the rest of your family?"

DEATH OF A JESTER

Now the boy on the row in front of him turned to Malachi and held out a crayon, inviting him to color. Malachi shook his head, got up abruptly and moved to the end of the row. The hand that held his coffee was trembling.

CHAPTER FIVE

When Branigan had finished talking to Kenisha and Cornel about the third clown sighting in three days, she drove to the *Rambler* office and updated Art. He asked her to post a few paragraphs online to supplement what he'd gleaned from the sheriff's office.

Then she called her mom and asked if she wanted to meet at Aunt Jeanie's.

"Yes, I do," her mother answered. "I'm just finishing a cake I want to take them, so give me thirty minutes."

Branigan wandered to the break area at the back of the newsroom, where soda and snack machines had replaced the cafeteria that once offered hot breakfast and lunch. She bought a Diet Pepsi and peanut butter crackers, waved goodbye to Art, and took the elevator. Outside the *Rambler* building, she chose an empty bench and sat down to eat.

Main Street gave her plenty to look at. The warm weather had brought out the Sunday brunchers and dog walkers and coffee drinkers. She could see that two art galleries in the next block had pulled easels and paintings onto the sidewalk. The restaurants with outside seating were doing a booming business, probably in Bloody Marys and mimosas. Older restaurants such as Marshall's closed after lunch on Sunday, refusing to get into the alcohol business.

City workers had replaced winter pansies with petunias in curbside beds and the hanging iron planters that swung from streetlights. Branigan noted that bushy red geraniums also sprouted from this year's planters, giving them height while the young petunias would soon spill over the sides in generous waves. The frost-free planting date of April 15 had come and gone, she realized with a start: she needed to set next Saturday aside to put out annuals in her yard.

She threw her trash into a receptacle and headed for her car.

Eileen Powers was pulling into her brother's driveway as Branigan arrived. Branigan took her mom's purse to free her to carry a coconut cake in a see-through plastic container.

Hearing voices in the kitchen, the women knocked on the screen door but didn't wait for an answer. As soon as Branigan stuck her head in, Isabella launched herself from a kitchen chair with a shriek. "Mom!" she called into the far reaches of the house. "Brani G and Aunt Eileen are here!"

She hugged them both as Jimmie Jean stood lazily and hugged Eileen as well. Branigan's Uncle Bobby, stocky, short-haired and dressed in the work pants and boots he wore every day of his life, solemnly hugged his sister.

"Bobby, I'm so sorry," she said, placing the cake on the kitchen table. "How is she?"

"You wouldn't know anything was wrong yet," he said. "We're just worried what the radiation and chemo will do."

Aunt Jeanie came through the doorway, her silver-streaked auburn hair cut fashionably short, a bright smile on her face. "So I have to get sick to qualify for Eileen's coconut cake?" She grabbed Eileen with one arm, Branigan with the other. "This is a treat indeed."

She bustled around the kitchen, setting out cups and dessert plates as Isabella made coffee and Branigan pulled out milk and sugar. Jeanie matter-of-factly gave them the details of her oncologist's diagnosis as her husband stared at his hands folded on the table.

"Tomorrow I start six weeks of chemo, then we'll see where we are. I'm sure I could drive myself, but Miss Jimmie Jean has offered so I'll take her up on it." She nudged her husband gently. "And I want this one to get back to his cattle and stop hovering." She smiled and covered his hands with her own.

Branigan swallowed. It was hard to see her roughneck Uncle Bobby so frightened. She'd never known Bobby without Jeanie and was sure none of them wanted to experience that. He'd been a good father to their five children, but Jeanie was the one who made this house a warm and fun-filled place. She'd even won over Gran Rickman, who'd not been sure how a Savannah beauty queen would take to country life. Family lore had it that Jeanie won her mother-in-law over the day her strawberry preserves won a blue ribbon at the county fair.

Eileen turned to Jimmie Jean. "Branigan tells me you might be acting at Theater on the Square this summer?"

Jimmie Jean stretched, fighting off a yawn. "I'm not sure what show they're doing. But my director sent an email in case they have a part."

"Well, let us know. We'll want to cheer you on. And Isabella – you're going to work with Liam?"

Isabella nodded. Her hair had always been lighter than her mother's or sister's and was now attractively sun-streaked. Her eyes too were lighter than their brown, somewhere between hazel and green. Her nose was lightly freckled, and her wide and generous mouth was curved into its habitual smile.

"I was hoping to get some crossover time with his social worker, Allison, but her baby's already past due. So I may have to simply dive in."

"He's lucky to have you. This is very close to what you do in Atlanta, isn't it?"

"Yes. I'm a counselor in a Title I school. I work with poor families, some of them moving a good deal, some of them homeless. Right now, I'm trying to line up children for summer lunch programs in nearby churches."

"That does sound similar to Liam's church."

"Only he's got tons less bureaucracy, from what I understand. Liam doesn't take government funding, so he's not big on paperwork. He said we'll be doing whatever we can to get people into doctor's offices, jobs and housing."

"But Jericho Road doesn't get many children, does it?" asked Branigan.

"I don't think so. Liam said there are occasionally families at the meals, but they're not living outside. So we'll see. I'm really looking forward to it."

She looked around and saw that everyone had finished their cake. "Anybody need seconds?" She refilled coffee cups as everyone declined another slice, then caught Branigan's eye. "Brani G, I told Mom I'd water her new flowers. Want to help me?"

"Sure. I want to see what you put out, Aunt Jeanie. I still have to do mine." Branigan stood and followed Isabella through the screen door.

"Can't kill marigolds," called her aunt.

As soon as Isabella uncoiled the hose and began watering her mother's newly planted verbena, salvia and marigolds, she shot a conspiratorial grin at Branigan. "I have to tell you this," she said, glancing to make sure no one had followed them outside. "We got a call last night from Theater on the Square. For Jamie Solesbee."

"Who the heck is that?"

Isabella was openly snickering. "You can't guess?"

Branigan knew Jimmie Jean's married name was Solesbee. But Jamie?

"She changed her name in West Palm Beach," said Isabella, grinning. "She thought Jimmie Jean was too hick. I thought Dad was going to blow a gasket."

Branigan laughed. "Jamie Solesbee, huh? I guess it does sound more West Palm Beach than Jimmie Jean."

"And she does too know what the summer play is. *Annie Get Your Gun*."

"Again? How many times can they do that show?"

"Well, apparently one too many for her. I guess it's better suited to a Jimmie Jean than a Jamie. She's trying to get them to change it."

Branigan stared at her cousin in disbelief. "She's been in town for two days and she's trying to get them to *change their show?*"

"Yep."

"Oh, my," she said, picturing the imperial director of Theater on the Square. "Lady Jamie Solesbee meets Sir Reginald Fortenberry. That's a show I'd pay to see."

For a moment, there was only the sound of water gushing as Isabella carefully watered around the roots. She glanced hesitantly at her cousin. "Did Jimmie Jean say anything to you about Jackson?"

"Not really," Branigan said. "She hinted at problems that could only be talked about over wine. And she flippantly mentioned divorce. Surely she wasn't serious... Was she?"

"I'm not sure. I just don't want *you* getting hurt. Again."

Branigan smiled gamely. "Water under the bridge. I'm way, way over that."

Isabella studied her cousin's face. "Okay. Good."

Isabella turned the hose onto her mother's rose bushes. "I mean, who'd give a drama queen like her a *gun*?"

Chapter Six

On Monday morning Branigan slid into a seat in the conference room, noting the smiles. In the empty seat at one end of the conference table leaned a painting of a clown on black velvet.

"Who invited our guest?" grumbled Tan-4, taking the seat at the head of the table, flanked by city editor Bert Feldspar and *Style* editor Julie Ames. When no one answered, he shook his head, apparently undecided on whether to growl or smile. Most of the city desk and *Style* reporters were assembled – Branigan, Jody Manson, Marjorie Gulledge, Harley Barnett, Art Whittaker, Lou Ann Gillespie, and arts writer Gerald Dubois. Branigan steeled herself for the sports metaphors that flew freely when Tan-4 and Bert conducted meetings.

"Okay, we're going into the ring on this one," Tan-4 began.

Branigan darted a look at Marjorie, who gazed toward the ceiling.

"Or three rings," deadpanned Art.

And so the clown jokes begin. Branigan sighed.

Bert ran a hand over his shaved head and waited for Tan to continue. Tan nodded at him. "Take the baton."

"Okaayyy. We've got three clown sightings in three days, all in the vicinity of little kids. Two were at low-income apartments. One was at an elementary school when school was out.

"A single witness in each case describes the clown similarly: white face, orange wig, red nose, red shoes, big old white pants with red stripes. Here's what we know: witnesses say he was trying to lure a child into the woods. But no child has been taken. The police seem to be leaning toward a hoax, though they haven't come out and said so. That about right, Jody? Branigan?"

The two nodded.

"The woman I spoke to, Kenisha Williams, seemed credible," Branigan said. "Very calm. Not attention-seeking. I can't say the same for her neighbors."

"My witnesses, not quite as much," Jody added. "The high school track guy was solid enough. The teen sister of the first boy seemed a little flaky. But I have to admit, she didn't back down."

"So all possibilities remain open," said Bert. "Questions so far?"

"Not a question," said Julie, "but I took a call from a newspaper in New Zealand, asking for a comment."

"Me too," added Lou Ann. "I was in early and took calls from TV stations in London and Sydney."

There was a moment's buzz around the table.

"I guess the police aren't giving them what they want," Tan said. "What did you tell them?"

"That we didn't know anything beyond what was online," Julie said. "But you know, we might want to think about letting a reporter go on air. Could be good PR."

Branigan met Marjorie's eyes again, and both of them cringed.

Tan was shaking his head. "Not until we know for sure if this is a real threat or a hoax. Opens us to ridicule."

Bert jumped back in. "The Grambling police chief and Cannon County sheriff are holding a joint press conference today. Jody, you grab that. I imagine that'll be our lead story.

"Lou Ann, want to see if Ringling Brothers has any runaway clowns?" The reporters laughed.

"And check the Volkswagen dealership for getaway Beetles," piped up Art.

"You're on a roll," Bert told him drily. "Seriously, Lou Ann, see if Ringling Brothers has any knowledge of this happening before, any firings, things like that. I know it's a long shot.

"And who wants to do the *Style* front on 'Clowns Are Our Friends'?"

Julie and Harley looked so startled that the older reporters laughed again.

"What he means," Branigan explained, "is we're going to get a call any minute from the clowning guild at the children's wing of St Joe's, complaining about the bad press. He wants to head them off with a story on what clowns do when they're not luring kids into the woods."

"Oh," said Harley, looking relieved. "I'll take that."

"Good. And Gerald, you want to do a piece on clowns in fine art?" Bert said, with a nod at the velvet canvas. Gerald looked horrified for a moment, until the reporters couldn't hold their laughter. Bert grinned. "Just kidding, man."

Branigan spoke up. "Bea Boswell reminded me of a clowning workshop that Theater on the Square put on last year. I thought I'd check and see if they're missing costumes, make-up, stuff like that."

Gerald looked up. "That reminds me. They also did *Clown Bar* maybe two years ago." When everyone looked blank, he added, "It's a recent play, a dark comedy, about a murder near this seedy bar where clowns go. There are a lot of clown characters and costumes in it."

"Sounds promising," said Bert. "Branigan, let me know what you find. Other ideas? Anything else?"

"Just one more thing," said Art, reaching for his bow tie and sending a stream of water onto Bert's shirt. "Beep! Beep!"

For a moment, there was no sound in the room as the other reporters stared wide-eyed at Art.

"Send in the clowns?" he asked weakly.

Bert groped for a tissue to dry himself. "Don't bother. They're here."

Branigan reached Reggie Fortenberry on the first ring. "Why are *you* calling rather than Gerald?" he demanded.

Branigan was accustomed to Reggie's flow from fulsome to despairing to disgusted, often within a single conversation. Heck, often within a single sentence. He'd been one year ahead of her at Grambling High East, the star of every play, winner of every state thespian award, terror of every drama teacher – and he went through three. After stints in San Francisco, then Los Angeles, then Atlanta, he announced that he was coming home to raise the standard of community theater, or as he called it "theater of the people". The longstanding Grambling Little Theatre on the Eastside wasn't in the market for a director, but downtown's Theater on the Square was in the midst of turmoil and snapped him up. That was six years ago. Somehow he'd managed to hang on to his job, though Branigan had noticed a quick turnover among board members when she got her season subscription notices.

Still, the level of community theater had risen markedly under his charge, aided at least in part by Gerald Dubois' enthusiastic reviews. Reggie regularly attracted singers and actors from Atlanta to fill roles that demanded more than Grambling could provide. *Oh, but he hasn't met Jimmie Jean Rickman Solesbee*, she thought wickedly.

"This isn't about a show," Branigan answered. "It's about these clown sightings."

"Ah, then how may I help you, Branigan?"

"I remember that you held a clowning workshop last winter. Are you missing any costumes, make-up, things like that?"

"I have no idea."

"That's what I figured. May I come over and have a look through your storage area?"

"Actually, my dear, you're the second person to call this morning about that. One of our dashing detectives is on his way over. I'll let you sit in, too, if you'll bring coffee."

"You got it. See you in twenty minutes."

She grabbed her purse and headed out. Gerald looked up as she passed his desk. "Going into the lion's den?" he asked.

"Anything I should know?"

"Only that Reggie thinks he has a lead on an out-of-town Annie for *Get Your Gun* this summer. I was hoping he'd try something written this century."

"Maybe he's going to make it a commentary on the Second Amendment."

Gerald laughed. "I guess there's always that possibility."

Branigan could have easily walked, but she didn't want Reggie and the detective, who was surely Chester, waiting for her. So she drove the six short blocks up Main to Bea's, dashed in and bought three coffees, then drove another three blocks east to where Theater on the Square reigned over one end of a city park.

The theater resided in a stately old stone mansion, gutted in the early 1950s and revamped for its current use. Its position in Grambling's reviving downtown allowed it latitude in fundraising; subsequent upgrades in the 90s and 2011 lifted the roof for expanded space above the stage, and added computer ticketing, a late-night bar and ornate restrooms. The theater's bread and butter consisted of lavish musicals, but its huge stage could be pared down for fringe productions, and the green space out front allowed for Shakespeare in the Park. Its versatility had successfully kept the newer Grambling Little Theatre focused on suburban supporters, even though the two theaters sometimes overlapped with big musical fare.

Branigan pulled around to the theater's rear parking lot that held only Chester's unmarked Crown Victoria and an ancient BMW she assumed belonged to Reggie. Slinging her purse over one shoulder, she balanced the three coffees in a cardboard tray and made her way to the side entrance that led to offices and the backstage area. A triangular wooden block was wedged in the doorway, so she elbowed her way in.

"Coffee!" she called.

Chester stuck his head out of a storage room. "We're in here," he said, coming to take the tray from her.

Reggie rushed from the same room in full host mode, having switched from peckish to effusive since she called. "Branigan! How delightful to see you, my dear! Detective Scovoy, do you know the delightful Miss Powers, the most gifted writer at our *Grambling Rambler*?"

Chester arched an eyebrow. "Um, yes, I do know Miss Powers."

"Of course! Of course! You would! All that nasty business last summer. Too, too ugly."

Branigan was accustomed to mention of the murders of homeless people that had engulfed her family the previous summer, but it still jolted. She drew a deep breath and silently handed the coffees around.

"So," she said. "Have you determined anything on the clown costumes?"

"No, we hadn't got that far," Reggie said. "Come." He led the way into a deep hallway that was wider than it appeared from the door and was crammed with a double row of vintage clothes. Branigan could see that bars had been hung at approximately five and ten feet off the ground to double the vertical storage space as well.

He pointed overhead. "Up there is nineteenth century. And earlier." He started walking, caressing the furs and silks and satins on the lower level. "We start here with the 1920s and 30s. Then the 40s and 50s. We have a large 60s section. *Hair. How to Succeed in Business.* Neil Simon."

He flapped a hand along the garments, screwing up his face at a lime green leisure suit. "Then those horrible 70s and 80s. Oh my, what were we thinking? Then a mash-up of 90s to now, not terribly distinctive.

"Down here at the end," he said, leading them into a side room, "are the more fanciful costumes. Cats. Insects. Horses. Winnie the Pooh. This is where the clowns would be."

He pushed impatiently through the racks, hangers squealing in protest as they scraped across metal rods. "Ah, here we go." He shoved a horse's rear end out of the way to reveal multiple pairs of expansive clown pants in bright red and orange and purple. A hanging plastic bag contained bulbous red noses and frizzy wigs in varying neon colors.

"We had the idea to do the clowning workshop because we had all these costumes from *Clown Bar.* We did it when it first came out. Did you see it?"

The other two shook their heads.

"Brilliant play. Dark comedy. It's about a former clown, Happy, whose druggie brother is murdered. Happy goes back to his clown life to investigate. So all this darkness surrounding clowning is really nothing new, is it?"

Reggie removed the hanging bag of noses and wigs to reveal floppy red shoes, their shoelaces tied together to hang from nails on the wall. Chester pointed to two empty nails on the bottom row.

"Are two pairs missing?" he asked. "From right there?"

Reggie tapped his lip with one finger. "Perhaps," he said. "I honestly don't know."

He returned to the rack once more, his face grim. "There are empty hangers here, too."

Branigan spoke up. "Do you have an inventory system? Any way of tracking what you have?"

"I don't. But our wardrobe mistress does. Barbara Wickenstall. Let me call her."

Reggie excused himself and they heard him talking on his cell phone. Chester spoke quietly. "Did you see his face when he saw those empty nails?"

"I did. He was surprised."

"Any idea what it means? You know this guy."

"I wouldn't say I know him well. I feel like I know more the character he plays, if you know what I mean. Kind of over-the-top male diva. What's the word? Divo. He was that way even in high school."

They quieted as Reggie walked back to join them. "Barbara will come in this afternoon and compare what's here with her computerized inventory."

"Reggie," said Branigan softly. "You looked like you noticed something a minute ago."

He turned a beaming smile on her. "Did I, love? Sorry, but I have absolutely no head for accounting or inventory or whatever it is Barbara does. All I do is shout out a decade, and she scurries in with the most magnificent attire and props. She really is amazing. I brought her with me, you know. We worked together in LA, but she was from the South and ready to come home."

49

Branigan looked at him for another moment and decided not to press. "Okay. The description we're getting from witnesses is billowy white pants with red pinstripes, white face, red shoes, red lips, orange wig. The only thing I don't see is the white pants. Did you have some?"

"I really don't remember." Reggie began walking out, head down, giving Branigan and Chester no choice but to follow. They exchanged glances.

Back near the side entrance, Reggie offered his hand for Chester to shake, effectively dismissing him.

"Shall we call you back this afternoon?" the detective asked.

"No, no, that won't be necessary. I'll have Barbara call you. No problem at all."

Branigan and Chester headed for the door, then Branigan turned. "Oh, one more thing. I hear you're looking at Jamie Solesbee for a summer production."

Reggie's face brightened, and he actually clapped his hands. "Yes! A colleague in south Florida recommends her highly."

"She's my cousin."

"Your *cousin*?" Reggie looked as if Branigan had thrown up on his shoes.

"She was Jimmie Jean Rickman then. She went to Grambling High West, so you probably didn't know her."

"Jimmie *Jean*?" Reggie looked horrified. Chester coughed, which Branigan suspected hid a laugh.

"Anyway, thank you again."

Out in the parking lot, with the side door closed firmly behind them, Chester and Branigan burst into laughter.

"I hope I didn't ruin Jimmie Jean's chance at stardom."

"It'll be a toss-up," said Chester. "He thought he had a big old celebrity from south Florida and now he finds out she's from north Georgia. I'm not sure he believes anything good can come out of Grambling – other than himself." He smiled at her. "But before you brought your cousin up, he sure was anxious to get rid of us."

"Yes, he was. But why?"

"No idea. I guess we have to wait for Barbara to see if anything's missing. But he saw something in there he wasn't expecting."

"Or didn't see something that he was," Branigan added.

CHAPTER SEVEN

Malachi and Slick sat on the hill overlooking Tent City 2 and passed a bottle of Jack Daniel's back and forth. Slick was celebrating a job that started tomorrow, building the stage in Reynolds Park for its summer Shakespeare.

Malachi had seen a couple of the plays in previous years, with girls dressed as boys and boys dressed as girls, which folks seemed to find hilarious. Malachi knew his Shakespeare as well as anyone who'd come through high school honors, but he still found the plays tedious.

Slick nodded toward the tent on the flat ground below.

"I seen that daddy and his oldest boy heading out this morning. And the mama taking those littl'uns to school, I reckon."

Malachi nodded, and took a sip. It went down smoothly. The thought of the youngest boy didn't bother him near as much now that he had a fifth of Jack in front of him.

"Pastor Liam done offer to help them if they want," he said. "Him and Miz Allison got that old cripple guy in a 'partment last month." Malachi's speech tended to reflect that of whomever he was talking to, and now it settled into Slick's cadence.

"What old cripple guy?"

"You know. He be staying in that camp behind the Walmart. Be at Jericho Road all the time, eating."

"White guy?"

"Yeah."

"Yeah, I think I know him."

Slick took the bottle back, and they sat in silence.

After awhile, Slick spoke again. "Where's his 'partment at?"

"Dunno."

"Pastor Liam pay for it?"

Malachi shrugged. "Dunno," he said again. "They pretty tight-lip 'bout folks they help. I think Jericho Road have some money and Miz Allison apply for government money and disability and she get vouchers. All that."

Slick took a sip. "Maybe get me a 'partment one of these days."

Malachi smiled slyly. "They make you quit drinking."

Slick guffawed. "Well then, maybe my tent ain't so bad." He took another drink, waved the bottle at the encampment below. "Least I ain't bringing no kids up in here."

A movement from the woods on the right caught Malachi's eye. He watched as a burly tanned man, mid-forties, scraggly white-blond hair to his shoulders, trudged into the camp. His arms were heavily tattooed where they emerged from a short-sleeved T-shirt. He was followed by a teen who looked to be seventeen or eighteen, his black hair frizzy, his skin darker. The boy carried a case of beer.

"Cheap stuff?" Slick asked.

"Sure look like it."

"Guess they couldn't find no work."

"Maybe he a pro wrestler."

Slick laughed, and choked on a sip of Jack. Malachi took the bottle he offered, sipped lightly and returned it. "You ain't got but a couple swallows left."

Slick looked at the bottle sorrowfully. "You been hearing 'bout those clowns trying to grab kids?" he demanded.

Malachi had read the paper over breakfast at Jericho Road. His friend, Miz Branigan, had a story this morning about the third sighting.

"Yeah. Don't make no sense."

"What don't?"

"I mean, you want a kid, why you dress so crazy you scare him? Why don't you dress like a po-lice or a fireman? Or heck, a kid would like Batman better than a clown."

Slick looked thoughtful. "Po-lice need to quit messing with Elise and find this guy," he said quietly. "You don't see Elise out here trying to hustle off no kids."

A flash of red and white appeared on the right side of the camp, and Malachi blinked, his mind on clowns. Then he saw the woman from yesterday in the same red dress and flat sandals, holding the hand of her youngest son. Why did he think he'd seen white? he wondered, straining to see into the woods beyond the woman.

"Guess he too little for school," Slick said, pointing the bottle at the boy.

"Guess so."

The men watched as the woman caught sight of her husband and older son coming out of their tent holding beer cans. The teen paused and looked to his father. Even from this distance, the woman appeared to be staring daggers at her husband as the boys looked from him to her.

Without speaking, the husband dropped onto the picnic table bench, leaned back and spread his arms wide on the table; he shrugged at the teen before upending his beer.

Slick laughed hoarsely. "Wouldn't wanna be him right now," he said.

Malachi didn't answer, only watched as the woman pushed past the teen and dragged the little boy into the tent behind her.

CHAPTER EIGHT

Barbara Wickenstall called Branigan mid-afternoon with the news that Theater on the Square was missing two pairs of white clown pants with red pinstripes and two sets of red shoes, round noses and bushy orange wigs. She didn't track make-up jars and had no way of knowing whether any of them were missing.

Branigan kept her on the phone for awhile, asking about her system and when she'd last seen the items.

"That I couldn't tell you," said the wardrobe mistress in a distinct Southern drawl. "We got them for *Clown Bar*, then used them again in last year's workshop. I'm showing that all of our clown items were checked back in before December of last year. So they disappeared sometime between December 1 and today. I wasn't looking for them any time in between."

"Who else has access to that wardrobe room?"

"Who doesn't? Casts and crews from three shows in the past six months. Board members. Audiences who come to greet the casts after shows. Volunteers. Cable guys. Phone guys. Pest control guys. And the five of us on staff."

"What kind of permanent staff do you have?"

"Well, Reggie, of course. Then an assistant director. Technical director and set builder and facilities manager. That's all one guy. Me. And box office handler/accountant. We hire musicians on a per-show basis."

"Pretty big outfit."

"Well, we do five major productions a year, plus six fringe and outdoor Shakespeares."

"Would it be possible for me to meet you in person?" Branigan asked. "This is a more complicated operation than I'd realized."

"Sure," said Barbara. "I'll be here every day this week. Want to come to my pitifully cramped office?"

"That'll be great. How's tomorrow morning at nine?"

"Surely you jest."

"What do you mean?"

"I have to stay for rehearsals most nights, so I don't come in until one."

"Ah, showbiz. Okay then, how's one o'clock tomorrow?"

"That's more like it. I look forward to meeting you."

Branigan twirled around in her rolling desk chair to tell Bert what she had coming. She saw the elevator door open across the hall and did a double take. It was bursting with clowns.

Beeps and honks and catcalls yanked up every head in the newsroom, and brought Tan-4 barreling out of his office. Harley stood, blushing furiously. "They're here for my hospital guild story," he mumbled, pointing the way to the conference room. But the five clowns weren't to be rushed.

Like puppies, they scattered to various points of the newsroom. "My name is Giggles!" shouted an obese woman with a garish yellow wig and Minnie Pearl hat. "And I'm looking for Harley!"

"Harley! Harley!" The other clowns took up the cry, looking under desks and in trashcans and inside telephone receivers. "Where's Harley?"

Harley looked as if he'd love to crawl under one of those desks. Instead, face beet red, he stood at the conference door. "Here, clowns. Here, clowns," he said, motioning them inside.

"Folks call me Ruggles!" shouted a tall man with green pants, yellow shirt, and red suspenders.

"And I'm his twin, Muggles!" called out a tiny woman dressed inversely in yellow pants, red shirt and green suspenders.

"Slippers!" screamed a man in a rainbow Afro with purple face paint. He lifted his leg to show gargantuan yellow bedroom slippers.

"And last but not least," yelled another fat woman, making a drum roll on Lou Ann's desk, "Flap-pers!" She flailed a pink fringed miniskirt that hung over red and green striped tights.

A silence fell over the newsroom as the clowns awaited applause. When none was forthcoming, they launched once more into beeps and honks and whistles, and ran toward the conference room. Three of them bumped into each other as they tried to enter, ran a figure eight and bumped again, until at last all lay sprawled on the carpeted floor. Harley stepped over them to take a seat at the head of the conference table. Finally realizing the reporters weren't going to respond, the clowns stood and scrambled into their seats.

Bert spun around to face Branigan. "Well, that was terrifying," he said.

Jody returned from the press conference held by Police Chief Marcus Warren and Cannon County Sheriff Clem Ocher. Bert called a quick meeting to let everyone compare notes. Harley was still closeted with the clowns. The reporters heard a thump and looked up to see Muggles – or was it Ruggles? – somersaulting down the conference table. They turned their backs and gathered around Bert's desk.

Jody started. "Chief Warren and Sheriff Ocher are being careful not to call it an out-and-out hoax," he said. "But they did reference incidents in Wisconsin and Alabama two years ago in which people admitted to 'creepy clown hoaxes'. And this spring, in Oregon and Indiana. They say they are taking our witness accounts seriously as abduction attempts, and if someone is goofing around, they will be charged for taking up law enforcement time."

Branigan jumped in. "Theater on the Square is missing two of the exact clown outfits that witnesses described."

Everyone turned to look at her. "Really?" Lou Ann asked. "That must mean something."

"But you could steal them as easily for a hoax as for a kidnapping," said Jody.

"Still," said Bert, "it indicates that we are probably dealing with someone local. Who else would be in that theater?" He thought for a moment. "Do the police know about this, Branigan?"

"Yes. They were talking to the wardrobe mistress at the same time I was."

He turned to Lou Ann. "You get anything from Ringling?"

"No, but they haven't been in this area anyway. A small circus named Broward & Sons was in Augusta in early April. And a rodeo was in Hartwell last week."

"A rodeo?" Bert exclaimed. "Good catch. I didn't think of that. Was anybody willing to comment?"

"Sort of the same thing Jody has. They're hearing about these sightings all over the country. Mr Broward gave me a statement about the dignity of professional clowning – as our friends in there are so aptly demonstrating."

As if on cue, one of Harley's guests went hurtling against the conference room glass, unleashing a quiver that ran down the entire wall of exterior rooms. Tan-4 exploded from his adjoining office. "That's enough!" he shouted, throwing open the conference room door. "Out! All you clowns! Out!"

"Not to put too fine a point on it," said Art, as the hospital clowns slunk for the elevator, "but those aren't pros."

Jody, Branigan and Lou Ann worked with Bert to weave a front-page story about the three clown sightings – and possible abduction attempts – in three days. Marjorie and Art combed the Internet to gather more sightings and make calls to the law enforcement agencies that handled them. Harley worked with a staff photographer to put together a quick *Style* front on the volunteer clowns of St Joe's pediatric wing.

"You guys owe me for this," he said wearily as he stood at Julie's shoulder for the edit.

"Somebody's gotta be the newbie, man," said Jody, clapping him on the back.

Branigan's cell phone rang, and she pushed aside papers to locate it on her desk. To her surprise, it was her cousin Isabella.

"Hey, I thought you'd be back in Atlanta."

"I have been, but I'm on I-85 right now heading toward you. Can you grab some dinner?"

"You bet. I'm actually free to leave the newsroom right this minute."

"How about the Italian restaurant at the Grambling exit? Is that too far for you to come?"

"No, that'll put us nearer the farm anyway. I can be there in ten minutes. How about you?"

"Maybe fifteen. Order me a Prosecco. I've got a lot to tell you."

"Will do."

Inside Caprisano's, a family-owned Italian restaurant that appealed to the Hartwell Lake crowd when they tired of fish camps, Branigan asked for a booth near the entrance so she could watch for her cousin. She ordered a bottle of Prosecco and had taken her first sip of the light and bubbly wine when Isabella walked in.

"Whew! From what I heard on the radio, I imagine your day was as busy as mine," she said, sliding in opposite Branigan. "Three clown sightings in three days? What kinda Bozo town is this?"

"Ha ha. I hear enough of that in my day job."

"Well, you may have the Atlanta TV crews heading this way soon."

"Unfortunately for the pretty boys, there's no video. They're being left high and dry. But I've had clowns to the left of me and jokers to the right all day. Tell me something new."

"I can do that," said Isabella, taking a long drink of wine. "Mmm. Good. So, first of all, Mom sailed through her first chemo treatment today. But I guess it's cumulative, isn't it?"

"Maybe. Or maybe it won't affect her badly. People seem to be all over the place these days on how they react to it."

"Right. Second, I'm officially back in Grambling."

Branigan sat back in surprise. "I thought you had three more weeks of school. You think it's that important you be with your mom?"

"It's not that."

Branigan waited.

"I don't want to tell Mom or Dad or Jimmie Jean," said Isabella. "They've got enough to worry about."

Branigan lifted an eyebrow, but still didn't speak.

"It seems," Isabella said, rolling the stem of her champagne glass in her hands, "I have a stalker." Now that it was out, she leaned back in the booth. She rolled her shoulders and sighed. "You're the only one in the family who knows."

Branigan was wide-eyed. "Who is he? Is it someone you know? Izzy B, is he dangerous?"

Isabella sighed. "He was a teacher at the middle school next to my elementary school. I dated him once, got a funny feeling and turned him down after that. Then I started getting notes on my car, tulips and roses sent to my office, rambling letters. I was pretty sure it was him, but everything was unsigned.

"That went on for three weeks or so. It was embarrassing, but seemed harmless. When the flowers became obvious to the school's staff, I told my principal, Dr Esperinza. She was great about it. After another week with no let-up, she shared with *his* principal. When his principal confronted him, he quit his job."

Isabella stopped for a moment and took another sip of wine. The waitress took that moment to return, so Branigan ordered vegetable lasagna and breadsticks without looking at the menu. Isabella asked for the same.

"So he quit his job," Branigan prompted.

"And it kind of escalated. I guess he had more time on his hands. The notes turned darker, more threatening. One day, I found a dead mouse on my windshield. The next day, a slashed tire. At that point, Dr Esperinza called the police."

"You hadn't done that before?"

"I'd thought about it. And I probably would have if it'd been a stranger. But knowing him, I guess it seemed more pathetic than scary." She shrugged. "In retrospect, I probably should have called them earlier."

"So what are they doing?"

"An officer visited him to let him know they have an eye on him. Which, of course, they don't because they can't afford the manpower for a dead mouse and a slashed tire. But they suggested I leave town for awhile, if possible. Then Dad called with the news about Mom, so it couldn't have come at a better time." She clapped a hand over her mouth. "I didn't mean that."

Branigan put a hand over her cousin's. "I know."

"As you know, I was going to wait until school was out to move here, but yesterday…" She hesitated, then drew a shaky breath. "Or last night, really, when I got home from Mom and Dad's, I could tell someone had been in my condo."

"*What?!*"

Isabella shivered. "I know. I called the officer I'd been dealing with, Lisa Gautier. She's the aunt of a kid in my school, so very sympathetic. She and her partner stopped by."

"Back up a minute," Branigan said. "How could you tell someone had been there?"

"Some mail had been opened that I'd not gotten around to. A pair of underwear had been moved to my pajama drawer. Toothpaste left beside the bathroom sink rather than in the drawer I keep it in. Nothing anyone else would notice but enough to send me a message."

"He was in your underwear drawer? Ewww. How'd he get in your condo?"

"That's the scary part. I have no idea. Officer Gautier suspects he had a key made."

"You didn't spend last night there, did you?"

Isabella shook her head. "No, I stayed with my neighbor. She's a retired teacher and we've been friends since I moved there, what, ten years ago? She went with me to change clothes this morning.

Then I went to school. I still hadn't decided anything for sure, but when Dr Esperinza found out, she got worried he might come to my office and endanger the children. So she suggested I go ahead and wind things up early. As a counselor, it's not as disruptive as it would be if I were teaching." She put her palms out. "So now I'm here. I called Liam. He said I sure won't be endangering anyone at Jericho Road, because all sorts of ex-felons hang out there. I hope he was just trying to make me feel better." She smiled weakly. "He said I can start this week."

"Izzy B, I'm so sorry. This is sick. And frightening."

"Tell me about it."

"You need one of Cleo's sisters."

"You know, I thought about that when I moved to Atlanta. But I didn't think it'd be fair to keep a dog all day in that little condo. My days can be long."

Branigan paused while the waitress brought their plates. She took a bite, swirling the melting cheese around her fork. "The good news is we have you back home for awhile. I can't tell you how excited I am about that."

Isabella smiled tiredly and raised her champagne glass. "Who's that sitting in my tree?"

Branigan grinned and finished with a flourish: "Izzy B and Brani G."

CHAPTER NINE

Here under the bridge, dusk fell earlier. Malachi found himself
seated on the hillside overlooking Tent City 2 once again.

The mom had been on the picnic table bench reading to the
younger boys until it got too dark. Well, that or it got too loud.
Malachi counted Wild Man and Butch and Randy and Shack passing
in and out of Wild Man's tent and diving into the groceries on the
picnic table. For some reason, Tent City 2 drew the younger men,
in their twenties or thirties, sometimes even their late teens. Some
of them, like Wild Man, had "issues", as Pastor Liam would say.
Meaning mental health issues. And some of them, like Shack, had
prison backgrounds. But Butch and Randy, near as Malachi could
tell, thought the whole homelessness thing was an adventure, a
camp-out, a way to live without following the rules of jobs and bills.
They'd find out soon enough how far that thinking got them.

To his surprise, he saw Slick walk out of the plywood bathroom
and join the others at the blackened fire pit on the far side of the
camp. Slick usually didn't have any use for those young men, but
they were openly passing around beer and whiskey, so maybe that
was what he was after. Malachi was pretty sure he saw a crack pipe
too, though the men tried a little harder to hide it.

This is no place for kids, he thought again. For the hundredth time.

He saw continuous movement in the family's tent, the sides
rippling with the bumps of knees and elbows, like the belly of a
pregnant woman. As he watched, the father and teenage son shoved
the tent flap aside and joined the circle of men around the fire.
Within moments, each took a pull from the whiskey bottle and
joined the noisy laughter.

No telling what trash talk coming outta that bunch, Malachi thought. He saw flashlights come on inside the family's tent and pictured young Mo sitting in his mother's lap. *No, wait, that isn't Mohamed. How silly.*

He looked again at the tent, where silhouettes could be seen. Sure enough, that mama was reading again to her kids, probably trying to take them to a place where they didn't sleep on the ground and eat out of boxes. Reading, like his granny used to do with young Malachi, back home in Hartwell. Reading, like he used to do with Mo, both of them pretending the young Bedouin understood English.

On the day of the sandstorm, Malachi stayed with the boy in the Opie Taylor shirt for most of the afternoon. Though the boy was alone in the house, he showed no fear, and was soon following Malachi from one room to the other. Malachi grew hungry and searched for food, but found none. The boy looked healthy enough. What was he eating?

On that first day, as they sat on the floor, the wind howling around them, the sand raising an unholy racket on the tiny house's concrete and aluminum exterior, Malachi pulled a pocket New Testament from his inside shirt pocket and read Matthew's account of Jesus calming the storm. The boy looked up at him, entranced, as if he understood this tale of the frightened disciples undone at learning their new friend had power over winds and waves.

When the Kuwaiti wind died down, Malachi took the boy by the hand and walked next door to the house where the old man had given him a tongue-lashing. Now an old woman ran out and hugged the boy, jerking him away from Malachi and pushing him toward her house. The boy turned at the doorway, grinned widely at Malachi and ran inside.

Malachi caught a ride on a passing Army Jeep and bounced and bumped the mile back to camp.

CHAPTER TEN

Branigan pulled into Theater on the Square's parking lot, surprised to see Jimmie Jean's white Range Rover. Instead of going in the side door, where she could see that Barbara Wickenstall had left the wooden wedge to hold the door open, she walked around to the lawn-facing front entrance. The heavy door of oak and beveled glass was unlocked, so she slipped in.

The theater foyer was a slightly grander version of the mansion's original entrance. A box office was tucked unobtrusively to one side, but otherwise the foyer's curving staircase, marble flooring and small but opulent wine bar gave Branigan the feeling she'd stepped into the home of a very wealthy neighbor. The foyer opened onto formal parlors on either side that handled overflow crowds on opening nights. Off one of those parlors was the theater's most recent addition – a full-service restaurant and bar with appetizers and small plate entrees available before shows. You could also order dessert and have it waiting at intermission. Branigan had recognized Bea Boswell's famous carrot cake on the tea cart the last time she was here with Aunt Jeanie.

The parlors were empty this Tuesday afternoon, but Branigan could hear music coming from the theater. She walked to the rear of the foyer and passed into the theater itself. Reggie Fortenberry sat at a grand piano and Jimmie Jean stood center stage, one boot-clad foot propped on an iron bench. She was dressed in slim-fitting black pants and a red-and-white gingham shirt, tied at the waist. She clutched a majorette's baton and pointed it as if to shoot; apparently, the *Annie* props weren't in yet. Branigan flattened herself against the back wall, hoping the stage lights would prevent the two from seeing into the audience.

Reggie finished his piano rippling and launched into "You Can't Get a Man with a Gun". Branigan watched in astonishment as Jimmie Jean *became* Annie Oakley. There was no other way to describe it. She stomped and danced and twirled over the bench, singing lustily about shooting cattle for steaks and quail in the tail, then wailing, "But you can't get a man with a gun!"

Her pretty cousin was the real thing. Reggie ended his accompaniment with a bang, and rose clapping. "Ah, my dear, dear Jamie! Roger was right. You are a wonder! We want you for our Annie."

Branigan had to admit that Reggie – and Roger down in south Florida – was right. She hadn't seen Jimmie Jean perform since high school, and she had grown into a major talent. Now that she had nailed the part, she was affecting modesty, head down, murmuring something Branigan couldn't hear from this distance.

Branigan didn't want to interrupt, so she slipped back through the foyer and around to the side entrance. She entered and called for Barbara, who answered from an office down the hall. Even in the woman's brief "Yoo hoo! Down here!" Branigan could hear the Deep South, deeper even than Georgia.

"What did this used to be?" Branigan asked as she walked into the cramped space, moving a crown wrapped in daisies in order to sit on a slim ladder-back chair, the only seating choice.

"Who knows? Butler's pantry? Breakfast room? Toy closet?" Barbara rose to shake hands, and Branigan could see that she was short, barely over five foot two. Her unruly hair had once been black, but was now liberally mixed with gray strands. Her handshake was firm and her gaze direct. The woman exuded competence.

"So tell me how you got to Grambling," Branigan invited. "I can hear by your accent you're not from too far away."

Barbara sat back down behind her desk because there was nowhere else to go. "Hattiesburg, Mississippi," she said. "I left right after college for New York and worked a good while on sets and costumes off-Broadway. Then I took a job in LA. That's where I met Reggie. But I didn't like California as much as everyone else did, so years later, when he called to ask me to take over the wardrobe for this place, I jumped at it." She eyed the restricted confines of her office. "You can see I landed in luxury."

Branigan smiled, liking Barbara Wickenstall. "Do you get home much?"

"Some. It's a seven-hour drive. That frigging Alabama's in the way. But at least I'm off the red-eye."

"I figured it had to be Alabama or Mississippi. So did it turn out to be a good move?"

"Oh, yes. I have to admit that out of all the theaters I've worked in, this is my favorite. I can't put my finger on what it is, but there's something very special here." She smiled, self-conscious at her effusiveness. "Or maybe it just feels like home." She cocked her head at Branigan. "So how about you? Reggie mentioned that he went to high school with you."

"Yes, I grew up just a few blocks from here." Branigan waved in the direction she thought was her parents' house. "I went to the University of Georgia, then spent a decade at *The Rambler* and several years at the *Detroit Free Press*. I never really got used to the weather up North and came back four years ago."

"It wasn't homesickness?" Barbara asked.

"Oh, yes, if I'm honest. I was plenty homesick." Branigan rummaged in her purse for a notebook and pen. "You?"

"Oh, yeah. I'm the oldest of five and all the rest settled right around Hattiesburg. So I knew I was missing fish fries and casino nights and frog-gigging with my nephews. But I've got to admit: Grambling feels a bit like Hattiesburg. That old Deep South. The good *and* the bad."

"I know what you mean," said Branigan, finding a pen at last. "I'm a little surprised we've never met," she continued. "I come to a good many shows here."

"Well, here's the only place you *would* meet me," Barbara said. "I've slept in this office many a night before an opening. My social network consists entirely of our staff and volunteers. And of course your Mr Dubois."

"Sounds rough." Branigan grinned. "Especially dealing with Gerald."

Barbara smiled. "He can be a little... precious. So how can I help you?"

"As we talked about yesterday, we're working on this story about clowns trying to lure kids into the woods. Or not. I wanted to see how you were able to come up with that answer for me so quickly."

Barbara made a few clicks on her laptop, then turned it for Branigan to see. "I've got our clothes listed by decades, then a whole separate section for specialty items. Animal costumes. Angel wings. Easter hats. Things like that.

"When you called, I went to clowns. As you can see, we are supposed to have three pairs of red pants, three yellow, two purple, and two white with red stripes. I checked the stock room and the whites were missing. Then I did the same thing with the shoes, wigs and noses. We're missing two full sets."

"So two of everything," Branigan mused. "How about shirts?"

"I haven't looked at those. Do you know a color?"

"I don't think the witnesses said. Can we work backwards from your list?"

"We should be able to." Barbara stared at the screen for a moment, then hit a key to print. A single page came out of a printer that teetered atop a rickety bookcase beside her desk. She stood. "We should have ten shirts of some sort. Let's go look."

Branigan followed her down the hall, noting how the smaller woman held herself erect and walked silently in ballet flats. They made their way through the vintage racks and into the side room she and Chester had visited yesterday. Barbara went directly to the rod holding the billowy pants and shoe bags. "Shirts should be nearby. Here we go."

She flipped quickly through the shirts in screaming stripes and raucous prints. Consulting her sheet, she eyed the rack, her lips moving. "One that is missing is a hibiscus floral in blue and green and purple," she finally said. "The other is a Hawaiian pineapple print in red and yellow. Truly hideous, as I recall." She flicked past the last shirt to another plastic bag that held suspenders. She unzipped it and rapidly pulled them out, counting as she went. "And we are missing two pairs of suspenders. I have no idea what color. I didn't record that specifically."

"I'm still impressed," said Branigan. "Your records are amazing." She thought for a moment. "Odd that no one mentioned a loud floral or pineapple shirt. Seems they would stand out."

"But paired with red shoes, red nose and orange wig?" Barbara asked. "Those ugly shirts might just fade away."

Branigan laughed. "You may be right." They walked back to Barbara's office, and Branigan gathered her things. "Thanks for taking the time to explain your system to me."

"No problem. It's kind of creeping me out to think that the person you're after was here."

Branigan paused. "Can you think of anyone it might be? Anyone who showed more than a passing interest in your clown workshop or costumes or anything like that?"

Barbara shook her head. "No, and that's what bothers me. You know, we have children in some of our productions. We're all hoping a stranger came in and stole the things; that it wasn't someone in the theater."

"How likely is that – that it was a stranger?"

"Well, it's not *unlikely*. I mean, you can see for yourself how we leave everything open. So anyone could come in."

"I hear a 'but'…"

"*But* they'd run the risk of me or Reggie or our assistant director Sam, or facilities manager Robert, or box office manager Camille seeing them. We talked about it last night after our Shakespeare rehearsal. None of us has seen anyone out of the ordinary."

"But does each of you know every volunteer?"

"Some of us do. Maybe Camille and Robert don't. Hard to say."

Branigan posed the question with which she always ended her interviews. "Is there anything else you can think of that I neglected to ask?"

"Not anything I can answer."

"What do you mean?"

"Well, the question I have is why? If you wanted to abduct a child, why would you dress in the most conspicuous way possible? Doesn't it strike you as bizarre?"

"Clowns in general strike me as bizarre. But to your point, I guess that's why the police think it's a hoax. For us, it's a story either way."

Barbara sighed. "Strange business you're in."

Jimmie Jean's Range Rover was gone by the time Branigan returned to the parking lot, but she found a note on her windshield: *"Cuz, that you? Mark June 9 on your calendar for opening night!!!!!"*

Branigan smiled. She and Mom and Aunt Jeanie and Isabella, and maybe even Dad and Uncle Bobby, would need to buy tickets early. Theater on the Square musicals routinely sold out, especially the war horses. Reggie wouldn't keep bringing rootin'-tootin' Annie Oakley back if she weren't such a draw.

With nothing new to add to the online clown coverage, Branigan decided to swing by Jericho Road before returning to the office. The sliding electric door alerted Dontegan to her entrance, and he stood up at the receptionist's window.

"Miz Branigan! Good to see you! How you been?"

"Good, Dontegan. Any new artwork I should see?"

"Not sure what we done added since you been up in here. You look round and see."

"I will. Is Liam in?"

"Uh huh. I speck in his office or the prayin' room."

Branigan wandered into the cavernous dining hall that served as both Sunday morning worship space and weekday soup kitchen. She spotted a battered coffee urn plugged in near the stage and helped herself to a cup. She then circled the hall, looking at the colorful canvases created in the Jericho Road art room.

She smiled appreciatively at the three-panel Good Samaritan mural that Tiffany Lynn had recently unveiled. With its movement of colors from dull to exuberant across the interaction between Samaritan and injured man, it was a stunningly sophisticated rejoinder to the clumsy mash-up of Old Testament characters on the opposite wall. Branigan knew that Liam kept both in a sly commentary: Tiffany Lynn was a homeless drug addict, while privileged high schoolers had painted the hopelessly inaccurate gathering of Moses, Joshua, Caleb and lions from the book of Daniel.

She stopped before a new landscape of Georgia farmland painted on a piece of aged and jagged wood. The artists of Jericho Road weren't picky about their canvases. They'd paint on the real thing or just as happily on scraps of tin, wood, cork, glass or cardboard.

This particular landscape was oddly beautiful, with a sun setting in clanging orange and red and purple over an otherwise muted hayfield. The colors in the sunset reminded her of the view from her back porch. She wondered if she had room for this piece in her office.

She looked in the right-hand corner and saw the name Jasper. Definitely worth considering, she thought as she headed for Liam's office. As she passed Dontegan, she saw him talking to a dark-skinned woman in a red dress, a small, lighter-skinned boy by her side. The boy looked up at Branigan and smiled, holding out a bag of gummy bears.

"Are you sharing?" she asked, kneeling at his level.

He nodded, offering her the bag. The mother glanced down, decided that Branigan was no threat, and continued her conversation with Dontegan.

Branigan smiled at the boy. "Thank you, but I don't want to take your bears. You might need them later."

He nodded seriously and withdrew his offer.

"What's your name?"

"Andre," he murmured, then moved behind his mother's legs and dug into his candy bag.

Branigan stood. "Bye-bye, Andre," she said, and headed for Liam's office. Before she reached it, she heard a familiar laugh. She stuck her head in the office marked *Social Worker* and saw Isabella seated behind the desk. Liam stood across the room, leaning against the wall with his arms folded.

"Brani G!" he said, coming forward to hug her. "You're here just in time to help your cousin settle in."

"What happened to Allison?"

"She was so glad to see Izzy B she nearly cried. Turns out she had wanted to take her last few days off, but didn't want to leave us without help."

Isabella grinned. "She gave me two hours of orientation and took off, poor thing. I expect she's in a recliner about now, sipping lemonade."

"Well, I'm glad that worked out. I think you've got your first customers, by the way."

"Really?"

"A mother and little boy are talking to Dontegan."

"I'll see what they want."

After Isabella had left, Liam led the way to his office, two doors down. Branigan took her favorite rocking chair, upholstered in green, leaving him the one with navy cushions. The chairs were from the nursery of Charlie and Chan, Liam's college-age children. He'd once told her he wanted to create the same sense of warmth and safety for the people who came to his office.

Jericho Road was a church that operated an eighteen-bed homeless shelter for men, a soup kitchen, and a mini-closet for work clothes. It was located in a former big box grocery store that had sat empty for seven years after a chain vacated it. Under Liam's leadership, it now sported flower gardens and an art program and housed offices for a social worker and mental health counselor. "Every person who comes in needs something different," she'd heard him say in countless speeches around Grambling. "It's not one-size-fits-all." Mostly through trial and error, he'd stumbled upon a constellation of services that offered people a gift they didn't know they were seeking – a way to belong.

"You lucked out on that one," Branigan said, nodding toward Isabella's office.

"I'm telling you, God brings people here at the most opportune times," Liam said, spreading his freckled hands in surrender. "If I didn't believe it when I started, I do now."

"I didn't know you had kids here."

"We don't have many. We see some at weekend meals and during the summer, but they've always seemed to have some kind of housing. But just this weekend, Malachi told me about a family who'd moved into the encampment under the Garner Bridge."

"Oh no. Is it the woman who's out there now?"

"What's she look like?"

"Very dark, pretty woman with a little boy named Andre. Three or four or five years old."

"That's them. She brought an older girl and another boy this weekend. Malachi told me there's a father and teenage brother in the camp too."

"Sheez. That's no place for children."

"I know. I'll see what information Izzy B can get from them, then we'll put our heads together. The problem is, Grambling doesn't have a family shelter. The dad and older boy would have to go one place – even here – and the mom and little kids someplace else. Which is probably why they're living in that camp."

The longtime friends were silent for a moment. Finally, Liam spoke again. "So what's going on in your world?"

"We're on clown watch."

Liam laughed. "I've been following that. Anything to it?"

Branigan shrugged. "Who knows? It seems to crop up across the country sporadically, though from the phone calls we're getting, Grambling may be the epicenter right now. The question is, are that many people dressing up as clowns and going into the woods? Or are that many alleged witnesses making up this urban legend at the same time?"

Liam smiled. "Fascinating."

"Make you wish you were a reporter again?"

"Heck, no. No reason to be back at Clown Central. Speaking of which, how's Tan-4?"

"Blustery. Harley had the clown guild from St Joe's in yesterday and they sent him over the edge."

Liam threw back his head and laughed. "I can picture it now."

"Yeah, five of them honking and whistling and crashing into things. We were afraid they were going to shatter that line of glass walls."

"I'd pay to watch Tan watching that."

Branigan stood. "Well, let me get out of your hair. I'm so glad you and Izzy B are working together. Two of my favorite people."

"Let's cook out one night soon. I'll have Liz call you."

"You got it. Did Isabella tell you that Jimmie Jean is back too?"

"She did. I'm not sure Grambling can handle all these Rickman women at one time."

Branigan passed Isabella's door as she walked out. Andre was sprawled full-length on her rug, coloring, while his mother used the phone on Isabella's desk. Branigan could see the woman's profile, staring straight ahead at the wall, while Isabella looked on, watching quizzically.

CHAPTER ELEVEN

Malachi walked into the Jericho Road parking lot just as Miz Branigan was leaving. He stood silently until she caught sight of him, her face splitting into a wide smile. Yeah, he figured she'd be happy to see him, and he was oddly pleased. They'd been through a lot this winter after Pastor Liam's girl Charlie had the wreck that killed her college friend.

"Malachi!" Branigan cried, reaching out to hug him. "I haven't seen you in weeks."

He ducked his head. "Miz Branigan."

"What you been up to?"

"Not much."

"Coming in for dinner?"

"Yep. Thought I'd see if the flowers need some weeding or watering before supper."

"Well, it's awfully good to see you, my friend."

Malachi dipped his head again to hide a smile, and Miz Branigan walked on to her car.

He headed for Pastor Liam's office to ask what gardening needed doing. But as he passed Miz Allison's office, he saw the boy from the bridge sprawled on the floor. Malachi stopped, then pulled back out of sight. He heard a woman's voice – it wasn't that nice Miz Allison – speaking softly. "Can you tell me what that is?"

The boy answered confidently. "It's a clown."

"Why are you drawing a clown?" came the voice.

Well, that was weird. The voice sounded like Miz Branigan. Only he knew it wasn't her.

"I saw him."

"At a circus?"

"No. At our camp-out."

"Andre, don't be telling the lady your silliness." This was another voice. Probably his mama.

"It's not silliness, Mama. I saw him when Stacy took me to the bafroom."

The Miz Branigan voice came again. "Do you think he's been hearing the news?"

The mama didn't answer immediately. Malachi pictured her shrugging. He leaned in more closely. "We don't have TV. Maybe he heard some of the peoples talking. They's a lot of talking under the bridge."

"No, Mama, I didn't hear nobody. I saw the clown. He had candy."

"Mrs Arneson, I think we need to call the police," said the Miz Branigan sound-alike. "There have been three sightings of clowns trying to lure children into the woods."

"No, Stacy would've said. That's my ten-year-old." A moment's silence.

"Still. What if he really did see someone?"

"No police!" The woman was almost hissing. No one said anything for awhile, then the mama spoke in a calmer voice. "And you know not to take candy from no stranger, right?"

"Yes, Mama."

No one had ever taught Mo that. Malachi guessed that before the Iraqis invaded Kuwait, there *were* no strangers in the boy's life. A week after the sandstorm, Malachi asked a fellow soldier to go with him to the Bedouin village. Khalid was from Washington, DC, where his parents had settled after emigrating from Jordan. Like Malachi, he was a private, but he had the skill of speaking Arabic; he had his eye on the State Department after the war. The two hitched a ride on an Army Jeep.

The old man was out in front of his house. Khalid approached him, speaking rapidly in Arabic. The old man responded in a torrent that sounded pretty much like what he'd hurled at Malachi the week before.

Khalid held up his hands in surrender. "He's speaking some dialect I don't understand," he said to Malachi. "And I don't think he's happy."

"Some of your words gotta be the same," Malachi pleaded. "Ask about the boy."

Khalid slowed down. He repeated the word for *boy* slowly, making hand motions to indicate someone waist high. The old man pointed to the house next door.

"The boy is in that house," Khalid reported, pointing to the concrete and aluminum dwelling where Malachi had first seen him.

"Does he live there by himself?"

Khalid tried again, speaking slowly and using hand motions. The old man calmed down when he realized Khalid could make out what he was saying if he spoke slowly. The two talked haltingly for some minutes, the old man gesturing repeatedly at the house next to his.

Finally Khalid turned to Malachi. "Okay, I think I'm getting this right. The boy's name is Mohamed. Sounds like maybe an IED in the road killed his mother and father. An older brother was taking care of him. Then the brother joined the fight against the Iraqis and left Mohamed with these neighbors. But the boy is afraid his brother will come back and not be able to find him. So he spends almost all day in his old house. This man's wife goes over and brings him here to eat. Some nights she can get him to spend the night with them."

Malachi sat back on his heels. "Poor little guy."

Khalid squatted beside Malachi. "He says the brother is about your age. That's why Mohamed took to you."

"Yeah, he warn't afraid." Malachi waited a moment. "Tell him I'm gonna see Mohamed."

Khalid said something to the man, who stood and nodded for Malachi to follow. Malachi and Khalid walked behind him, the man's knee-length white shirt billowing over baggy white pants and brown sandals. The man walked right into the empty front room without knocking. They passed into the sleeping room and found

Mohamed sitting on the same mat where Malachi had originally found him. The boy stood with a shout and ran to Malachi, hugging his legs. He then pulled away, taking Malachi's hand and looking curiously at Khalid.

The boy and the old man spoke briefly. "Mohamed says he wants you to read to him," Khalid smiled. "You read Arabic, do you?"

Malachi pulled the New Testament from his shirt pocket. "He fine with English."

He allowed the boy to pull him to his mat and both of them sat with their backs pressed against the wall. The old man squatted to watch as Malachi flipped to Luke's story of Jesus sending demons into a herd of pigs. The boy never took his eyes from Malachi's face.

When he had finished, Mohamed pointed to the little New Testament again.

"You want another one?" So Malachi kept reading, about Jesus healing a twelve-year-old girl and a bleeding woman, sending out the twelve disciples, feeding the five thousand.

The old man and Khalid wandered outside, and still Mohamed wanted more. So Malachi read about the transfiguration and about a father who brought his demon-possessed son for Jesus to heal.

But that one had to be the last, for in reading the story of the desperate father seeking healing for his son, Malachi's eyes began to fill, paining him in much the same way the sand had done the week before.

Now he passed the back of his hand over his eyes and knocked on Pastor Liam's door, asking if he needed the church's flowers tended before supper.

That night Malachi had trouble sleeping. He hadn't thought of Mo in awhile, not while awake anyway, but now the face of the small, grinning boy was before him every time he closed his eyes. He thought maybe it was the nearness of young Andre, but really, if he was honest, the nightmares had returned before he ever saw the little boy in Tent City 2. Maybe it was the return of the Southern

78

heat, a reminder of the relentless Arabian sun. Or maybe it was the grit in his food, his coffee, his socks, his sleeping bag. Whatever the reason, his mind was flashing back to Mo, and that wasn't good.

This happened every few years, and when it did, his drinking got worse. Yeah, he'd admit that. He never knew for sure what triggered the memories, the nightmares, or for that matter what made them recede again. He just knew that when they came, he was in for some rough nights, some puking days, some blank spots in his memory.

Tonight he was in and out of sleep, or maybe in and out of blackouts. Hard to tell. He groped around his sleeping bag and hit a pile of empty King Cobras that clattered in the stillness. His hand closed on the neck of a bottle – not one of the forty-ounce malt liquors, but the more squared off Jim Beam he'd bought yesterday. He shook it and felt the welcome weight of liquid sloshing. He grasped it and stumbled through his tent flap, padding over the hard red earth in bare feet. He knew that wasn't a good idea – there could be anything from copperheads to rusty nails to metal rings from pop-top cans. He walked gingerly, in case he needed to snatch his foot back.

He left the shelter of the bridge and walked onto the litter-strewn path outside. A half moon lit discarded mattresses, knee-high weeds, piles of empty beer bottles and orange juice cartons. He unzipped his camo pants and peed for a long time. Sighing, he rezipped and, grasping the quart of Jim, made his way between the tents, where he could hear snoring. He climbed the hill and hopped across the railroad tracks, cringing as his feet hit gravel. He cursed himself for not grabbing his boots before leaving his tent. Oh well, he was almost across now. One more sharp rock to his heel, and he was over the tracks and back onto the cool, packed earth. He sat at the top of the hill and twisted the lid on his bottle. The whiskey slid down his throat, smooth and familiar and welcome.

Tent City 2 was quiet, so it must be very late, maybe even close to dawn. Malachi drank and drifted, drifted and drank. He was on his grandparents' farm one minute, in a tent in Kuwait the next, the

Bedouin village the next. Mo's face appeared before him. Or was it Andre's? He hadn't saved the boy. That was the problem. He was a soldier in the all-powerful US Army and he couldn't save one little Kuwaiti boy. What good was he?

A light flickered in the Arneson tent. Even in his hazy state, Malachi remembered the name he'd heard from Miz Allison's office. Seconds after the light flared, two people stumbled through the flap. The taller figure held a flashlight in one hand, and the hand of his tiny companion in the other. Malachi guessed it was the teenage son and Andre. They headed for the plywood-walled latrine in the back of the camp.

He watched blearily for a moment as the tall figure slumped to the ground in front of the makeshift bathroom and the little figure disappeared inside. Malachi stood to return to his tent, but once on his feet he swayed and staggered. He remembered the punishing gravel he'd have to cross, and sat back down abruptly, then toppled onto his side.

Wouldn't be the first time he'd slept on the hard ground.

Malachi had no idea how much later it was when the screams woke him. The screams of a hysterical, panicked mother who'd realized her child was gone. He kept thinking she'd stop; that the screams couldn't continue at that volume, that intensity, that level of sheer madness. But he was wrong.

It was the early morning of Wednesday, May 3.

CHAPTER TWELVE

Branigan stood beneath the towering Michael Garner Memorial Bridge and shivered, though the sun had been up for two hours, dissipating the morning chill. The homeless encampment was littered and squalid, and for the first time, she was struck by the desperation of those who lived there; she was glad to have Marjorie and Harley with her.

Jody was with the Grambling police over the hill in Tent City 2, and they were allowing no more reporters in. A TV news crew was climbing the hill to shoot footage from above. Here in Malachi's camp, two officers were interviewing residents, but they weren't bothering with reporters, so Branigan, Marjorie and Harley spread out.

Branigan headed straight for Malachi's tent. "Knock, knock," she whispered, since there was nothing to rap on. She waggled his tent flap. "Malachi! Are you in there?"

She saw a dark hand unzip the tent, ground to waist height, and then flip a canvas flap until it rested on the tent's roof. An overpowering smell of liquor hit her. Branigan stopped, embarrassed. She'd guessed that Malachi had a drinking problem or he wouldn't be living out here. But she'd never faced it up close. Now his clothes and tent and very body reeked of alcohol, and when he stood to face her, his eyes were bloodshot.

"Are you all right?" she asked, gently touching his arm.

He nodded, embarrassed too. "Headed to Jericho Road," he mumbled. "Shower and coffee."

"You've heard?" she asked. "The youngest boy in that family has disappeared."

81

Malachi nodded. "Yeah. Hard to miss with his mama yelling like that."

Branigan raised her eyebrows, but Malachi lowered his head and walked away. Her eyes followed him and she saw him pause for a moment at the river birch that guarded the camp's entrance, one arm reaching out as if for support.

She turned to find a man with a thinning gray ponytail balance a grill on uneven rocks over an open fire. He carefully added a dented coffee pot, and to Branigan's surprise, it stayed upright.

"Aren't you Slick?" she asked, remembering Malachi's neighbor from previous visits. "May I talk to you?"

He shrugged.

"Did you see or hear anything last night?"

"Nah, I was asleep until I heard that lady start yelling. Come up outta my sleeping bag so fast I fell into the tent wall." He laughed.

"Had you met the family? The Arnesons?"

"Yeah. But I didn't like it a bit they was here."

"Because?"

"Because this ain't no place for kids. Anybody tell you that."

Branigan looked at him thoughtfully, waited to see if he'd say anything else.

He leaned over to stir the fire. "Any man bring a kid out here ain't got no business having kids."

When he said nothing more, she thanked him and looked around for Marjorie and Harley. Marjorie was speaking to a woman with greasy brown hair piled atop her head. Harley was surrounded by three young men close to his age, all of them smoking and gesturing animatedly.

From what Malachi had told her, Tent City 2 tended to attract the young residents. She wondered if they had already spoken to the police, or if they'd sneaked away. If they had outstanding warrants, they'd be avoiding law officers.

She drew closer to Harley, knowing he'd have trouble taking notes from all three as they talked over each other. He flashed a grateful smile. "Branigan, this is Randy, Butch and, um, Wild Man. Guys, this is my colleague, Branigan."

She pretended to ignore Randy and Butch's ogling, focusing instead on Wild Man, who was in constant motion. Besides a jerkiness in his muscles, there was something wrong around the eyes.

"Gentlemen," she said. She looked at Harley, silently inviting him to continue his interview.

"Go on, Randy," he said. "You were telling me about Shack."

The young man had a pierced eyebrow, a stud through his upper lip and a tattooed snake winding around his neck. He wore a Florida Marlins baseball cap over his shaved head. "Yeah," he said, looking at Branigan. "Butch and me share a tent. Wild Man's on one side of us and Shack on the other. But sometimes Shack sleeps outside, on a piece of carpet."

He paused and looked at his blond tent mate. "Butch and me didn't hear nothing, least not till the boy's mama started crying. But Shack, he saw what happened. The police took him down for questioning."

"And what did happen?"

Randy and Butch looked at her. "A clown got him. A clown got that kid."

Branigan heard a sharp intake of breath, and the one they called Wild Man began gesticulating uncontrollably. He stepped closer, too close, invading her personal space. She took a step backward and he followed.

"A clown!" he said excitedly. "Shack saw the clown."

"What is your name?" Branigan asked. "I know they call you Wild Man, but what's your real name?"

When he didn't answer, she asked, "What does your mother call you?"

Wild Man's face relaxed slightly, though it was still uncomfortably near Branigan's and his spittle sprayed her when he spoke.

"Edward!" he said loudly. "She calls me Edward." He shuffled his feet and rolled his shoulders. He seemed incapable of standing still.

"Edward what?"

"Edward Richard Oliver." He was fairly shouting.

"Okay, Edward. Did you see anything last night?" Branigan asked quietly.

He nodded vigorously. "Shack saw the clown. He told me he saw the clown."

"We'll talk to Shack," she said. "But you? What did you see?"

Wild Man dropped his voice, looked over his shoulder. "I saw Andre. Andre's a nice kid."

"When did you see Andre?"

Harley and Randy and Butch leaned in to listen.

Wild Man's speech was rapid fire. "In the middle of the night. I got up and Shack was outside his tent drinking beer. So we started talking about this job he's trying to get over at the park like Slick. I might want to build the stage too, like Shack and..."

Butch interrupted. "You didn't say you were awake too." Harley signaled him to be quiet. Wild Man was focused on Branigan's face, barely six inches from his own. She forced herself to remain in place.

"So you and Shack were talking during the night?"

"Yeah. And Andre came out of his tent with his biggest brother. Jaquan." Wild Man was nodding excitedly. "Jaquan took him to the bathroom and sat down out front. I think he fell asleep. Andre was in there a long time. And then next thing we know, Andre's mama, she's hollering and yelling."

Branigan glanced at Harley. "Edward, there are some things missing. First of all, did you see Jaquan get up?"

Wild Man gazed over Branigan's shoulder. "No-oo-oo," he said slowly. "That was later. When his mama ran out."

"Who told the mother? Why did she start yelling?"

"I don't know."

Branigan decided to back up. "Did the mother go to the bathroom?"

Wild Man's face brightened. "Yes! That's when she started yelling."

"Okay. So did you see her come out of her tent?"

"Yeah. She come out of her tent and ran to the bathroom. And she yelled 'Jaquan!' But she didn't stop. She ran straight in the bathroom." He looked at Branigan, waiting for her approval.

"Very good, Edward. How long did she stay in the bathroom?"

"She didn't stay. She started hollering in there and ran out and never stopped hollering. 'Andre! Andre! Andre!' That woke everybody up. Then she yelled, 'He's gone! Andre's gone!'" Wild Man beamed at Branigan, scuffling his feet.

She nodded to keep him talking. "And the father? Where was he?"

"He was tearing round the camp, looking in everybody's tent. I don't know if he said anything or not, because the mama was making so much noise."

"And Jaquan? When did you see Jaquan again?"

Wild Man looked helplessly at Butch and Randy. "Did you see Jaquan?" he asked them.

Butch shook his head and Randy shrugged. "Not till the police took him."

Branigan and Harley and Marjorie stepped away from the bridge's shelter to compare notes. A few minutes later Jody joined them.

"The police took the entire family to the Law Enforcement Center," Jody reported, jerking a thumb at Tent City 2. "They're posting an officer over there in case the boy comes back."

"They don't believe a clown snatched him?" Marjorie asked in disbelief.

"No, they do. I guess I should've said 'in case someone brings him back'. They really don't know what happened and are trying to cover all their bases. What'd you guys get?"

Harley spoke up. "We got comments from the three guys who live in the tents nearest the family. And Branigan got some good details from Wild Man."

"How dependable is he?" Jody asked.

Branigan looked at Marjorie, who had written most of the background stories on people in the camps the preceding year. "Do you know him?"

Marjorie nodded. "Schizophrenic. Sweet guy when he's on his meds. But I have seen him off them and he talks non-stop right in your face and you can't understand a word. Pastor Liam or Allison from Jericho Road hustles him down to the mental health clinic to get a shot."

"We could understand him fine," Branigan said. "Odd and jerky but coherent. He said the older brother, Jaquan, took Andre to the bathroom in the middle of the night. Apparently he fell asleep while the boy was in there. Then it sounds like the mom woke up and found that Andre wasn't in the tent, so she went to the bathroom looking for him. She had to wake Jaquan up. When she didn't find Andre, she started screaming."

"Did this Wild Man see a clown?" asked Jody.

"No, he says someone named Shack did. So where was this Shack, anyway, when he saw him?"

Jody flipped his notebook closed. "Don't know. The police whisked him out of here. I'm headed to the Law Enforcement Center now."

"Send Bert what you have and we'll fill in," ordered Marjorie. "I'm sure he'll want to meet with all of us after we post online."

Branigan placed a hand on Jody's sleeve and waited for Marjorie and Harley to walk ahead. "Are the police thinking pedophile?" she asked quietly.

"What else? You couldn't get a ransom out of that family."

Branigan remembered the child shyly offering her his gummy bears and hiding behind his mother's legs. She remembered the faces of those clowns, so eerily weird, in the videos from across the country. She felt sick as she followed Jody from the camp.

CHAPTER THIRTEEN

As soon as Bert had finished editing the kidnapping story for the paper's website, Tan called him and the reporters into the conference room. The clown painting, subject of jokes two days earlier, was turned to face the wall.

The publisher appeared shaken. "I have to admit," he started off, "I favored the hoax theory in the beginning." He ran a hand through his thick hair. "I mean, with all those similar sightings across the country, it sounded hokey. But now... that little boy..." He didn't finish his thought, looked around. "Where's Branigan?"

"Finishing up a phone call," Harley said. "She'll be right in."

"Jody," Bert opened. "What are the police saying?"

"Same thing as Tan. Clown sightings may or may not be real in other places, but here a clown really was trying to take a kid. And did. The strange part of this, of course, is that the family's homeless, so there's no likelihood of ransom."

Branigan walked in.

"Anything?" Bert asked her.

"Yeah. Andre and his mother were at Jericho Road with my cousin Isabella yesterday. She's filling in for Liam's social worker this summer. She said Andre drew a picture of a clown and said he'd seen him when his sister took him to the camp bathroom."

Jody scraped his chair back. "When?"

"Isabella saw the boy yesterday afternoon. She's not sure when he saw the clown though. She wanted to call the police on the spot, but the mother resisted. Isabella feels bad she didn't insist and is calling Detective Scovoy now."

Bert spoke up. "Branigan, update the online story with what you've got. And see if you can get that drawing the kid made. Jody, stay with the police. Marjorie, can you give us a better description of that bathroom in the camp? And take a photographer over there. None of our previous shots showed it."

Marjorie nodded. "It's basically a bench over a hole in the ground with plywood walls around it."

"But is there a window? Is there room for more than one person? Did the boy see a clown inside with him, or in the distance, or what? Just get more specifics."

"Will do."

"Anything else?" Bert asked.

"One thing," said Tan. "After Channel 5 ran their story this morning, viewers started bringing money and food to the station. We've had three pledges since our story went online, all for the family. This may become a sidebar."

Bert nodded. "Okay, everybody move."

The *Rambler* staff had seen outpourings of sympathy every time they had written about the encampments under the Garner Bridge. In the past, Grambling citizens had sent in truckloads of clothing and food and toiletries. Malachi told Branigan that maybe a quarter of the items were used; the rest mildewed, rotted or were traded for drugs.

But this time, the city's compassion had a more localized target – the Arneson family. Money poured into the local TV station, the *Rambler* office, Jericho Road and even some local churches, earmarked for the family.

Tan Grambling called Liam Delaney and asked him to oversee the account. "We can't cover the story and hand out money," Tan growled. The TV station and local pastors were grateful to follow suit, knowing that Liam dealt with these issues daily. Liam reluctantly agreed.

Late Wednesday afternoon, he met with the Arnesons. Isabella took Jaquan and the two younger children to the church kitchen for a snack, while the parents sat in Liam's office. Oren Arneson perched in the navy rocker, his eyes angrily roaming Liam's office. Flora sat in the green chair, staring straight ahead, disengaged. Liam wondered if she'd taken something for her nerves.

He started gently. "People are very concerned about Andre – and about you. They have sent contributions to move you out of Tent City. There's enough money to pay a security deposit and a few months' rent."

"How much money?" demanded Oren.

Liam hesitated. "A little over four thousand dollars."

"Can we just take it?"

Liam made a quick decision and unapologetically lied. "No, the money was given specifically for housing while the search is going on for Andre. I've been instructed to pay it directly to a landlord."

Oren glared at him for a moment, and Liam met his gaze.

"We may not want to stay in Grambling after all this," the father said.

"But you'll want to stay until Andre is found."

"Oh, sure."

The silence stretched between them. "Would you rather the money be used for a couple of motel rooms until you reach a decision?" Liam asked.

For the first time, Oren smiled. "Yeah, that'd be good," he said.

"Okay," said Liam, standing. "You choose a motel and I'll send a staff member over with a week's rent. After a week, you can let me know where to go from there. Sound good?"

Flora's eyes flicked to the pastor, and she spoke for the first time. "That's very kind of you," she said softly. "Thank you."

"I can't take the credit," he said. "It's from the people who read about you or saw you on TV. They want to find Andre and to ease you of some worry."

Oren stood abruptly and took the notepaper on which Liam had scrawled his phone number. He looked almost happy. "We 'preciate it, Padre. Come on, Flora. Let's get the kids and find us a place."

After they had left, Liam stood for a long time at his office door, hoping the situation would turn out well but aware of a creeping fear that it wouldn't.

Branigan and Isabella and Jimmie Jean met for dinner at the Nicholas Inn, a plan they'd made earlier in the week because Jimmie Jean wanted to see the renovation of the grand old hotel. Branigan doubted Isabella was in the mood to follow through, but she didn't cancel.

Instead, Isabella hugged her sister and cousin and slid into a chair with a sigh. While it was still light outside, the inn's dining room was intentionally dim, with rich woods and glittery chandeliers; a single silver candle sat on each damask-topped table. Jimmie Jean ordered a good cabernet sauvignon, and the sommelier uncorked the bottle with a flourish.

Branigan waited until they were alone to address Isabella. "Thanks so much for the tip on Andre's clown drawing," she said softly. "I know it wasn't easy to tell us, but you never know what can be helpful for the public to know in a case like this."

Isabella swallowed, looking close to tears. "Your Detective Scovoy couldn't have been nicer. He said even if I'd called earlier and they'd interviewed the boy, he doubts anything would have turned out differently."

"Sure," said Jimmie Jean. "I mean, they'd had sightings at the apartments and the school, Izzy B. It wasn't like this came out of the blue."

A waiter solicitously took their orders – a salad for Jimmie Jean, who claimed the theater's Annie Oakley costume had to be let out, grilled salmon for Isabella, vegetable stir-fry for Branigan. When he left, Isabella let out another shaky sigh.

"So how are you doing?" Branigan asked.

"All right. It was just a hard way to start a new job, you know? Knowing what falls under a client's privacy and what to report is the hardest part of this job anyway. I didn't feel comfortable reporting something ten minutes after I'd met Mrs Arneson. That would've been a good way to never see her again."

"All you can do is use your best judgment."

"That's exactly what Liam said."

"So where are the Arnesons now?"

"In the Heart of Grambling, that motel off North Main."

"Really? That's like ninety dollars a night, isn't it?"

"Eighty a night, and they got two rooms."

"That's not a place homeless people usually go," said Branigan.

"What do you mean?" asked Jimmie Jean.

"Well, there are motels that cater to people right on the edge, who pay by the day or week. But they're usually thirty-nine to fifty-nine dollars a night, or two hundred for a week."

"That's eight hundred dollars a month," said Jimmie Jean. "Surely they could get an apartment for that."

"They could if they could get ahead enough to pay a security deposit and the first month's rent, plus deposits for water and power. But very few can do that."

Isabella nodded in agreement. "So they pay those high costs, dribbling it out a day or a week at a time. In Atlanta we say, 'It's very expensive to be poor.' The poor pay all kinds of costs we wouldn't think of paying."

Jimmie Jean stopped with her wine glass halfway to her lips. "Like what?"

"Like paying to cash checks at a convenience store," said Isabella.

"Or getting a pay day loan at three hundred percent rather than a bank loan for six percent," added Branigan.

"Buying marked-up groceries at a convenience store."

"Paying top dollar for a roach-infested apartment near downtown because they don't have transportation for a cheaper apartment in the suburbs."

Jimmie Jean held up her hands. "Sheesh, I get it."

Branigan turned back to Isabella. "So Liam was okay with the Heart of Grambling?"

"I wouldn't go that far. He was uncomfortable paying for a motel, period. Apparently Jericho Road never does that. He got stuck with handling all the money coming in from the public, and it had to go to the Arnesons. And the Arnesons understandably aren't ready to pull the trigger on an apartment. The motel is a temporary compromise."

"Did you take them?"

Isabella nodded unhappily. "Liam and I helped get their clothes from under the bridge. The father and Jaquan took one room, the mother, Flora and the two younger children, the other. After Liam left, I spent a few minutes showing the kids the swimming pool. As I was leaving, I saw Oren – that's the father – coming out of the convenience store across the street with a case of beer." She shrugged. "I know I'm not their probation officer, but still…"

"Yeah. I wonder how the good citizens of Grambling would feel to know they're financing Mr Arneson's drinking." Branigan took a sip of water. "Did Liam leave money for food?"

"He bought gift certificates for two fast-food places nearby, and arranged unlimited meals at the motel restaurant." Isabella shrugged. "We'll see."

"Wait a minute," said Jimmie Jean. "Liam didn't give him any cash, right? So how's he buying beer?"

Branigan held up her hands. "He could have a disability check or work day labor or panhandle. The point is these donors are providing everything else, so he's free to use his money for beer."

The women ceased talking long enough to allow the waiter to place their salads before them. They ate for a moment in silence, the Rickman sisters indicating their pleasure with the historic hotel's renovation. Jimmie Jean put down her fork and raised her wine glass. "To finding the kid," she said. "Now let's talk about something else."

"Like you?" teased her sister.

"That'd be good."

"Fair enough," said Branigan. "How are rehearsals going?"

"Smashingly. I came in early today to work on my solos with Reggie. He's really talented. Very good eye and ear. Good suggestions on blocking."

"How's the rest of the cast?" asked Isabella. "Who's your love interest? Buffalo Bill?"

"No," Jimmie Jean laughed. "Buffalo Bill is the old codger who heads the Wild West Show. Annie's love interest is a fellow sharpshooter named Frank Butler."

"Who's playing him?" asked Branigan. "Is Sir Reggie himself stepping in? He does that sometimes."

"No, this is a newcomer from Atlanta who showed up and auditioned. Reggie was blown away." She smiled coyly. "Nearly as blown away as he was by yours truly."

Isabella rolled her eyes. "JJ, your talent is surpassed only by your modesty."

"So we don't know him then?" Branigan asked.

"I wouldn't think so. He's a public school drama teacher off for the summer. Colin Buckner."

Isabella dropped her fork onto her plate with a clatter, and it bounced to the floor. The waiter hurried over to replace it. Isabella was staring at her sister, so Branigan took the utensil. Even in the candlelight, she could see that her cousin's face had paled.

"Izzy B, what's the matter?" Branigan whispered.

"Colin Buckner," she said. "That's my stalker."

CHAPTER FOURTEEN

Wednesday night supper at Jericho Road consisted of beef stew, salad, rolls and iced tea. Sixty homeless people mixed with the servers from Covenant United Methodist Church, eating together and talking at the round tables. Not all the church volunteers ate with the Jericho Road folks, but Pastor Liam encouraged it. You had to hand it to the Methodists – they were trying.

Malachi asked for an extra roll. It had taken most of the day to get over his queasiness, and the bread, he knew from long experience, would help. Other homeless people spoke to him, nodding their heads, some even touching the peaks of their baseball caps as he passed their tables with his plate. "Mr Malachi," they said, as if he were deserving of some special respect. He knew it was because of the gossip about his military service. Rumors ran wild on the streets and Malachi had heard them all. He had been a paratrooper. A tank gunner. A sniper. A helicopter pilot. The attention made Malachi feel worse. The last thing he deserved was their respect.

He remembered Miz Branigan's face this morning, when she came to his tent. He saw her all but invisible recoil at the way he'd looked, the way he'd smelled. For the first time since he'd known her, he'd seen her shock. And he was ashamed.

He had a choice. He could finish this supper and go back to his tent, sit with Slick and whoever else was around, and finish off one or two or five giant malt liquors as he'd done every night for the past few weeks. Add a pint of Jack Daniel's for dessert. Or he could stop. Right now. He could stop and concentrate on Mo. No, no, not Mo. Andre. He could concentrate on Andre.

That Detective Scovoy he'd helped before was working the case. And Miz Branigan was working it for the newspaper. The three of them had broken two cases – one involving the murders of homeless people last summer, the other involving the murders of college girls around Christmas. He'd helped them find the truth. Yeah, he'd helped them a lot.

That's why Miz Branigan had been looking for him this morning, to help with Andre's kidnapping. After all, it'd happened right under his nose. But her face showed her shock when she saw him. He'd thrown up as soon as he got past the river birch. He hoped she hadn't seen *that*.

So yeah, he had a choice to make. Go back to the comfort of malt liquor and whiskey. Or pull himself out of this mess and think. Think about why a clown would snatch a boy from a homeless camp.

CHAPTER FIFTEEN

A silence descended on the table at the Nicholas Inn. Branigan glanced around to make sure no one at the other tables had heard Isabella.

Jimmie Jean was the first to find her voice. "Isabella, honey, what do you mean by 'my stalker'?"

When Isabella didn't answer, Jimmie Jean turned to Branigan. "You know what she's talking about, don't you?"

"It's her news to tell."

Jimmie Jean leaned across the table. "Izzy B?"

Isabella pushed her salad to one side. "I didn't want to worry Mom and Dad with all they've got on them. So please don't tell them."

Jimmie Jean nodded.

Isabella poured out the story of the middle school teacher who had sent her letters and flowers, left a dead mouse, slashed her tires, and, she was pretty sure, entered her condominium. "My principal was concerned enough that she sent me home three weeks early. That's why I'm here."

"But he never signed a letter and you never saw him do those things, right?" Jimmie Jean asked.

"Right."

"Could it have been someone else?"

Isabella looked dubious. "Pretty coincidental if it was."

Jimmie Jean leaned back in her chair. "But Colin seems so... so normal. I mean, he's good looking and talented and obviously experienced in musical theater. I can't imagine him having to *stalk* someone to get a date."

"Think what you like," Isabella snapped. "I'm telling you what happened. And when his principal confronted him, he didn't deny it."

"How do you know that?"

"Dr Esperinza told me. She's my principal."

Jimmie Jean shook her head as if to clear it. "Do you want me to confront him?"

"No! I don't know." She turned pleading eyes to Branigan. "What do you think?"

"I think you need to tell your Atlanta cops and Chester. Even put them in touch with each other. If this guy followed you to Grambling, that's escalation."

Isabella shuddered. "I was feeling so safe to be at home. Just to think he's here makes me sick."

"Well, I can't imagine a safer place than Uncle Bobby's house," Branigan said. "But Izzy B, you need to tell your dad. Don't let him and Aunt Jeanie be caught by surprise."

"She's right," said Jimmie Jean. "I understand you not wanting to worry Mom, but they need to know to keep the burglar alarm activated, put Dad's shotgun in his bedroom, things like that."

For the first time, Isabella smiled. "Dad's shotgun? You might want to mention that during rehearsal some night."

Jimmie Jean smiled grimly. "You can count on it."

The women's conversation was desultory as they ate their entrees, the pall of Andre's kidnapping and Isabella's stalker weighing upon them. They turned down dessert and sat quietly as they finished the wine, each caught up in her own thoughts.

"Well," said Branigan finally, "let's work out a plan of action on Andre Arneson. Izzy B, you're at Ground Zero on all this. What do you and Liam have planned?"

"Obviously, it's a police case. They've asked if they can work with the family from Jericho Road rather than the motel, so Liam gave them an office. Having the Arnesons there will allow me to work with them on housing, if that's what they decide to do. And I guess eventually jobs, but that's not going to happen until Andre is found."

Jimmie Jean put her glass down. "So you think he'll be found?"

"I sure hope so."

Jimmie Jean didn't say anything for a moment.

Isabella tilted her head. "Why? You don't?"

"It's just that…" She glanced at Branigan. "I mean, he's homeless, right? So there's no chance of ransom. What else would you kidnap a child for?"

Isabella put her head in her hands. "Believe me, we've thought of that. But let's not go there yet."

"Yeah, the police do have witnesses," added Branigan. "And a pretty massive manhunt is underway. It's way too early to assume he's dead. Or sold. Or whatever."

"Okay," said Jimmie Jean. "And the other? Izzy B's stalker? The more I think about it, the more I think I should say something right away. Let Colin know we're on to him. Though the fact that he's using his real name says that's what he intended."

Branigan turned to Isabella. "I think she's right, Izzy B. Let him know that we and the police are watching him."

Isabella shrugged. "All right. And I'll report it to the Atlanta and Grambling police first thing in the morning." She looked at her sister. "So much for a quiet summer while we take care of Mom."

The next morning, Branigan drove to Jericho Road. Lily of the Valley Baptist Church was taking a turn serving breakfast, with its customary pancakes, sausage and bacon. Branigan grabbed a cup of coffee from the urn and turned down a plate. She scanned the room, filled with men and women, some laughing and talking, some with their heads hung morosely over their plates. Most seats had backpacks hanging off them, or duffle bags stuffed under the tables.

Volunteers from Lily of the Valley passed among the tables with coffee refills and baskets of biscuits. She didn't expect to see Liam or Isabella, and didn't; the staff rarely came in early enough for breakfast, letting the serving church handle the meal.

She located Malachi sitting alone at the table farthest from the door. She slid into a chair near him, leaving an open seat between them. After yesterday's run-in, she wasn't sure what his reaction would be.

"Good morning," she said.

"Mornin'." He picked up his coffee and Branigan saw that his hand shook.

"You feeling better?"

He grunted in a way that could have meant yes or no.

Branigan could tell he'd showered and changed into clean clothes, but the scent of alcohol still emanated from his pores. "I wanted to ask you to point out Shack to me. Apparently, he saw the clown who took Andre."

Malachi twisted in his seat. "Table by the wall," he murmured. "Red cap and black T-shirt."

She looked and saw a tanned face, clean shaven and handsome, maybe late twenties. Thick brown hair curled underneath the baseball cap. He was the kind of person she'd overheard visitors ask Liam about – *He could be on the cover of* GQ. *What's he doing here?*

Liam always shrugged, and responded, "There's a reason, even if we can't see it."

Shack laughed suddenly at something one of his tablemates said, and Branigan noted his even white teeth. If he had a drug habit, it wasn't crystal meth.

"He's popular," she commented.

"Ever'body want to know what happen," Malachi said.

"Why's he called Shack?"

"'Cause people dumb asses."

Branigan looked up in surprise. She was unaccustomed to this side of Malachi and wondered if he was experiencing alcohol withdrawal. She watched as he emptied four sugar packets into his coffee; she had her answer. She remained silent until he looked at her again.

He finally spoke. "His nickname was Shakes, not Shack," he said. "As in Shakes-peare. When he first come to Grambling, he work at that summer Shakespeare over in the park and be quoting all the time. So folks called him Shakes. But after while, people moved on, and new people thought he was saying Shacks, then Shack. He just let it go."

It was a long speech for Malachi, and Branigan laughed appreciatively. "Weird story. I figured he lived in a shack in the woods."

Malachi shrugged. For the first time, Branigan caught the hint of a smile. "Yeah, he did for awhile. Then a storm got it and he came up under the bridge."

Branigan changed tack. "Have you talked to him about what he saw night before last?"

"Nah, I ain't. But I'm 'bout ready to start." He seemed embarrassed, and looked at a point over her shoulder. "I ain't had a drink in twenty-four hours."

"Good for you, my friend." She hesitated a moment, then plunged ahead. "Are you okay? I've never seen you like you were yesterday."

He kept his eyes on his coffee. "I usu'ly control it a little better."

"Has something happened?" she pressed. "Something to upset you?"

Malachi raised his gaze to meet hers. "Nothing I can't handle," he said in a way that told her the subject was closed.

"Well," she said, "I'm going to see if I can catch Shack after breakfast. Want to sit in?"

Malachi thought for a moment. "Nah, don't want him thinking I'm hanging round reporters. You go on, and I'll catch him back at camp."

Branigan nodded, and swiveled around to watch Shack as he held his friends enthralled, no doubt with the story of a clown lurking outside Tent City.

She waited at her table alone, sipping coffee, until she saw Shack and his friends stand. She walked quickly to their table and introduced herself as a *Rambler* reporter, requesting a few minutes of Shack's time.

"Well, sure," he said, smirking for his friends' benefit. "I've always got time for a pretty lady."

Branigan smiled woodenly, and motioned for him to join her at the table Malachi had vacated. "I know you've spoken to the police," she began, as he settled his backpack on the seat between them. "And it looks like a lot of your friends have been asking as well, so I apologize for making you repeat yourself. But can you start at the beginning and tell me what happened on the night of the kidnapping?"

"Sure thing," he said, seeming to relish his time in the spotlight. "Where do you want me to start?"

"Your real name."

"You can call me Shack. Everyone does."

"Sorry, but that's not good enough for the paper. I need your real name."

"Bradley Drucker. Brad." He smiled ruefully. "It sounds funny to say it. I've been Shakes or Shack for so long."

"And where are you from, Brad?"

"South Florida, originally. Orlando awhile. Valdosta. Macon."

"You've been making your way steadily north."

"Well, if you can call anywhere in Georgia 'north'." He smiled, and Branigan was struck again by his straight white teeth. It looked as though there had been braces in his past.

"So tell me about the night of the kidnapping. I'll interrupt if I have questions."

"We'd been sitting around the fire, drinking a little. Me, Wild Man, Randy and Butch. Slick from the other side of the tracks. And that new guy and his son who moved in."

"The Arnesons."

"Right. The fire burned down, and everybody went back to their tents. I went to mine, but it was hot in there, so I pulled my sleeping bag outside. Then I was wide awake again, so I got a beer and sat outside drinking it."

Branigan nodded encouragingly.

"Wild Man came out after a little while and sat with me. We

talked and drank some more. Then we saw Jaquan – that's the oldest boy – come out of his tent with his little brother. Andre."

"What time of night was this?"

"No idea. 2 a.m.? 3? I just know it was way late."

"Okay. Go on."

"Jaquan took Andre to the latrine. We built it out of plywood when some women was living on our side of Tent City a year or so ago. It looked like Jaquan sat down outside the latrine and sent Andre in with the flashlight, but it was so dark, it was hard to see exactly. I never saw them come back, and then I think I dozed off, and then I had to pee. I figured surely that kid was finished by then, but I found Jaquan sitting up, asleep, outside the latrine."

He looked away from Branigan and seemed to be concentrating on his hands, folded on the table. "Before I went inside, I heard something, kind of a rustling, in the woods. Then I heard Andre talking, and I saw those big old white clown pants everybody's been talking about. At least, that's what I *thought* I saw. But I'd been drinking a lot. I wasn't too sure about what I was seeing."

He raised his eyes and looked at Branigan. "I was about to turn around and start yelling, but then I got dizzy, and then I got sick, down-on-my-hands-and-knees sick. After I threw up, I wasn't sure if I'd heard Andre in the latrine or in the woods. So I ran in the latrine to look. It was empty. I came back out and ran in the woods, but wasn't nobody there and I didn't have a light or nothing. I was still deciding what to do when the boy's mama come running outta her tent. Before I know what's happening, she starts screaming and wakes everybody up. Then the dad's tearing around, about to rip our tents down. I was basically trying to stay outta their way."

Branigan looked at Shack incredulously. "Let's back up a minute. You saw the clown and Andre in the woods and you didn't go after them? You didn't call out to Andre?"

Shack looked sheepish. "I know it sounds bad," he said. "But like I said, I was sorta seeing double and not at all sure *what* I was seeing. And then I got sick."

Branigan knew from Jody that someone had indeed been sick outside the latrine. But not to raise an alarm at seeing the boy being led into the woods?

Shack met her gaze for a moment, then looked down at his hands again. He picked up a basket of biscuits left over from breakfast and twirled it around.

Branigan gave him some more time, but he didn't say anything else. So she changed gear. "Well, as you may have read in this morning's paper, little Andre told a social worker at Jericho Road that he'd seen a clown in the camp sometime before his kidnapping. Did you ever see a clown around there before Tuesday night?"

Shack shook his head. "No, but I work most of the time."

"Doing what?"

"Day labor, mostly. I get sent out most days on construction sites. I can do anything – roofing, carpentry, electrical, painting."

Branigan hesitated a moment, wondering why he was homeless if he was so proficient. "Do you mind if I ask why you're living in Tent City?"

"I got a felony. Won't nobody hire me permanent."

"Drug charge?"

"CDV," he said. Branigan raised her eyebrows, knowing this meant criminal domestic violence. He added hastily, "My ex-wife tried to tell the judge she'd lied, but he didn't believe her. I did eighteen months and haven't had a permanent job since."

"I heard you got your nickname working at Shakespeare in the Park."

Shack grinned and grabbed a biscuit. Holding it aloft in his open palm, he affected a booming baritone. "'Alas, poor Yorick! I knew him, Horatio: a fellow of infinite jest, of most excellent fancy: he hath borne me on his back a thousand times; and now, how abhorred my imagination is!'"

Branigan grinned despite her misgivings about him. "Bravo, Hamlet. So did you build the stage, or what?"

"Built the stage, the sets, you name it," he said. "I'm building the stage this week, in fact. Soon's we're finished here. I watched lots of rehearsals along the way."

Branigan's mind flashed to her freshman year in college, when her dorm mates on Hall 2B had argued over whether to allow men in their rooms or make the hall off limits. She had offered the slogan: *2B chased or 2B chaste, that is the question.* The fledgling English majors found it hilarious, the others not so much.

Shack was watching her, thinking her private smile was related to his performance. He flipped the biscuit back into the basket and grinned.

"Have you thought of auditioning for a play?" she asked, imagining the story possibilities of a homeless man taking part in a Theater on the Square production. Reggie could get a lot of mileage out of the publicity.

"I thought about it," Shack said. "But from what I've seen, that director is a piece of work. I'm not sure I could work with him for five weeks, or however long it took."

"Still, it might be worth it. Those shows get a lot of attention. Maybe it could lead to a job."

"Yeah, maybe. But the actors volunteer. I get paid to build the stage, and sometimes the sets if they can't get nobody else."

Shack turned and glanced toward the Jericho Road door. Branigan could see that he was ready to leave. She wanted to ask him something else, something about Shakespeare maybe, or *Hamlet*, but the question danced maddeningly outside her grasp. So instead she asked, "Is there anything else you can think of that I neglected to ask about the clown or the kidnapping?"

He turned back toward her. "No, but I may think of something. I'll get back to you if I do." He hoisted his backpack onto his shoulders, not noticing Branigan's puzzled expression.

That was a strange answer, she thought. *Does he know something else or doesn't he?*

Branigan figured Isabella and Liam would be in by now, so she walked down the hall and knocked on Isabella's open door.

"Any news about Andre?" her cousin greeted her.

"No, sorry," Branigan said. "I was just talking to the guy who saw the clown that night."

"What'd he say?"

"Well, it was odd. He says he saw the clown and heard Andre in the woods, but he didn't go after them because he was drunk and not sure what he was seeing. Then he got sick, and then he ran into the latrine. By the time he did go into the woods, the clown and Andre were gone. I mean, I know he was drinking, but still..."

"Do you think he was lying?"

Branigan shrugged. "Hard to say. Where does impairment end and lying begin?"

"Ah, that is the question."

Branigan cocked her head. There was that tantalizing thought again – a question or a memory lying just outside her reach. "What did you say?"

"That is the question."

"Oh, right. That reminds me: this guy quoted Shakespeare rather impressively. And he was good looking."

"So you're wondering why he's on the street?"

"Well, yeah. And he claims to have all kinds of construction skills."

"Sounds like a question for Liam."

"Is he in yet?"

"No, he had an early meeting with some colleagues from other agencies. But he told me to ask if you and Chester can come to his house to cook out tomorrow night. Along with me and Jimmie Jean."

"Absolutely for me, and I'll check with Chester. We were planning to get together Friday night. I've got my fingers crossed this kidnapping hasn't changed things."

"I sure hope the police solve this soon," Isabella said. "I can't stop thinking about how scared the little guy must be."

Branigan was silent.

"What?" asked Isabella.

"I just remembered something Shack – that's the guy who saw the clown – said. He said he heard Andre talking to the clown. Not screaming or fighting, or anything like that. His word was 'talking'."

"Isn't that the whole point of the clown? So the victim's *not* afraid? At least, not in the beginning?"

"Maybe," said Branigan, still unsettled by a niggling thought she couldn't identify. She knew from experience that she wouldn't capture it by dwelling on it. Best to head back to the newsroom and work on something else. "I'm heading out. I'll see you at Liam and Liz's tomorrow night."

Branigan walked down the hall and veered once more into the dining room, where the shelter residents were finishing the morning's clean-up. She sought out the landscape artwork with the brown hay fields and the red-orange sky, and stood before it. She knew exactly the place in her office where it would hang. Only now there was another irregular wooden scrap right below it. This one showed white puffs of cotton in a field with a barn in the distance, again in somber colors, while the sky exploded into a pink and purple and magenta sunset. It looked so much like the view from Branigan's farm that her breath caught. She glanced in the corner, and wasn't surprised to see the name: Jasper. The same as on the sister painting.

Now that she'd decided to buy one, she was going to have trouble deciding which one. She signaled to Dontegan, who was overseeing the clean-up.

"Dontegan, do you know this Jasper who painted these wood pieces?"

"Sho. He finishing up in the kitchen right now."

She walked to the kitchen and peered through the large casement that allowed cafeteria-style service. A short black man in an apron was wiping down the island. She noticed that he limped as he made his way around it.

"Are you Jasper?" she asked, entering the airy kitchen.

He looked up. "Yes, ma'am. Can I help you? All the pancakes are gone, but we still got biscuits and bacon."

"No, no," she assured him. "I wanted to talk to you about your art."

A grin split his thin face. "Always glad to talk about that."

"First of all, I love your work. Are those paintings in the dining hall a specific place?"

"Yep, that's where I grew up. Little place you ain't never heard of, I imagine. Abvul, South Carolina."

"Sure I have," she said. "Ab-be-ville" – she accented all three syllables – "to us outsiders." She motioned toward the dining hall. "But I didn't realize its farmland looks so identical to ours. I'd like to buy a piece, but I can't decide which one."

"Buy 'em both," he said.

"Don't tempt me." She leaned against the kitchen counter. "Is Jasper your first or last name?"

"Last. It's Alphonse Jasper."

"It's nice to meet you, Alphonse," she said, holding out her hand and introducing herself. "What brought you to Grambling?"

"The rodeo finished in Hartwell and I didn't feel up to going with them. So I caught a ride here and got a job in the chicken plant."

"The rodeo?" Branigan asked, remembering Lou Ann's reporting. "What did you do in the rodeo?"

He smiled again, showing such perfect teeth that they were surely dentures. "I'm a clown."

Branigan was dumbfounded. "A clown? When did you get into town?"

"Last week."

She drew a deep breath. "I guess you've been hearing about the clown sightings and the kidnapping of a boy from our homeless camp?"

Alphonse flapped his cleaning rag in disgust. "Ain't no real clown done that," he said adamantly. "A real clown would never hurt a kid any more than a real doctor or a real policeman would."

"Where have you done rodeo clowning?" she persisted.

"Everywhere. Texas. Oklahoma. Arkansas. South Carolina. Georgia." He laughed, warming to his subject. "I was a rider in my younger days. That's where I got this." He pulled open his shirt to expose a long white scar along his collarbone. "And this." He rolled up a sleeve to show another.

"You rode bulls?" she asked. "Or broncos?"

"Both. But it was bulls did that damage. When I couldn't ride no more, I became a clown. Lot of riders do. But when I got this while clowning" – he pushed his apron aside and pulled up a pants leg to show the widest and longest scar yet – "I figured I better be hanging it up soon. Got more than a little arthritis, too."

"But you said you were a clown in Hartwell recently?"

"Yep. A quick job for a week. I shouldn't have, but the pay's better than the chicken plant."

"So now you're working in a chicken plant and painting on the side?"

"I always painted," he said, "even when I was in the rodeo."

"Well, you're very talented," she said. "I'll let Dontegan or Liam know when I decide on a painting."

The silent doors of Jericho Road whisked open to let Branigan pass. Once outside, she called Jody to let him know about Alphonse Jasper's presence in the shelter. She'd let him alert the police that a rodeo clown had moved to town at the exact time the clown sightings began. It might mean nothing. But it was an odd coincidence, especially given the kidnapping of a homeless boy.

As she crossed the parking lot, her mind wandered from the little-known Alphonse to Shack to Malachi. She wondered if Alphonse had the same drinking problem as the other two. He didn't seem to have a mental illness, though he probably had plenty of physical impairments by now. What led to his homelessness? As Isabella would say, "That is the question."

Branigan stopped. *Hamlet.* That was what had been tickling her memory. She pictured a fellow student in her college theater class holding up a plaster skull. *Alas, poor Yorick! I knew him, Horatio: a fellow of infinite jest....*

The doomed Yorick was a court jester.

A clown.

CHAPTER SIXTEEN

Malachi pulled a sagging lawn chair, one strap busted, into the shade of the river birch that stood sentinel over Tent City. It wasn't quite as depressing here in the dappled sunlight as it was in the dimness under the bridge. It was also warmer, which somehow made his shakiness easier to tolerate.

A whole day sober, and he was already feeling a little of the queasiness subside. He wasn't going into *re-covery*, as Pastor Liam preached about constantly. All he wanted was a little clarity. A little clarity so he could think. He might allow himself a couple of beers later, which would actually help his clarity. He'd just lay off the hard stuff for awhile.

He wanted to talk to Shack, but Shack was over at Reynolds Park with Slick. Both men had snagged jobs with the theater, building the stage for Shakespeare in the Park. Shack oughta be in his element, having an excuse to quote Shakespeare without getting his ass whipped. That theater director would eat it up – if, that is, he didn't have an underling dealing with the hired help. Which he probably did.

Reggie Fortenberry. Malachi knew him in a way most people in Grambling didn't. He'd seen the director more than once under the broken streetlight outside Ricky's Quick Mart, a notorious spot where the city's uppity east-siders met its drug-dealing west-siders. If Malachi left his spot under this tree and walked up to the street, he'd be able to throw a rock and hit the shabby convenience store.

Reggie Fortenberry had never seen Malachi; Malachi would bet his life on that. If the homeless were invisible to most people, they were downright non-existent to the theater director. They couldn't support his theater, buy tickets or act. Therefore, they didn't exist.

But Malachi had seen Reggie buying coke late at night, probably after rehearsal. He noticed a pattern, and reading the *Style* and *Arts* sections of *The Grambling Rambler*, put two and two together: Reggie bought cocaine in the days before an opening. Malachi imagined it helped him stay awake, to focus. Or at least that's what the director told himself.

Malachi stretched his arms above his head. He was getting sleepy sitting here all warm with a belly full of pancakes and bacon. Maybe he'd grab a nap before going over to talk to Shack.

Tent City was quiet enough for Malachi to sleep. Deep into a sunny spring, its residents left during the day – for the public library or day labor or courthouse benches or panhandling spots. You had to be careful panhandling on Main Street, though, because city cops would arrest you. Randy and Butch claimed they'd had better luck lately on the interstate ramp.

Lying on top of his sleeping bag, Malachi allowed his mind to drift to the Arnesons, to think about what might have happened to little Andre.

But his mind wouldn't cooperate: Mo in his Opie Taylor shirt was the face in front of him. Malachi dozed and was back in the desert, bumping along in an Army Jeep, his rifle held loosely, pointing heavenward. He was with his granny, and he turned to her in astonishment. *Granny, what you doin' in the Army?* She laughed. *Never you mind.* He knew something was wrong and tried to wake up, and thought he did.

But then he was running, running, running toward Mo's house, an unnamed fear deep in his gut. As he entered the doorway, heart pounding, the house exploded, all four walls blasting away in a fireball of heat and blinding light. Malachi fell on his face and covered his head, though his helmet was strapped on tight.

From behind him, he heard the slamming of feet and then the

shrieks of the old man and woman next door. He wanted to shout too, to scream Mo's name, but he was rooted to the sandy ground and couldn't make a sound.

Finally, he jerked awake to the sound of his own whimpers, the sleeping bag beneath him slick with sweat.

That's not how it happened, he thought groggily. But it was close enough to make him remember why he'd needed the Jack and the Jim and the malt liquor. Without giving himself time to think, he pushed out of the tent and walked to the Quick Mart. He went inside and bought a single beer. And then another.

CHAPTER SEVENTEEN

Style editor Julie Ames looked around the newsroom. Normally, Theater on the Square was Gerald Dubois' beat, but he was tied up with the symphony's spring concert and an art gallery opening. Andre Arneson's kidnapping was occupying Jody, Branigan and Marjorie, and she'd just asked Lou Ann for a sidebar to accompany her Sunday front on bathing suit cover-ups.

Her eyes landed on Harley Barnett, and she started his way. He saw her and snatched up his phone.

"Too late," she said. "It didn't ring."

Harley sighed and put it down. "What fresh hell do you have for me?"

"Carpenters are building the stage for Shakespeare in the Park," she said. "That's always good for a photo and short piece. Gerald will preview the season next week, but the stage going up signals summer."

"As opposed to temperatures in the 80s signaling summer."

"Sarcasm doesn't become you."

"Your wish is my command," Harley said, standing and grabbing a pad and digital recorder.

Arriving at the city park commanded by the graceful mansion-turned-theater, Harley was surprised to recognize two workers from Tent City. The guy in the gray ponytail – Slick, they called him – hadn't had a lot to say during yesterday's interviews. But the guy in the baseball cap – Shack – was the one police took in as a witness. Branigan was supposed to grab him this morning, but Harley didn't know if she'd located him. It wouldn't hurt to double-team the only witness to the kidnapping. Harley headed for him.

"Shack, isn't it?" Harley introduced himself and explained he was doing a short feature for *The Rambler*. That was all the prompting the carpenter needed. Tossing his hammer on the grass, he flipped an imaginary robe aside and intoned, "'One may smile, and smile, and be a villain. At least I'm sure it may be so in Denmark.'"

Harley didn't know whether to applaud, and settled for an uneasy smile.

Shack bowed nonetheless. "I talked to your colleague at Jericho Road," he said, taking up his hammer once more. "Good-looking blonde chick."

"That was Branigan," Harley said. "Were you able to help her?"

Shack shrugged. "Guess so. I just told her what I told the police – about seeing a clown take that kid."

Harley cringed inwardly, remembering the jokes that surrounded the early sightings. If they'd taken the story more seriously from the start, would it have changed the outcome? He couldn't see how, but that didn't do much to assuage his disquiet. "Well, if she's got all that, let's talk about this stage then."

After speaking with Shack for a few minutes, Harley had him point out the project supervisor. That was the theater's facilities manager, Robert Mangione, a large man whose belt was lost in the folds of a rolling stomach. Harley introduced himself and got more information about the construction project.

"But let me get our director for you," Robert said. "He always wants to speak to the press."

The man kept his voice even, but Harley detected a hint of something, maybe the tonal equivalent of an eye roll. While he waited, Harley wandered around the well-kept park, dodging dog-walking retirees and young mothers with strollers.

He returned in time to see Reggie Fortenberry round the corner of the skeletal stage in full flamboyance mode. Harley could tell he was on the verge of gushing a greeting when his eyes fell on a workman with a gray ponytail, holding a two-by-four. Slick turned and met Reggie's gaze, and the director stopped abruptly. Then he slapped a welcoming smile on his face and accosted Harley so quickly that the reporter wondered if he'd really seen anything at all.

Reggie steered Harley away from the noisy workmen, talking vociferously about his Shakespeare season. "We've got *A Midsummer Night's Dream* and *Hamlet*," he enthused. "My dear boy, it doesn't get any better than that. They'll be running out here while *Annie Get Your Gun* runs inside. Summertime is quite mad."

"How do you do all that?" Harley asked. "Gerald probably knows, but I don't."

"Sam – that's our assistant director, marvelous talent – is in charge of Shakespeare this year. I've done simultaneous shows in the past, but I don't recommend it. Something has to give, and it's usually my sleep. Or my sanity." He laughed heartily, then rubbed his hands together. "So, what do you need?"

"Just our annual building-the-stage-to-welcome-summer story," Harley said with a nod at the workmen busily hammering. He pretended to listen as Reggie went over much the same territory as his facilities manager had covered. But he kept his eye on Slick and Shack, looking for all the world like experienced carpenters. Harley wondered if it was because both Robert and Reggie were watching. He couldn't imagine the two being quite so gung-ho otherwise.

Reggie was winding up his monologue about the importance of a stable and well-constructed stage. "Of course, that's really not my bailiwick," he trilled. "I am the artistic director. I wouldn't know a hammer from a screwdriver."

Harley fixed him with a tired stare. "Right," he said, closing his notebook with a snap. Gerald might have to put up with this twit, but he didn't. He took one last look at the workmen hoisting two-by-fours into place and wondered what the connection between Reggie Fortenberry and the homeless Slick could possibly be.

Reggie signaled for Robert Mangione to follow him back to his office. Unlike Barbara Wickenstall's closet-size space, Reggie operated out of a former second-floor bedroom of the mansion, complete with fireplace, marble mantel and private bath.

With his staff, he dropped his effusive manner and talked in a more normal tone. "Where did you find your construction workers?" he asked.

The facilities manager looked at him in surprise. "The day labor place. Like I always do."

"I don't remember them sending us homeless people before."

"I didn't know they *were* homeless. What makes you think that?"

"I saw two of them interviewed on the news last night. About that boy missing from the homeless camp."

"Really? Which two?"

"I don't know their names," Reggie snapped. "But one has a long gray ponytail and one quotes Shakespeare – badly – every time I walk past." He looked out of his window at the stage taking shape below. He saw his leading man from *Annie Get Your Gun* amble across the park and approach the carpenters. Colin Buckner. What a gift he was, landing smack in Reggie's lap. He'd been negotiating for another Frank Butler from Atlanta when Colin walked in for an audition. The theater was saving thousands of dollars, and the middle school drama teacher was a match for the professional he'd been ready to hire. Win, win, win.

Reggie yanked his attention back to the matter at hand: his facilities manager with sweat stains under both arms of his yellow T-shirt. While the rest of his staff was proficient – he wouldn't have it any other way – they couldn't match Reggie sartorially. He pointed out of his window to the workers below. "You know, they're wearing the same clothes they wore on TV last night."

Robert hid a smile. "Do you want me to get rid of them?"

"Are they decent workers?" At Robert's nod, Reggie turned from the window, decision made. "No, we need to get that stage finished. I was just startled to see them. That's all."

Robert left the office for the workshop, shaking his head. Who did Reggie think worked day labor? He'd be surprised if anyone on the stage crew *wasn't* homeless. It wasn't the kind of thing you asked, any more than you'd ask if they had felonies on their records. *Sheesh,* did Reggie think people waited all year to spend four days building his frigging stage?

With Robert gone, Reggie stood awhile longer at the window. He was not pleased to have his two lives overlap like this. Not pleased at all.

What kind of drug dealer was homeless, for goodness' sakes? Not a very good one, obviously. Reggie alone had given him enough money for an apartment – heck, many, many months in an apartment. Clearly, he was using his own product.

Reggie had bought cocaine for years on the city's west side, but had confined his use to the nights before an opening. Lately, though, he'd needed something a little earlier in a production. The schedule was relentless, with one show's performances rolling into the next show's auditions and no downtime at all. Who wouldn't need something to take the edge off? And then Slick had suggested something beyond coke. And then someone else had found out.

Reggie had it under control – he was sure he did – but it wouldn't do for his board to learn of his little habit. He had enough trouble with them as it was. Certain members would relish the chance to get rid of him, to send this theater sliding into the backwater from whence he'd hauled it.

He'd already fielded three calls about those blasted clown costumes. He'd talked with Barbara and they'd agreed that anyone with enough nerve could have marched right in and taken them.

He turned to his window again and looked at Slick, whose name he certainly did know, and the ridiculously named Shack, hoisting and hammering and shouting. He looked at Colin Buckner, trying to chat with them. Was he trying to score?

Hmm. Anyone with enough nerve.

CHAPTER EIGHTEEN

Rather than going to Liam and Liz Delaney's cook-out straight from the newsroom on Friday, Branigan returned to the farm to exercise Cleo. Only, once more the dog wasn't at the house and didn't come when called. Branigan changed into shorts and a T-shirt, pulled on her running shoes, and swept her hair into a high ponytail. Locking the side door, she sat on the stoop and punched in Chester's number. She wasn't surprised to find him at the Law Enforcement Center.

"I'm so sorry, but I'm not going to be able to get to Liam's," he said.

With the search for Andre Arneson still within a seventy-two-hour window, she couldn't say she was surprised about that either.

"But I've slept at the LEC the past two nights, and I'm fading," Chester said. "I can drive out to your place when we're through tonight."

"Absolutely. Call me when you leave so I can be sure to get home before you."

Pocketing the phone, she called once more for Cleo. She heard barking from far off. That goofball. Was she hanging out with Uncle Bobby's cows? In a moment, the rattle of old cotton husks announced the German shepherd's return, and Cleo leapt from the cotton patch and into the grassy back yard. Branigan laughed and ran from her, the dog barking excitedly and trying to jump onto her mistress.

"Okay, that's enough," Branigan wheezed finally. "Let's hit the pasture."

After jogging on the path through the cotton patch, passing

the barn and two empty chicken houses, Branigan picked her way carefully through the barbed-wire fence that bounded the pasture, while Cleo scooted underneath like a soldier on an obstacle course. Branigan had two routes. If she went right, she'd enter the flat pastures behind Uncle Bobby and Aunt Jeanie's house. If she went left, she'd pass woods, two lakes and an old vine-covered shed where Pa and his buddies had played poker – the one thing Gran didn't allow in her house. And if she went far enough in that leftward direction, she'd eventually encounter more barbed wire and the adjacent pastures of the Satterfield family. Mr Satterfield had died a decade ago, and Mrs Satterfield eight years later. Their non-farming children were still trying to decide what to do with the property. As far as Branigan knew, their house, a half mile from her own, stood empty.

Cleo headed left. "No, let's go behind Uncle Bobby's," Branigan said. "We haven't run this way in awhile."

The dog hesitated for a moment, then whined. Branigan remembered her coming home wet and muddy last week. "I don't want you near those lakes anyway, so come on." She began jogging along the fence line to her right, and after a few moments Cleo followed. They passed Uncle Bobby's house off in the distance, and spotted his cattle in the farthest pasture. Branigan cut her circle short of the cows, though the young woman and farm dog were such a familiar sight to them, the big animals weren't fazed. Even with the cows eating their fill, these fields were at the height of their springtime green. This was the countryside Branigan loved, at its most lush season.

She looped the large acreage contentedly, enjoying the scenery and the heat.

After showering and dressing in close-fitting coral pants, a white eyelet top and sandals, Branigan grabbed a bottle of sauvignon blanc and a light pinot noir to take to the Delaneys' house. She opened the windows of her Civic, allowing the fragrant spring air to finish drying her hair. Driving up the rural road a quarter mile, she turned into her Uncle Bobby's driveway. Isabella was outside waiting, a pie in her hands.

"Is that Aunt Jeanie's famous lemon meringue?" Branigan asked as she pulled up.

"Nope. Isabella's not-so-famous apple." Isabella slid into the passenger seat.

"Where's Jamie Solesbee?"

"She's going to meet us there. She was rehearsing with Reggie this afternoon."

"And your folks?"

"Out to dinner, if you can believe it. Dad's really making an effort to do everything Mom wants while her energy is still up. He even bought opening night tickets for *Annie Get Your Gun*. Enough for you and your mom and dad, too."

"That was a sacrifice," Branigan said, "knowing what he thinks of live theater."

"I think he figures it won't be so bad with your dad there. And Jimmie Jean in the lead. Though I'm sure he'll get mad all over again when he sees her listed in the program as Jamie."

Branigan grinned. "The man simply doesn't understand high art, does he?"

"Apparently not." Isabella changed the subject. "So what have you heard from Detective Scovoy about the kidnapping?"

"Precious little. As you know, I can't cover the Grambling Police Department, so Jody is handling that side of things. I've only talked to Chester once a day, briefly, since Wednesday. They're all hands on deck right now, looking for Andre. What's going on with the family?"

Isabella sighed. "It's like three *different* families. Flora and the daughter, Stacy, are barely holding on. Stacy thinks the kidnapping is her fault because Andre saw the clown once before when she took him to that camp bathroom. But she never even knew it."

"She's too young to shoulder that kind of guilt."

"Javion, that's the seven-year-old," Isabella continued, "thinks he's landed at Disney World, with a bed and a pool and all he wants to eat. And the father and Jaquan have hardly been sober for the past three days."

"Uh-oh."

"Tell me about it. With the community picking up the tab for the motel and meals, that leaves whatever cash Oren has for cigarettes and beer and liquor. And I hope that's all he's buying."

"Does Liam know that?"

"Oh, yeah. But his hands are tied. Your boss and the TV station and the other preachers insisted that money was given for the Arnesons."

"That's got to be killing Liam. He talks about 'empowering' rather than 'enabling' all the time."

"And he's right. But it's hard to stop a train like this."

The cousins drove in silence. Isabella lowered her window and turned up the radio.

"Even with all the uproar," she yelled over the wind, "I love being back here. Without all the others, Jimmie Jean and I don't even have to fight over a bathroom."

"How nice for Aunt Jeanie!"

They arrived at Liam and Liz's two-story brick house set in a rapidly gentrifying neighborhood on downtown's Oakley Avenue. The front yard was already blooming with early roses, yellow coreopsis and white geraniums, along with the fading pink and white azaleas that had blanketed Grambling in April. Liz was a designer, and Branigan credited her with starting the renaissance of this neighborhood twenty years earlier.

She and Isabella eschewed the front door and went through the carport to the kitchen. Liz hugged them both, and pointed to the back deck where they could see Jimmie Jean and Liam. "There's beer and wine and Diet Coke out there," she said. "Help yourselves while I finish this salad. I'll join you in two shakes of a lamb's tail."

The women left their wine and pie on the kitchen counter and headed for the deck, which also showed Liz's gardening expertise.

Boxes attached to the deck rail burst with petunias and marigolds and trailing English ivy that curled into the latticework. In the yard beyond, huge hydrangea bushes and towering hardwoods gave a feeling of privacy even though neighboring houses were close on this city street.

"So glad you could come," Liam said. "Am I going to be the only male?"

Branigan poured herself white wine from a bottle chilling in an ice bucket, and Isabella nodded for the same. "Looks like it," she said. "Chester is caught up with the search for Andre."

"Am I ever going to meet this detective of yours?" asked Jimmie Jean with a toss of her head.

Isabella looked at her sister sharply, before her eyes darted to Branigan's face, gone deadly still. The women all knew what had happened the last time Jimmie Jean met one of Branigan's boyfriends, though their perspectives were decidedly different.

Bending to get a beer, Liam missed the exchange. "One way or another, I guess we're all caught up with this search for Andre," he said.

Jimmie Jean smoothly changed direction. "Liam's been telling me about the money coming in," she said. "Over eight thousand dollars."

Isabella grimaced. "That's even more since this morning," she said, accepting a glass of cold pinot grigio.

"People want to help," Liam said.

"But...?" Branigan prompted.

"I don't have to tell this group what comes after the 'but'."

"You sort of do," said Jimmie Jean. "Branigan and Izzy B have been filling me in on enabling, but what's wrong with people giving money for the family to get a place?"

The other three exchanged glances. Isabella shook her head from side to side to indicate ambivalence. "It's not so much the place to stay," she said, "as it is the choices certain family members are making."

"Like what?"

"Well, the police have set up temporary headquarters at Jericho Road because we have more room than the motel does. Flora comes every day with Stacy and Javion. But the police haven't been able to get the father to come in."

"Why in the world not?"

"Because he's by the motel pool drinking."

Jimmie Jean's eyebrows shot up. "You're kidding."

Liam and Isabella shook their heads. "With Jaquan," Isabella added.

"Is that even legal? For a teenager to drink?"

"As long as a parent allows it." Liam shrugged. "Technically, they can't have it by the pool, but I assume they're drinking in their rooms then coming out. And the police aren't looking for a reason to arrest them while Andre is missing."

"What a nightmare!" said Jimmie Jean.

Liam rolled his eyes at Branigan. "'If it ain't a mess…'" he fed her the line.

"'It'll do till the mess gets here.'"

Isabella laughed. "Don't tell me. I know this." Then after a moment, "Tommy Lee Jones in *No Country for Old Men*."

"Very good," said Liz, joining them on the deck. "All the Rickmans are up on their movie trivia."

"Speaking of movies, kind of," Branigan said, "how goes it with Annie Oakley?"

"Fine, I think," said Jimmie Jean. "A heck of a lot of dialogue and lyrics. If I forget something, I just yell, 'Ah, shoot!' or 'Hell's bells!' or 'My foot!' and stomp around until I remember."

The friends laughed, and Jimmie Jean turned to her sister. "And Izzy B, I was finally alone with Colin this afternoon. I told him I knew what he'd done in Atlanta and why he was in Grambling."

Isabella visibly tensed. "What'd he say?"

"You were right, Sis. He didn't deny it."

"But what'd he say?" she repeated.

"He was sort of abashed, I guess you'd say. Embarrassed. He admitted he'd had a bad crush on you, but said he'd gotten over it."

"He's over it?" Branigan hooted. "So what's he doing here?"

Jimmie Jean shrugged. "Exactly. That's what I asked him. He said he'd originally come because of Isabella, but that he's over it. Over her. He even asked out a girl in the cast. He doesn't want to let Reggie down at this point, so he plans to stick with the show through June."

Liam turned from the ribs he was basting on the grill. "And you believe him?"

"Well, it's not a case of believing him. I mean, a week ago he's so smitten with Izzy that he moves here and now he's over her? That's a little lame. But an Atlanta policewoman called him, and Detective Scovoy sent an officer to talk to him. So I don't think he'd dare try anything."

Isabella blew out a long breath. "That's good news," she said. She laughed and held up her glass for everyone to clink. "That's really good news!"

A few hours later, the five friends sat around a dining room table littered with cloth napkins and glasses, but cleared of barbecue-smeared plates and gnawed corn cobs. They passed around Branigan's bottle of pinot noir, interspersed with Isabella's apple pie and mugs of coffee. Branigan loved the Delaney house. It reminded her of the one she had grown up in a few streets over. It was good to be with people you'd known since childhood, she mused, as she watched their beloved faces deep in conversation. Good to be with people who knew you so well that a misstatement or a stupid remark was laughed at and forgotten. She wondered how newcomers ever established the deep-rooted friendships that were so important to her. She'd had acquaintances during her time in Detroit, but no one she kept up with. No one she'd really considered a friend.

Her gaze fell on Jimmie Jean. Growing up, she and Isabella and even their mothers had laughed good-naturedly at JJ's over-the-top antics, her need for attention, her propensity for drama. That was why Branigan had been so blindsided by what happened with Jackson. When she'd introduced her boyfriend – her first boyfriend, in fact – to her cousin, she'd expected him to join her as a spectator to the performance that was Jimmie Jean's life. But it hadn't worked out that way.

The opening of the front door interrupted her reverie. Charlie, Liam and Liz's teenage daughter, smiled broadly at seeing the guests. Branigan stood to hug her. "You finished with classes?" she asked.

Branigan had known Charlie since the girl was born, visiting the hospital and seeing Liam's red gold hair on the baby almost before she could open those blue eyes. Charlie had started her freshman year at the University of Georgia but was seriously injured in a wreck while driving home for Christmas. She had elected to take two classes online during the spring while undergoing dental surgeries; she planned to return to Athens in the fall.

"Done and done," she pronounced. "But I've still got summer school at Grambling Tech. Hey, Izzy B and Jimmie Jean." She made her way around the table, giving hugs. "The gang's all here."

"Let's see that smile," said Jimmie Jean.

Charlie grinned obligingly.

"Wow, you're still a knock-out."

Charlie blushed. "And did I hear that Theater on the Square has a new star?"

"Well, a new rootin' tootin' sharpshooter anyway."

"So when is your brother headed home?" Isabella asked. Liam and Liz's adopted son Chandler was finishing his freshman year at Furman University in nearby South Carolina.

"He's headed to North Myrtle for a beach week," Charlie replied. "But then he'll be here for the summer." She directed an exaggerated smile at Liam and Liz. "It'll be good to get all this parental attention off me."

"You wish," said her mother. "We can double our efforts."

When Charlie went up to bed, the party broke up. Branigan

still hadn't heard from Chester and wondered if he was going to spend yet another night in the uncomfortable bunk room of the Law Enforcement Center.

She got her answer before she was halfway home. He was headed to her farm.

Chester was waiting in her driveway when she arrived. "You didn't leave Cleo in the house, did you?" he asked as he opened her car door.

"No, she's out. She didn't greet you, huh?"

She scanned the cotton patch but could make out nothing in the inky dark. The cicadas in the pecan trees boomed in her ear. Cupping her hands to her mouth, she called, "CLEO!"

Turning to Chester, she said, "I don't know what's up with her. She's developed a fondness for the pasture she never used to have."

They listened intently for a moment.

"I hear her," Chester said. "Way off."

"Let's go on in," Branigan said. "She'll come in when she's ready. I want to hear all about your week."

They left the stoop light on and walked into the den, Branigan punching in the alarm code, Chester falling wearily onto the sofa. "I've had enough to drink," she said, "but can I get you a beer or a glass of wine?"

"I'd love a beer," he said. "I don't think I can move."

She fetched a beer from the refrigerator and opened it for him, then made a cup of hot chocolate for herself. Kicking off her sandals, she turned on a lamp in the den, and sat at one end of the couch, pulling her feet under her.

"So what's going on with the search?" she asked. "Any progress?"

Chester shook his head wearily. "The mom's been real involved. She's beating herself up for not letting Isabella call us the first time Andre mentioned a clown. Turns out Oren has an outstanding warrant in North Carolina, and she was afraid any police involvement would get him arrested."

"Liam says that happens all the time. That's why homeless people rarely report crimes."

"Right.. We're holding off right now, but the minute we find that boy, we'll contact North Carolina." He paused. "We're off the record, right? Even to the point of not telling Jody?"

Branigan held up her hands. "Totally off the record. Tan knows we're dating and I'm off the story as far as you and the Grambling PD are concerned. Even if it means we miss something, that's how it is."

He relaxed.

"Isabella said the dad and older brother haven't come in to Jericho Road at all," she said.

"Yeah, we've interviewed them at the motel. That is, when we could find them sober, which has basically been around 7 a.m. The dad's a real piece of work."

"I know you guys have to look at the families," she said. "But with the whole clown thing, what are you thinking?"

"We *have* to assume it's a stranger abduction," Chester agreed. "We owe that to the little guy. But we've got two detectives looking into the dad's background, to see if there are any cheated acquaintances, offended victims, people like that." He yawned. "The one I feel bad for – besides Andre, I mean – is Jaquan. He's got a dad in the picture, but he's such a bad influence, you have to wonder if he'd be better off without him."

"But you can see why Flora would be afraid to have him arrested," Branigan said. "She has four kids to support."

"I guess," sighed Chester. He closed his eyes for a moment, and Branigan wondered if he'd fallen asleep. Then he stirred, and put a hand on her thigh.

"Brani G, there is nowhere else I want to be right now. I guess you know by now that I am crazy about you. But I gotta get some sleep."

Branigan laughed. "No problem. Let's get you to bed."

Hours later, she awoke and tiptoed outside to see if Cleo had returned. She called softly, but the dog didn't appear. That had never happened before, though the shepherd had the run of the farm. Branigan relocked the side door and returned to bed.

CHAPTER NINETEEN

Malachi slouched in his tattered lawn chair in the moonlight. Every little while he could hear a laugh echo across the railroad tracks. Those young men didn't know crap. It looked like fun – no rent, no bills, no jobs, no curfews – on a warm spring night like this. But then the cold would set in. The cold and the sickness and the shakes and the bug bites and the grime and the begging. And then the invisibility.

He finished his fourth beer of the day, and crumpled the can with resolve. *And only a twelve-ouncer*, he thought with satisfaction.

He had no intention of going cold turkey, but he wasn't drunk and hadn't been all day. He'd spread the beers out like meals, one every few hours. His hands were steady and his mind was clear. So what was bothering him? What thought couldn't he quite reach?

He leaned his head against the chair's aluminum frame and looked at the stars. The woods were alive with cicadas and tree frogs, but the mosquitoes weren't bad yet. It was a beautiful night, almost beautiful enough to make you forget you lived under a bridge.

Aw, he didn't want to go there.

Andre. He needed to concentrate on Andre. He'd walked to the Heart of Grambling this afternoon and seen Oren snoring by the pool. Jaquan was laid out too, eyes closed, foot moving to whatever he was hearing through his ear buds. Malachi watched them for awhile, and realizing Oren wasn't going to wake up, he nudged Jaquan.

The boy's eyes shot open, and he sat up, jerking out his ear buds. "Mr Malachi?"

He pulled a chair close to the teen. "Just Malachi."

The boy nodded, watching him.

"You got a nice place here," Malachi opened. "Where your mama?"

"Her and Stacy and Javion down at Jericho Road, working with the police."

"You don't wanna be there?"

Jaquan looked at his sleeping father. "Dad says they don't need all us getting in the way."

"Hmm." Malachi let the silence stretch out. Jaquan leaped to fill it, as Malachi figured he would.

"Anyway, I done told them all I know. I was asleep by the latrine when that clown got Andre. It wasn't my fault. I was asleep."

Jaquan's eyes belied his words. They slid away from Malachi, and he reached for his sunglasses. Malachi knew a little something about guilt, and he saw it all over Jaquan. He waited a few more moments, then spoke softly. "Guilt don't follow logic, son. And beer and liquor don't do a thing to fix it."

Jaquan's face took on a steely calm behind the sunglasses, and he murmured something Malachi didn't catch.

"What's that?"

"I said, you should know."

Malachi nodded slowly. "Yeah, I should. And I'd sure like to save you ending up like me if I could."

Jaquan swallowed. "Is it true you killed people in the Gulf War?"

Malachi shrugged. "That's what a soldier do." He stood. "If they's something you saw or you know about your brother, you best tell somebody. And not your daddy."

It was as if Jaquan hadn't heard him. "Is that why you drink?" he asked. "Because you killed people?"

Malachi shook his head, didn't bother to answer. No, it wasn't that he'd killed people. Not in the way Jaquan meant. Not soldiers.

He was pretty sure he drank because he hadn't *kept* someone from being killed. A small Bedouin boy in a striped T-shirt. But he sure hadn't wanted to talk about it with Jaquan, so he'd left.

Now Malachi jerked from a doze at the sound of cans rattling in a trash pile next to the bridge. Had to be a raccoon or a possum. He hurled his crumpled beer can into the pile. "Get!"

More rustling followed, then silence.

It was past midnight, the first midnight he'd seen sober for longer than he cared to think about. Mostly, by this time of night, he was unconscious.

Unconscious. Or blacked out. Malachi's eyes opened wide. The elusive thought he'd been trying to catch clicked into place.

Was he always unconscious during those blackouts? Or could he just not remember what he'd done?

Once when he was in Atlanta, he woke up with a busted hand and no memory of how it'd happened. Another time in Hartwell, he'd found wet clothes on his tent floor, and no memory of being in the rain or getting in a shower, or heck, even falling in the lake.

The night Andre disappeared, the night he woke up to the mad cries of Flora Arneson, he was on the hill above their campsite with only the foggiest notion of how he got there. It would've been dark, of course, but he had a full view of their tent, the latrine, the woods. Had he seen something? *Think, Malachi, think*, he pushed himself.

Had he noticed something out of place? Seen someone who shouldn't have been there?

Or more frightening, had he done something?

He hadn't been able to talk to Shack yesterday or today. He knew Shack was working on that Shakespeare stage, but still: where was he? Malachi hadn't seen him come in last night or go out this morning or come in tonight. He hadn't been at Jericho Road for dinner. And his bike was gone. Something was up with that one, that was for sure.

Malachi squirmed to relieve the stiffness in his back. The half-busted straps on this chair weren't helping.

He wanted another beer. He hadn't bought another one for this very reason. To get one, he'd have to walk to Ricky's Quick Mart. And he wanted something else more. He wanted to find Mo. No, not Mo, *Andre*. He wanted to find Andre.

He closed his eyes. *What did you see, Malachi?* But faced with the black hole of three nights ago, his mind wandered. Damn, he wanted a beer. He'd never been much of a drinker growing up. His granny wasn't having those shenanigans in her house. That's what she'd called it when Malachi's high school friends got into trouble for drinking. *Those shenanigans.* He'd snuck a few beers, sure. But nothing like he'd had in the Army.

The beer flowed freely there. At first, he wasn't any more interested than he'd been in high school. But then came the trek to join another company for a sortie inside Basra, Iraq. Two weeks later, he and his buddies returned to base camp, sun-stricken and exhausted. After a day's rest, he'd snagged Khalid for a return trip to the Bedouin village to see how Mohamed was doing.

They bounced along in the borrowed Jeep, the mile of desert road looking like every other mile of desert road from Kuwait to Iraq. As they approached the edge of Mo's village, Malachi saw a house half standing, its roof and upper walls blown off. On the next street, a pile of rubble marked the site of another bombed house. Malachi's heart began to thud. This village had seen the same sort of firefight that Basra had.

Two skinny dogs roamed the streets, but it was clear of people. Khalid pulled the Jeep into the old couple's non-existent yard and surveyed their intact dwelling, a single jagged hole on one side the only sign of violence. But that's not what drew Malachi's attention. The hole was on the side next to Mo's house, except there was no longer a house there.

Malachi leapt from the Jeep and ran into the heap of smashed concrete and twisted aluminum and white dust – all that white dust. For the rest of his life, he'd remember the sight of that white dust that covered everything.

He looked around wildly for something, anything: a sleeping mat, a tiny sandal, a striped shirt. He was vaguely aware of the old couple coming out of their house and speaking softly to Khalid. He saw the old man make a motion with his hands, guttural noises coming from deep in his throat, then lifting his arms to indicate *it went away, it all went away.*

Malachi scarcely recognized his own voice. "Mo was inside?" he asked Khalid.

"Yeah."

"Where he at now?"

Khalid spoke quietly, then listened. "They buried what they could find within twenty-four hours. That's their custom." He listened for another moment. "Do you want them to show you?"

"No," Malachi said in the voice that wasn't his. "Please thank them. And let's go."

That night, Malachi did get hold of the beer that flowed freely at the Army camp. As he had every night since.

It didn't take long to graduate to the harder stuff, the King Cobra and the Jack and the Jim and everything in between. But it took years for the blackouts to take hold. He remembered the first one because it was so scary, waking up on a bulldozer on a construction site in Gainesville, Florida. He'd lived in a boarding house then, and the last thing he remembered was sitting at the kitchen table with his co-workers, passing around a bottle. Or four. Fortunately, he woke up around dawn before the job foreman got there. He climbed down from the bulldozer, shaking, retching, thankful he hadn't had the means to start it up.

From then on, the blackouts were too numerous to count. The broken hand, the wet clothes, and oh, yeah, once he woke up in a public bathroom with a swollen eye that didn't open for a week. He never did know if he'd fallen or been beaten.

So the idea that he could do things, and endure things, while completely out of it was nothing new. The question was: what was he capable of? He'd been dreaming of Mo for weeks now. Could he have taken Andre in a misguided attempt to save him? If so, where was the boy?

Damn, he wanted a beer. Maybe it was worth a walk to Ricky's.

Chapter Twenty

On Saturday morning, Branigan woke before Chester. She went outside immediately and was happy to find Cleo in the driveway. She hugged the dog's neck; Cleo whined a greeting and bumped against Branigan's legs, then shot into the cotton patch and out of sight. What the heck was up with that dog?

Branigan collected the newspaper and made a pot of coffee before quietly pulling on shorts and a T-shirt, washing her face and adding sunscreen and a touch of mascara. She felt exhilarated and anxious at the same time, and knew she'd need to burn off some nervous energy today.

She was on her second cup of coffee when Chester came into the kitchen, barefoot and wearing his khakis from the night before and one of her extra-large T-shirts advertising the Salty Dog Café on Hilton Head.

"Hope you don't mind," he said, with a tug at the navy shirt.

"Not at all. The Salty Dog suits you."

He came around the island and scooped her into his arms, burying his face in her hair. "Believe me when I tell you you're the only thing keeping me sane right now."

She hugged him tightly. "I'm glad."

A moment later, she pulled from his embrace. "How about some coffee? And pancakes? Or cereal?"

"Cereal's fine. And lots of coffee. I'll need to head back to work before noon, but being here helps clear my head."

"If you like, after we eat, we can walk. That always helps me think."

"Sounds like a plan."

"Oh, and by the way, thank you for sending an officer to check out Izzy B's stalker. Jimmie Jean thinks he was appropriately scared."

"You're welcome, though I'm sorry to say I never checked back. When that kid was snatched, everything else got pushed aside."

"Understandably so. I'm just glad your officer made time for it."

Thirty minutes later, Branigan and Chester headed into the sunny morning. She called for Cleo and heard nothing in response.

"If you don't mind, let's head toward the lakes," she said. "I want to see what is so interesting to that dog."

"Lead the way."

They walked single file through the cotton patch, and past the barn and chicken houses. Branigan held the strand of barbed wire so it didn't snag Chester's shirt, then he returned the favor.

"Man," he said appreciatively once he'd straightened and looked out over the pasture. "This is beautiful. No wonder you're willing to live this far out of town."

She pointed right. "That's my Uncle Bobby and Aunt Jeanie's land. I spent a lot of time there with Izzy B and Jimmie Jean growing up." She swept her arm straight ahead and left. "And this was Gran and Pa's land. They pretty much shared all their acreage with Uncle Bobby and let the cows roam between the farms."

"I see your Uncle Bobby has a separate barn."

"Yeah, he mostly keeps tractors in it. He keeps his cattle in Pa's old barn. There's no such thing as a farm without barns and sheds and shacks all over the place."

They walked left toward a shimmering lake.

"Any fish in there?" Chester asked.

"Sure. At least, I guess they're still there. Pa used to stock it." She pointed to a green mound at the edge of the lake. "See that shed? There is actually one under all those vines. It started out as a fishing shed, where Pa cleaned them. Later he brought in a table and chairs and made it a poker parlor."

Chester laughed. "Your grandfather was into illegal gambling?"

"You bet. Quarter ante. Big money. Though I think the real draw was for all the local farmers to have a place where their wives couldn't find them."

Chester pointed. "Hey, I think I see Miss Cleo."

Branigan looked and saw the shepherd emerging from the shed. As they got closer, they could see the rickety porch jutting out from its canopy of vegetation.

"How did she get in there?" she said. "She's lucky she didn't get trapped inside. Cleo!" she called, but the dog ignored her, and went back into the shed. "What the..." Branigan's eyes widened, and she and Chester stared at the doorway where Cleo emerged once more. Or rather, stared at the small figure that the dog nudged through the doorway.

Andre Arneson.

Branigan and Chester began running for the boy, but stopped simultaneously when they saw a look of fear cross his face. By silent consent, they approached him slowly, holding hands to keep themselves from bolting forward.

"He knows you, right?" Chester whispered, never taking his eyes off the boy.

"Maybe. I met him once. Let me try to talk to him." She stopped a few feet from the small figure, and knelt. "Hi, Andre. Do you remember me?"

He shook his head.

"I'm Cleo's mom. This is Cleo." As if the dog understood, she walked over and licked Branigan's face. Branigan hugged the big dog's neck, and saw Andre relax.

"He likes you!" he beamed.

"She," Branigan said. "Cleo is a girl. And I think she must like you, too."

"She does."

Branigan scarcely knew where to begin. "Andre, I met you and your mom at Jericho Road. You offered me your gummy bears. Do you remember that?"

He nodded.

"Your mom has been looking everywhere for you. Do you know who brought you here?"

"A clown," he said confidently.

Branigan could see in her peripheral vision that Chester was creeping quietly to the shed's side window. She remembered the gun he'd left in her bedroom. "Is the clown still here?" she whispered.

"No. Another clown bopped him on the head and he fell down and went to sleep."

"Another clown?"

Andre nodded. "I'm hungry," he said.

Chester shook his head at her. "No one here," he said, and entered the shed.

"Andre, we'll take you up to my house and get you something to eat," she said. "But can you tell me how long you've been here?"

"One sleep," he said. "Mama told me how to count. One day, one sleep, two days, two sleeps, three days, three sleeps."

"Good boy. So you've been here just one sleep?"

"What do you have to eat at your house?"

"Cereal. Pop-Tarts. Pancakes. Whatever you want."

Chester came out, speaking into his cell phone. "Branigan, the chief wants to know if Andre needs paramedics."

"Andre, do you hurt anywhere, honey?"

"No, ma'am. Except my stomach. I think it'll feel better when it gets some pancakes."

She smiled. "Well, then pancakes it is." She turned to Chester. "I don't think he needs paramedics. Just food. Can you come with us or do you need to stay here?"

"No, I'm staying with you in case someone comes back for him. The crime scene isn't going anywhere."

Branigan and Chester each took one of Andre's hands and they began walking back to the house, Cleo leaping happily in front of them. When the boy complained that his legs were tired, Chester swung him onto his shoulders, his little tennis shoes banging the detective's chest with every step. Branigan was bursting with questions, but she held off, unsure of how traumatized the boy might be. He seemed okay, but it was hard to tell.

Then she remembered someone who was trained to talk to children. She pulled her cell phone from her shorts pocket and called her cousin next door.

Members of both the Grambling Police Department and the Cannon County Sheriff's Office were gathered in Branigan's front yard and driveway, at least thirty officers in all. Another three were going over Pa's poker shed, seeking fibers, fingerprints, clues. So far, they'd bagged two empty water bottles and two cinnamon bun wrappers.

Because the kidnapping had occurred within the city limits, Police Chief Marcus Warren had taken charge, and his colleague Sheriff Clem Ocher was providing back-up. Based upon Detective Scovoy's opinion that the boy had been on Branigan's property only one night, the chief was organizing teams to search outbuildings on neighboring farms.

Some of the teams were already heading out, but the chief held a few back to see what Isabella could learn. Right now she was in Branigan's kitchen with the entire Arneson clan as the boy wolfed down pancakes. But Chief Warren had asked that she question him as soon as he was able to talk about something other than breakfast. And since the chief noted that the huge German shepherd seemed to make the boy feel safe, he'd told Branigan she could sit in with Isabella and Detective Jim Rogerson if she'd handle Cleo. From the look on Branigan's face, the chief knew he'd tossed her, Br'er Rabbit-like, into a delectable briar patch.

It wasn't easy getting Andre away from Flora and Oren. Andre's father grabbed him and kept his face buried in the child's neck for so long that Branigan began to question her earlier opinion of him. His mother refused to let him out of her sight.

Finally the officers compromised and allowed the parents to sit at the dining room table where they could see Andre in the adjoining living room. Isabella placed Andre on a sofa with his back to his mom and dad so he wouldn't be distracted. Cleo lay at his feet, and Isabella tugged a comfortable wing chair to within a few feet of the boy. Detective Rogerson sat unobtrusively to her left, and Branigan remained behind him.

"So are you full now?" Isabella asked Andre with a smile.

"Yes, ma'am. Can I take Cleo home with me?"

Isabella laughed softly. "I don't think Cleo's mom would like that any better than your mom would like it if you moved away. Besides, Cleo likes living on the farm, where she can run."

The boy nodded seriously.

"Andre, I want to ask you some questions about the person who took you from your camp. Can you tell me about that?"

"It was a clown. I saw two clowns."

"Two? Are you sure?"

He held up two fingers.

"You saw two clowns?" Isabella seemed bewildered, and didn't know what to ask next. Detective Rogerson passed her a note.

"When Miss Branigan and Detective Chester found you in the shed, you told them that one clown bopped another clown on the head and he fell down. Is that right?"

"Yeah."

"Where was that?"

"I don't know."

"Do you know what he bopped the clown with?"

"A funny hammer."

"A funny hammer. Okay. Did the clown get back up?"

"No, he went to sleep."

Isabella glanced at the detective, who passed her another note. "How did you know he was asleep?"

"The other clown said."

"What did you do when he went to sleep?"

"We went to Cleo's house."

Isabella took a note from the detective. "Can you tell me what a funny hammer looks like?"

The boy screwed up his face. "It was big and red like the clown's nose."

Isabella read from a steady stream of notes that Jim Rogerson scribbled and passed to her.

"Andre, can you think about where this clown got hit and fell asleep? Was it inside or outside?"

"Inside. But not at Cleo's house."

"Okay, good. Did you sleep inside that house? I mean, before the clown went to sleep?"

His face lit up. "Yeah, two sleeps." He seemed glad to be helpful.

"Did you have a bed?"

"No, a sleeping bag on the floor. Like at our camp." He turned and when he couldn't see his parents, stood up and looked over the back of Branigan's couch. Seeing them, he waved and sat back down. "It smelled funny," he added.

"Smelled funny how?"

He shrugged.

"Did it smell bad?"

"No, just funny. And there was brown grass under my sleeping bag."

"Brown grass. All right. That's good remembering." Isabella glanced at the detective, who was taking rapid notes.

"Andre, can you tell us about the night you left camp?" Isabella asked. "What do you remember about that?"

"I went to the bafroom. With Jaquan. He lets me go by myself 'cause I'm a big boy."

"Did a clown come into the bathroom?"

"Yeah. He was funny."

"How was he funny?"

"He was tiptoeing and trying to climb up the walls to get out. I pointed to the door and he fell on the ground and shook his hands and feet in the air."

"That *is* funny. Did he ask you to go with him?"

The boy thought. "No, he didn't talk."

"So why did you go with him?"

"He pointed to me and the door. He made me laugh."

"And so you went with him into the woods?"

"Yeah."

"Were you scared?"

The boy looked puzzled. "No. He said he had a puppy that needed a family. He asked me if Mama would let me have it."

"So he *did* start talking to you."

"Yeah, in the woods. I wanted to wake up Jaquan and the clown said the puppy might be scared and we didn't have time."

"Was there a puppy?"

"Not at first. But then we found Cleo." The boy grinned and reached down to pet the shepherd. "She's waaaay better."

"Yes, Cleo is a good dog," Isabella confirmed. "And she likes you."

She glanced at the latest note Detective Rogerson handed her.

"Andre, this clown you went with. Was it a man clown or a woman clown?"

"A man clown," Andre said confidently.

"Was it anybody you'd ever seen before?"

The boy shrugged.

"You don't know or you don't want to tell us?"

"I don't know. Can I go outside and play with Cleo?"

Isabella sat back and raised her eyebrows at the police detective, who spoke softly. "That may be all he's going to give us for now. But try to find out how he got from the camp to way out here."

Isabella nodded. "Andre, you've been a very brave young man. But I need to know one more thing. Did you ride in a car with the clown?"

He frowned and shook his head.

"Then how did you get from your camp to the place with brown grass?"

Andre's face brightened. "We rode a bike."

"A bike? Or a motorcycle?"

"A bike like Jaquan had one time. It was a long way, and it was dark. I got tired. We had to rest lots of times. Can I go outside and play with Cleo now?"

The detective nodded his assent. Isabella held out her hand for Andre to shake. "You are a good answerer. We're happy you're home."

But he was already crouched on the floor, his arms around the black and tan shepherd, whispering in her ear. Flora joined him, pulling him into her lap beside the dog. Oren came over and placed a large hand on his son's head, patting him in much the same way that Andre was patting Cleo. As Isabella and Jim Rogerson exited Branigan's little-used front door to join officers in the yard, Branigan hung back to escort the Arnesons out. Even with all the police officers on site, she didn't trust Oren Arneson in her house. She felt bad about her unease, but not bad enough to leave him inside. When she finally got the family to the front yard, they heard radios squawk to life. Branigan made her way to Chief Warren just in time to hear Chester's voice rise above the crackle.

"Chief, we've found a body."

For a moment, everyone in Branigan's yard fell silent.

"Can you ID it?" Chief Warren asked.

There was silence for a moment on Chester's end. "Well, he has on an orange wig and face paint and wild clothes. I need to wait for the crime scene techs before touching anything. But you know who I think it is?"

Branigan, Isabella and the officers strained to hear.

"I think it's that homeless guy we interviewed. The witness."

Branigan looked at Chief Warren, stunned. "He goes by Shack," she told him. "But his real name is Bradley Drucker."

Warren handed the radio to another officer, instructing him to get Chester's position and to send a crime scene team in. He pulled out a cell phone and ordered another team to begin assembling information on Bradley Drucker, who'd been interviewed three days before at the Law Enforcement Center. "Don't contact the family until we have a positive ID, but I want to know everything there is to know about him. Hometown, education, family, jobs, previous felonies, the works. And find out why he was homeless in Grambling."

The chief called Detective Scovoy again, and consulted with Sheriff Ocher and Isabella. Then he returned to Branigan. "You got anything else on this guy Drucker?"

"He was building the stage for Shakespeare in the Park," she said. "And he quoted Shakespeare a lot. His nickname, Shack, was a bastardization of Shakes." She thought for a moment. "He told me he was from Florida originally, south Florida. He'd been in prison for domestic violence. Oh, and he had awfully good teeth to be living on the street."

Warren frowned. "So either he hadn't been out there long, or he wasn't into crystal meth. Very good, Miss Powers."

"Can I ask you something, Chief? Not for *The Rambler.* Jody Manson will be calling you on that."

"Go ahead."

"Where *is* Detective Scovoy? Where did he find the body?"

"In a barn on the Satterfield farm." He waved a hand to indicate the land adjacent to Branigan's. "Sheriff Ocher tells me the property's been vacant for two years."

"That's right. Is that where Andre was taken?"

"We can't say for sure yet, but that's what it looks like. And Miss Powers?"

"Yes?"

"Detective Scovoy said there's black and tan dog hair all over the place."

CHAPTER TWENTY-ONE

Once the city police officers, sheriff's deputies and Arnesons had cleared out, Branigan called the *Rambler* newsroom to make sure a reporter was en route to the Satterfield farm. Bert assured her that Jody was already there with a photographer – unusual in this day when reporters shot most of their own photos and videos. Bert also asked if she could come in and write a first-person account of finding Andre Arneson in the fishing shack on her farm.

As if on cue, Branigan heard the ping of another call on her cell. "Uh-oh. If you know that already, the TV stations do, too. I bet that's who's calling."

"Don't answer until we get our story online," he instructed.

"Will do. I'll file from here, then come into the office. I'll also send you a picture of Cleo. She's the one who found him. I take it we're meeting later?"

"Yeah, a few of the reporters are out of town, but everyone else is headed in. Call me when you're ready to post, and let me read over it."

"Okay."

Branigan opened her laptop at the desk in her home office. A sliding glass door opened to a back porch and offered a view all the way to the pasture. From here, trees and blackberry bushes hid the mound of greenery that covered Pa's fishing shack, but she could picture the exact spot where it sat by the lake.

Only now Branigan saw more than the bucolic scene she'd known all her life. In her mind, she saw a clown walking her pastures, gripping some sort of hammer. What was he doing way out here on her land, this kidnapper and killer? Clearly something had disrupted the kidnapping. What was it?

She got up and locked the doors she had left open when the officers left, pushing down the oily knot of trepidation in her stomach. She returned to the office, where Cleo lay sleeping beside her desk, and began writing about the dog's odd behavior of the past few days and her morning walk to find the shepherd, editing out Detective Scovoy's presence. "No use waving that red flag in Tan's face," she said aloud. It was uncomfortable writing in the first person; reporters were trained to keep themselves out of stories. Nonetheless, she plunged ahead. Getting this story online fast was the priority. She could tweak the writing for tomorrow's print edition when she got to the office.

Forty minutes later, she called Bert to alert him that the story was ready. "If I sound like too much of a goober, change it," she told him. "I'm on my way in."

She took a quick shower, dressed, woke Cleo from a deep sleep and set the alarm. The dog trotted outside and nosed around the yard where all the officers had been. She seemed to understand that her little friend was no longer in the pasture and didn't seem inclined to head that way.

Branigan gave her a hug. "You're a good dog – you know that? And you're going to be famous soon. I hope it doesn't go to your head."

She glanced uneasily once more toward her pasture, then hopped into the Civic and drove to the newspaper office, not realizing until she was nearly there that she was famished. She'd long missed lunch, and now it looked as if supper would be another Diet Pepsi and pack of crackers.

The *Rambling* staff assembled an entire front page of stories and sidebars on the finding of Andre Arneson and the murder of Bradley "Shack" Drucker, who'd been positively identified by police. Jody handled the law enforcement angle, Marjorie contributed a piece on Tent City 2, and Harley interviewed Flora Arneson and Liam for an update on the financial support from readers. Besides her first-person sidebar, Branigan wrote part of the lead story about the family's reunion at her house. Normally, the reporters wouldn't have access to a counselor's interview of the victim, but Tan took Cleo's involvement as a lucky break that got them an inside track. The tricky part came with some of Andre's assertions – for instance, that Shack "went to sleep" after being bopped with "a funny hammer". Branigan and Bert agreed to withhold the statement.

Jody reported that indeed the handsome young man had been killed by a blow to the head. No murder weapon, funny or otherwise, was found.

They couldn't speculate in the story, but Branigan's head was spinning with theories. Had Shack kidnapped Andre? Would there have been time for him to bike out to the Satterfield barn, leave the boy, and get back to Tent City 2 before Flora's screaming discovery that her son was missing? Surely the police would time such a ride in the next day or so, but it seemed unlikely.

Which meant there was a second kidnapper. Had he dressed as a clown, too? Andre said there were two. Had the second clown and Shack fought over the kidnapping to the point that he murdered Shack?

With a jolt, Branigan remembered something else that belonged in the story, and hurriedly rewrote a few paragraphs. Shakes-turned-Shack would appreciate being remembered with his quote about poor dead Yorick. The court jester.

The clown.

After Bert and Tan had wrapped up the editing, Jody, Marjorie and Harley headed to Zorina's, the newspaper staff's favorite bar located on a section of South Main far below the fashionable area. But Branigan was restless and didn't feel like drinking. She told her colleagues she might join them later.

An hour of daylight remained on this mid-spring Saturday. Branigan hopped into her Civic and headed into the countryside, no destination in mind. Now that the kidnapping had turned into a murder, she wouldn't see Chester for awhile, so she wasn't eager to go home.

She wanted time to think – to think about him, about her feelings for him, about what she wanted from this relationship. She was forty-two, and had always wanted a family. That time was past, she feared, but marriage…that was still a possibility. Was it something she'd consider with Chester? Was it something Chester would ever consider?

The thought of him, of his strong arms wrapped protectively around her – was that just last night? – sent her stomach into an excited tumble. She told herself she was being silly, downright school-girlish. She fumbled for a CD in the soft case on her passenger seat, and without looking, popped one in. When she heard the beginning strains of Chris Isaak's "Wicked Game", she knew where she was headed. She lowered her window to take advantage of the cooling evening air and belted out the song that had remained popular from high school through her college years.

She turned onto a familiar pockmarked road, one of scores that led to the shoreline of Lake Hartwell. Leafy hardwoods and fields of soybeans and aging farmhouses whipped by on both sides, but she didn't see a single person. Some dogs, cows, a horse, two mules, and that was about it.

She was on autopilot, this bumpy road as recognizable to her as the in-town street she grew up on, as familiar as the rural road that ran in front of Gran and Pa's farmhouse. She'd first visited the sprawling lake shared by Georgia and South Carolina as a toddler, riding on her Grandfather Ira's boat. Her dad had gotten a ski boat when she and her brother Davison were eleven. Some of her friends' parents had lake houses and double-decker docks, curving sliding boards and pontoons and jet skis. Almost every summer party during high school was held out here.

As soon as "Wicked Game" ended, she punched it to play again. In her mind, it was the soulful song of *that* summer. The temperature coming through the car window dropped slightly, signaling that she was nearing the water. Up ahead was the dirt turn-off that led to a boat ramp. She turned in, expecting to encounter traffic as weekend boaters left the lake. Instead, she found a faded yellow metal barrier lowered across the unpaved lane. A mud-spattered sign read "Ramp Closed for Repairs. Next Nearest Ramp is Don's Landing".

Branigan turned off the Civic motor and Chris Isaak's haunting voice, and sat in the sudden silence, broken only by cicadas and crickets and an occasional tree frog gearing up for nightfall. It was darker here under the trees, shadowy and brooding.

She left the car, ducked under the barrier and walked along the deserted track, undergrowth threatening to take it over now that cars weren't using it daily. She reached the boat ramp and saw that its concrete was broken, a piece jutting haphazardly skyward before dipping into the lake's serene waters. The US Army Corps of Engineers had gotten to the "closed" part of the project, just not the "repairs" part. There were no boats on this finger of the vast lake, undoubtedly because they were lined up to get off at some other ramp. She'd been here when it was similarly placid, when the lake was like glass, when just she and Jackson Solesbee had taken advantage of water skiing at its best, at dusk.

She'd been nineteen, home after her freshman year at the University of Georgia, working a summer job as a waitress in a pizza parlor. She'd said no to the invitation to an early June lake party from a fellow waiter because she wouldn't know anyone. But at the last minute she changed her mind.

Her colleague's parents had a ramshackle cabin but an impressive extended boat dock with a ski boat, a pontoon and a flotilla of jet skis. Most of the partygoers had attended Grambling High West, so many of them knew her cousin Robert Jr. As they talked, Branigan realized they were at least his age – twenty-two. The casual way they pulled out coolers of beer also told her they were of legal drinking age. Nonetheless, they'd made her feel welcome and she'd enjoyed the afternoon of boating and sunning and water skiing.

They'd come in around twilight, pleasantly tired, for the host to grill burgers and hot dogs. They were halfway through eating when a man drove up in a black pick-up truck with another cooler of beer. Everyone seemed to know the good-looking newcomer in worn jeans, T-shirt and John Deere cap, his dark hair curling nearly to his shoulders. His brown eyes flicked to Branigan immediately, and widened slightly.

After greeting everyone, he helped himself to a burger and beer and made his way to her, eyeing her straight blonde hair and tanned legs. Branigan silently wished she'd brought make-up to reapply; her lake-scrubbed face probably looked twelve years old.

Indeed, that was the first thing he'd said. "You don't look old enough for a beer."

She colored, avoided his implied question. "I've had some at college." She didn't tell him she far preferred wine coolers or sweet frozen daiquiris.

"College girl, huh?" He smiled and called out to his host, "Chris, where'd you find a college girl?"

"Pizza Rio," he answered. "Where else?"

He turned back to Branigan, a small smirk on his lips. "Studying the culinary arts, are you?"

She raised her chin. "No, just slumming."

He laughed. "Fair enough." He held out his hand. "I'm Jackson Solesbee."

"Branigan Powers."

"Tell me about yourself, Branigan Powers. What are you studying for real?"

Branigan and Jackson spent the next three hours deep in conversation on the cabin's lakeside porch, the surrounding woods alive with night sounds and the intoxicating smell of honeysuckle. She learned all about Jackson Solesbee, about his childhood in nearby Royston, how he'd worked summers in his uncle's construction company, how he'd attended one year of technical school, how he had dreams to run his own company. He was twenty-three and had moved to Grambling because of its building boom as international companies discovered the former textile town.

He listened intently as she told about growing up on a tree-lined street with her mom and dad and twin brother Davison, about how they were both at the University of Georgia, about how she was studying journalism and planned to be a reporter.

"What's it like having a twin?" he asked.

"A year ago I would've said great," she answered. "But now, he's never around. I never saw him at UGA. I thought we'd catch up this summer, but he's always spending nights at his buddies' houses." She shrugged. "I gotta admit, it makes me sad."

"We can't have that now, can we?" he asked, pulling her to her feet. "Let's go down to the lake."

Sitting at the end of the dock with their feet in the water, moonlight glittering like sapphires, their muted conversation continuing non-stop, Branigan had one of those moments of complete contentment. Every once in awhile a fish jumped, breaking the surface with a gentle plop. Branigan wondered if Jackson Solesbee was going to kiss her. She wondered if she was going to let him.

But he didn't, not that first night. "This is why we live in the South," he murmured.

She turned to him in surprise. "Funny you should say that. I never realized it until this year when I met a lot of people from up North and out West. They told me all their reasons for coming to UGA, and it made me realize we do have something kinda special. I'd always thought it was just… home."

"Do you like the beach?" he asked.

"More than anything," she replied.

"Maybe we can go camping later this summer."

And just like that, her magical summer began.

Branigan looked around at the gathering dark. Her perch on the cracked concrete was growing uncomfortable. She ran her hand over the rough boat ramp, site of a dozen, two dozen, launchings of Jackson's boat that summer.

She'd since learned that most people have one summer they remember for the rest of their lives; one summer that stands out as a pinnacle of youthful yearning and exhilaration. But at the time, it felt like something no one had ever experienced before. Gazing out over the water, she could almost hear their laughter as they slid the boat off the trailer, Jackson splashing to hop in before she let it drift. Sometimes, they'd make a party of it, inviting Chris and Isabella, her old high school buddies Liam and Liz, colleagues from Jackson's construction project. Sometimes, they'd go alone, hauling the boat onto a deserted island and spreading a blanket to spend a languid afternoon, then pulling each other on water skis when the sun turned the lake into a fiery reflecting pool.

Jackson picked Branigan up every evening at her parents' house, and they went out to dinner or for drives or to this very boat ramp to gaze at the stars and talk about the future. On nights she worked at the pizza parlor, he showed up with a friend from work, ordering pizza and beer so her manager wouldn't complain. Then she'd leave with him, not getting home until two or three in the morning.

At first, Branigan's parents were apprehensive about Jackson, wary of the age difference and afraid his lack of a college education might persuade her to drop out, get serious too early. But once they spent time around him, they recognized his ambition. He was as serious about a career in construction and real estate development as she was about journalism.

True to his word, he borrowed his parents' camper and took Branigan to Edisto Beach State Park on the South Carolina coast. They woke early to watch the sun rise, huddled together under a blanket with cups of coffee. By day, they swam in the ocean and discovered that surfing was nothing like water skiing. At night, they returned to look at the stars, packed absurdly close over the dark, heaving ocean.

On the last night before their return to Grambling, Jackson pulled the blanket around Branigan's shoulders. The only sound was waves lapping on the beach and palm fronds whisking together in the breeze. He leaned in close. "Hey, College Girl, I think I'm falling in love with you."

Branigan froze. She'd not expected this and didn't know what to say. It had happened so unexpectedly, so stealthily. She thought it was love, but what did that mean for them, for her?

He laughed at her silence. "Don't worry. I'm not going to ask you to leave that college of yours."

She turned, a feeling of relief and something else flooding through her. He knew her so well, respected her dreams. "I love you, too," she said.

The summer passed in a blur until, too soon, it was mid-August and time to return to school. Jackson wanted to drive her, saving her parents from having to follow her Toyota Corolla – which didn't come close to holding her belongings. They packed his truck with bedding, clothes, shoes, books, dishes, fridge – all the accoutrements of dorm life.

As they drove separately to Athens, Branigan was aware that things between them would inevitably alter. Jackson wouldn't be free to come down every weekend. With term papers and exams, she wouldn't be as carefree as she'd been this summer. She steeled herself for change, negative change. But to her surprise, they made it work. Or, if she was honest, Jackson made it work. He drove down every other weekend, a schedule that allowed her to cram her work into the days he wasn't there and to enjoy him when he was.

He joined her family for Thanksgiving, further winning her banker dad over with extensive questions about how Grambling's real estate development was being financed. Gran and Pa were pushovers, impressed with any young man as good with his hands as Jackson was.

During Christmas break, he was so excited about his present for her – a new slalom – that he gave it to her on her first night back in town.

She laughed delightedly. "Didn't take you long to figure out I'm not a jewelry and fur kind of girl."

"Thank goodness for that," he said, kissing her.

He planned to return to Royston to spend Christmas with his family, but Branigan invited him to her family's annual gathering at Uncle Bobby and Aunt Jeanie's two days earlier. "You've met Izzy B," she said, "but now you can meet the rest of the clan. Including Miss Jimmie Jean, family diva."

"So there is a jewelry and fur girl somewhere in the gene pool."

"Oh, there is."

"I can't wait to meet Her Majesty."

The Rickmans' kitchen was full to overflowing with Gran and Pa and all three of their children's families. Uncle Bobby and Aunt Jeanie's brood were home – three from college, two still in high school. Isabella ran to hug Branigan and Jackson, then turned to introduce him to the rest of the family.

In retrospect, Branigan remembered the exact moment Jackson's eyes alighted on Jimmie Jean, in a tight sweater and pencil skirt, holding a cigarette and looking as if she'd just stepped from a 1940s movie poster. His eyes widened slightly, but Branigan was too busy exchanging grins with Isabella to take note. Jimmie Jean was outdoing herself by flaunting that cigarette in front of Uncle Bobby, and the girls waited for the explosion.

As soon as everyone's attention had turned elsewhere, Jackson turned to Branigan and mouthed, "Wooh, you were right."

After a long dinner and dessert, necessarily eaten in three different rooms, Jimmie Jean sidled up to Branigan. "Wow, Cuz, you done all right."

"Thanks. I think."

"I mean it. He's a dish. Izzy B said he's a construction worker, right?"

"Well, he's saving up to start his own company." Branigan inwardly cringed at her rush to boost Jackson's status.

"Nothing wrong with that."

"So what's up with you, anyway?" Branigan asked. "Everything going all right at Auburn?"

"Actually, no. I'm going to sit out this semester."

Branigan was shocked. "You're kidding!"

Jimmie bit her lip. "I'll probably go back. I just need some time off."

"What'd Uncle Bobby say?"

"Not much. Just gave me that disappointed look that I hate. Mom's afraid I won't finish. We've been having a bit of a hullabaloo all day. I was glad to have the family over to take the focus off me."

Branigan smiled to herself. That was a first.

"Well, I hope it works out, JJ."

Branigan looked around, surprised to find that full darkness had fallen over the lake. An owl hooted eerily, and uneasiness set in. After all, there was an active search for a murderer underway. She wished Cleo was here, though the dog would be thoroughly soaked by now. Branigan stood, arching her back to relieve the stiffness, glancing around at the woods that had grown inky during her mental wanderings. She spared one last thought for the brightness of her nineteen-year-old self. She had been so innocent, so naïve. Chris Isaak's soaring voice rang in her ears, as it had so many times that year. Wicked game, indeed.

She tentatively made her way through the pitch blackness, tripping twice over fallen limbs she hadn't noticed on her way in. She reached the Civic and got in with relief, locking her doors and punching the CD player's eject button before she could hear those wounding words again.

Better to ride home in silence.

CHAPTER TWENTY-TWO

Malachi finished his eggs and bacon at St James AME, and carried his coffee out the door. He usually helped with clean-up, but not today. He was in a hurry to get a newspaper.

He walked down South Main, quiet before folks headed to church. He passed in front of the *Rambler* building, quiet, too, now that the morning edition had been delivered. He ducked into a side alley, where a recycle barrel beside the loading dock held discarded papers – ones not good enough to throw on driveways. He helped himself.

He took the paper to a bench on South Main and read every word about Miz Branigan and Cleo finding Andre Arneson on their farm, the boy's return to his family, Shack's murder. Of course, he knew a good bit of the story already. TV had it last night, and details had whipped through Tent City like a tornado.

Still, the paper had some stuff he didn't know. How the boy said a clown had biked him to the first place, which turned out to be the barn of someone named Satterfield. How he claimed he'd seen *two* clowns. Nothing about the boy seeing the murder, though.

Malachi read on to see if the reporters had the part about Andre seeing a clown in the homeless camp days *before* his kidnapping – the part he'd overheard at Miz Isabella's office door. Yep, there it was. He sat back. Miz Branigan and her friends had done a good job.

Malachi let out a long sigh. Truth was, he was relieved. Immensely relieved. He laughed out loud when he flipped inside to see a picture of Cleo, sitting like a queen on Miz Branigan's side steps. He was acquainted with the big shepherd and appreciated how protective she was of Miz Branigan.

Now that he knew he'd had nothing to do with the kidnapping – that his blackout on the hill above Tent City 2 was unconsciousness and nothing else – he was eager to talk to Miz Branigan and Detective Scovoy.

Because, despite his drunkenness, maybe he'd seen something the night of the kidnapping.

Okay, but where to start? Twice Malachi thought he'd seen swirls of white in the woods outside Tent City 2: once, before he ever heard about any clowns, and once when Miz Arneson came in, dragging Andre with her. He'd dismissed it at the time. But could it have been those giant white clown pants the reporters wrote about?

Also, Andre said a clown had approached him with candy when he was alone in the camp bathroom with his sister Stacy outside. Was that when the kidnapping was supposed to take place? Did the kidnapper see Stacy and fear she'd raise a ruckus?

A thought occurred to him, and his eyes shot open. Was Andre even the specific target? There'd been clown sightings at Oliver Creek Apartments, the elementary school and Glenden Arms. Was the kidnapper simply seeking a kid, any kid?

Surely he could've got more in ransom by snatching another kid. But ransom didn't seem to be the point. Andre had been missing for three and a half days, and no one had asked for money. Or if they did, the newspaper didn't have it. And those reporters were all over the story.

Malachi flipped back to Harley's sidebar on the family and how much money the community had raised. Over ten thousand dollars. Now that Andre had been returned, Flora Arneson told the reporter she hoped to move out of the motel and into an apartment, one with a fence all around and a playground for Stacy and Javion and Andre. No mention of her husband or Jaquan.

An idea took seed in Malachi's brain. Who benefitted from this whole kidnapping thing? As far as he could tell, only the family. What did you call that? He tried to remember his granny's vocabulary drills. *Ironic.* Yes, ironic. The very people who appeared to be suffering the most over Andre's kidnapping ended up benefitting the most. Coincidence? Maybe.

And the murder. Shack, who was the only witness to the kidnapping, was killed in the barn where the boy was first held. Dressed as a clown, yet clearly he was involved in the kidnapping. But he couldn't have been the only one. Shack had worked every day last week putting up the stage for Shakespeare in the Park. Slick said as much. Surely someone else stayed with the boy during the day. They couldn't risk him wandering around the countryside.

Slick? Nah, that didn't make sense. He was working on that stage, too.

Malachi closed his eyes and went back to the night he sat on the hill above Tent City 2, bare feet sore from the gravel, a bottle of Jim in one hand, bleary images of Mo flashing through his brain. The fire below was dying down. Earlier that night, he'd seen Oren and Jaquan Arneson join Wild Man, Butch, Randy, Shack, even Slick, around the circle, drinking and laughing.

When Miz Arneson woke everyone with her screaming, he'd seen them all again, hadn't he? Not Slick, but Slick didn't live on that side. Was someone else missing?

Malachi stood. He wanted to see if Miz Branigan was at Jericho Road this morning.

CHAPTER TWENTY-THREE

Branigan thought about sleeping in, but she was wide awake by 8 a.m. When Chester called and asked if she wanted to go to church, that sealed it. They agreed to meet at Liam's eleven o'clock service.

"I'm surprised you're not working," she said before hanging up.

"I am. I'm meeting the Arnesons and Andre at Jericho Road at noon. Isabella has agreed to sit in."

"You think Andre's got more to tell you?"

"I know he does. It's just how far and how hard we can push a four-year-old, you know? I sure don't want to do any more damage than has already been done."

"I know what you mean. But honestly, Andre doesn't seem to be traumatized. Izzy B would tell you if he was."

"Doesn't that tell you something?" Chester asked. "I mean, I get that he loved being with Cleo and all, but the boy was taken away from his mother for three days."

"Yeah, I guess I'm just grateful."

"That's what I love about you, Brani G. See you in awhile."

Branigan showered and dressed in a multicolored sundress and teal sandals. She poured a bowl of cereal and ate while rereading the morning's coverage of the kidnapping. Shack's murder got little shrift because Jody had been unable to learn much about the homeless man beyond his criminal record. She knew that whoever was assigned the Sunday desk would be working that story today, trying to track down Shack's family and interviewing people in Tent City.

She'd give anything to sit in on the interview with the Arnesons,

158

but it was a Grambling PD interrogation and she had no business there. She'd also love to talk to Malachi, hear the gossip that was undoubtedly flying around Tent City. Where was he, anyway? It broke her heart that his drinking had gotten so out of hand. She'd known, of course, there had to be a reason he was homeless. But during the year she'd known him, she hadn't seen it up close. She missed his clarity, his insight. Heck, she missed his friendship, she realized.

She drank a last cup of coffee, hugged Cleo and headed out of the door. She stood by her car and took a lingering last look at the idyllic view of her land. Who else had looked over this same view and determined it was suitable for a vile scheme?

In the dining-hall-turned-sanctuary, Branigan saw Flora, Stacy, Javion and Andre on the front row, Flora gripping Andre tightly enough to make him squirm. She didn't see Oren or Jaquan.

Liam gave thanks for Andre's safe return and asked for prayers for Shack's friends and loved ones. If the police couldn't locate Shack's family, he said, Jericho Road would hold a memorial service sometime this month.

After the opening hymn and prayer, Liam announced with a grin that his music director had prepared a special song. The director, his black eyes twinkling, hopped on the electronic keyboard and signaled to the drummer and bass player. Within a few notes, the congregation recognized Paul Simon's "Mother and Child Reunion" and laughed appreciatively.

Branigan reached to squeeze Chester's hand that rested on her shoulder. He smiled as she swayed in her seat. "We wouldn't be hearing *this* at First Baptist," she whispered.

After the service, many in the congregation stayed behind to drag folded round tables from the hallway and return the sanctuary to a dining space. It was Third Presbyterian's turn to serve, and they were ready with plates of fried chicken, okra, squash and cornbread as soon as the tables were erected. Branigan watched as the Arnesons took their plates and followed Isabella and Chester into the conference room.

Shortly afterward, she saw Oren and Jaquan standing uncertainly just inside the shelter's electric door. She hurried to show them the way to the conference room, peeking inside as she dropped them off. The children were happily digging into their chicken, but Flora ignored the plate in front of her, looking nearly as tense as Oren and Jaquan.

Upon returning to the dining hall, Branigan was delighted to see Liam talking to Malachi, who looked like the friend she remembered, showered, shaved, meeting Liam's eyes. The hand that accepted a plate of food was steady. She slipped into a seat at their table and made small talk with the parishioners, housed and homeless, as she ate the lunch a volunteer slid in front of her. She caught Malachi's eye and asked if he had time to talk afterward.

"Sure do," he said.

"You can use my office," Liam offered. "I need to see some folks out here."

After the meal, Branigan and Malachi passed the conference room in silence, then closed Liam's door and settled into his rocking chairs.

"Detective Scovoy questioning the family?" Malachi asked, with a nod at the room next door.

"Trying to get more information from Andre about his kidnappers, I think."

"I been studying on that."

Branigan leaned forward, her silence inviting him to continue.

"Your reporters wrote how much money going to Andre's family, right?"

She nodded.

"You see anything suspicious about that?" he asked.

"Predictable," she said. "Every time we write about the homeless or Tent City, donations pour in. You know that."

"Yeah, but they been food and clothes and firewood and

kerosene heaters. Stuff like that. This time it's cash money – ten thousand dollars – for one family."

"Well, people were concerned about them living under that bridge while going through the trauma of the kidnapping. And the Arnesons can't get their hands on the cash. Liam's got it."

"But now they getting an apartment – maybe a full year's rent."

She sat back. "What are you saying?"

"I ain't sure, Miz Branigan. But don't people say 'follow the money'? It seem strange no one asked for any money for that boy. Or that a homeless boy got kidnapped to begin with. But now the only place money turn up is with his family."

She thought for a moment, considering what she knew of Flora and Oren. Precious little. Oren had been buying alcohol before the kidnapping, but that wasn't unusual for someone on the street. He could've sold food stamps, for all she knew. Could the couple have known that serious money would come in after the kidnapping? And even if they had, could a parent do that?

"Plus," Malachi continued, "Shack had to be in on it, right? To be dressed up like a clown in the same spot you find Andre? I saw him talking to the daddy and Jaquan plenty of times."

"But there were clown sightings all over town."

Malachi waved the comment away. "Coulda set them up ahead of time. Or coulda hopped on the crazy clown bandwagon."

Branigan snorted. Malachi's use of language cracked her up.

They heard chairs scraping in the room next door, and she held up her hand for silence. "Sounds like they're breaking up," she whispered. "Tell Detective Scovoy what you've told me."

Before they could move, a knock sounded on Liam's door, and Chester stuck his head in. "Liam said you two were in here." Without waiting for an invitation, he took a wing chair. Isabella followed him in and rolled Liam's desk chair to join the circle.

"Malachi's got something to tell you," Branigan said.

"Okay, shoot." Over the past year, Chester had grown to respect Malachi's insights as much as Branigan did.

Malachi went over the same ground he'd broached with Branigan. Chester stared at the ceiling, visibly rearranging facts in his head. "We've had our eye on Oren," he agreed. "He's doing his level best to get his hands on that ten thousand dollars, threatening to tell the media that Liam is withholding it from his family."

Branigan looked from Chester to Isabella in astonishment, but Isabella backed him up with a nod. "Before Oren was in the room," she added, "Flora asked me if Liam could pay up as many months of rent as the money allowed. She wanted to make sure Oren didn't get hold of it."

Chester continued. "So I could definitely see Oren involved. We contacted law enforcement in Raleigh. They're the ones who have a warrant, and it turns out it's for a scam. Different, but he's definitely capable of scamming."

"What was it?" asked Branigan. "In Raleigh, I mean."

"He and a young man – maybe Jaquan, I don't know – posed as firemen checking homeowners' smoke detectors. They got inside, one distracted the owner, and the other stole jewelry, cash, whatever they could find. Nothing sophisticated."

Chester paused, and no one interrupted his pondering. "But Flora?" he said. "I have to admit, I haven't seriously considered her. Oren doesn't know it yet, but he's going to jail in North Carolina. We've been holding off, trying to get more information on this kidnapping and murder." It was obvious the detective was thinking out loud, testing Malachi's idea. "So when all is said and done, Flora's the one who comes out ahead. Gets rid of a no-good husband *and* gets an apartment for her and her kids."

Isabella interrupted. "The only thing is..."

Chester finished for her. "She seemed genuinely distraught while Andre was missing, didn't she?"

Isabella nodded. "Definitely. Could she be that good an actress?"

The four sat for awhile longer, each puzzling on the little they knew of the Arneson family, wondering about the lengths to which they might go to escape homelessness.

"Oh, one more thing," Isabella said, pulling a sheet of drawing paper from her oversized purse. "While you were talking to his parents, Andre drew me a picture of the clown that took him. I don't think it'll be much help."

"Let's see," said Chester.

It was a crude drawing in red and black crayon. The red hair and round red nose were impossibly out of scale, taking up half the page. A black squiggly line was just under the face, between it and the dwarf body.

"What's that?" asked Branigan.

"He said it was a snake," Isabella said. "Maybe from the barn or your fishing shack?"

Branigan and Malachi stared at the drawing.

"It's on the clown's neck," murmured Malachi.

Branigan's heart began to race. "A snake tattoo?" she said, her voice rising in excitement. "We know someone with a snake tattoo!"

Chester was already pulling out his cell phone. "The guy from Tent City. What's his name, Malachi?"

"Randy," he answered. "Name's Randy."

CHAPTER TWENTY-FOUR

Chester hit Liam's office door on the run, talking to a colleague as he sprinted down the hall. "Pick up Oren Arneson at the Heart of Grambling," he said. "No arrest. Person of interest. And send back-up to Tent City, the side where the kidnapping took place."

Shoving his phone back in a holster, he jumped into his car and began shouting into the radio. Branigan hoped someone was in the newsroom to hear the police scanner. She turned to Malachi. "Randy? I didn't see that coming."

"Me neither. But I been thinking about that night of the kidnapping. I'd been drinking some." He looked embarrassed.

Branigan nodded, unsurprised. "And?"

"And earlier, I saw the daddy and Jaquan talking to Wild Man, Shack, Butch and Randy. But after it happened, with all the running around and yelling, I couldn't remember who was there. Now I think of it, I didn't see Randy. He coulda been in his tent. But he wasn't out there with everybody else."

"Sounds like Detective Scovoy is on the right track then."

"Guess I'll mosey on over and see what happen."

"I'll come with you," she said. "Not for *The Rambler*. Just visiting my buddy Malachi. You can ride with me." She turned to Isabella. "You working today?"

"Yeah, Sunday's a work day for us. Want to grab dinner later?"

"Sure. Caprisano's okay? That's the nearest for me."

"Fine. I can meet you at 6:30."

She hugged Isabella. "See you then."

She parked the Civic on the side of the road nearest Tent City, and she and Malachi walked along the trash-strewn path to the camp.

When they couldn't hear anything, they tiptoed up the hill and across the railroad tracks. A Grambling police car was parked nose-to-nose with Chester's Crown Vic, blocking the dirt path out of Tent City 2.

Malachi pointed out Butch and Randy's tent, where Chester was talking to someone.

"Is that Randy?" Branigan asked. "I can't tell from here."

"Nah, that's Butch," Malachi said. Two uniformed officers were making their way around the campsite, looking inside every tent. With Jericho Road serving lunch and the public library open, the rest of the camp appeared to be vacant.

Branigan saw Chester slap his leg in frustration, then look up and catch sight of them. He shook his head, and Butch joined him in his car.

"It look like Randy done took off," Malachi said.

Branigan pulled out her cell phone and called Jody. "Are you working today?"

"Yeah, on my way to the LEC. Heard some chatter about officers headed to Tent City."

"Okay, good. Then you didn't hear anything from me."

"Who is this?"

"Atta boy. See you tomorrow."

With the situation in police hands, Branigan headed back to the farm. It was still early afternoon when she pulled within sight of her driveway and spied a new-model metallic red truck. She glanced in her mirror and saw the empty country road stretching both ways. It was lonely enough out here that kidnappers had held Andre for three nights with no one hearing the slightest sound. She was reluctant to confront a stranger in her driveway, and started to make a U-turn and go back to her Uncle Bobby's. But then she glimpsed Cleo racing across the front yard in pursuit of a tennis ball. The visitor had won her dog over.

For goodness' sakes, she chastised herself, *it's broad daylight*. She veered into the driveway just as the figure threw the ball again.

She parked beside the truck. Almost before her eyes could

register who he was, her heart caught on, slamming into her ribs.

"Brani G," said the voice, so foreign, so familiar.

"Hello, Jackson."

She hadn't seen him in the four years she'd been back in Grambling or during all the years she'd lived in Detroit. He didn't often spend Christmas with Uncle Bobby and Aunt Jeanie, but when he did, her mom forewarned her. She'd been able to avoid him other than at a handful of weddings and funerals.

But here he was, not so very much changed from the man he was at twenty-three. He was a little thicker through the shoulders and torso, and his hair was shorter with as much gray as brown. He hadn't shaved in a couple of days, and the lines around his brown eyes were pronounced from years in the Florida sun. But those eyes glittered with the same sad warmth as his smile. Despite the years, despite the relationships she'd known since, her heart pinched.

"How are you?" he asked. "I've wanted to ask you that a thousand times."

"Just fine," she said with a shaky wave at the farmhouse. "I moved back here four years ago. It was time to come home." She brought her hand to her side, willing the trembling to stop.

"I wonder about that every time I'm in Royston," he said, gazing over her fields. "But West Palm is where the work is." He leaned against his truck. "I like your dog. She looks like the ones your grandparents had."

Branigan fought to keep her tone breezy. "Yeah, Cleo's from the same line." She patted the dog, then pulled her hand back when she saw the tremor. Why was her body reacting this way? "What are you doing here?"

He turned, and smiled sadly again. "On my way to Bobby and Jeanie's. Not sure how welcome I'll be."

She didn't answer.

"Can I come in?" he asked.

"No, I don't think so," she said. "Anything you want to say, you can say out here." She hadn't meant to sound sharp, but it came out that way. When he looked abashed, she added, "And Jimmie Jean might see your truck."

He smiled. "Fair enough." He sighed deeply. "I owe you an apology."

She laughed without amusement. "I hope you're kidding."

He looked at her. "No, I'm not. That was a crappy thing I did and I've never felt right about it." He looked down and kicked at the driveway, seemingly trying to gather his courage. "I loved you. You know I did. But you were so... so *driven*. I knew you were going places and I didn't know if I could keep up." He finally pulled his eyes back up to meet hers.

Was she hearing this right? "That is the stupidest thing I ever heard," she said flatly. She noted that her hands had stopped shaking.

She recalled the morning after the family dinner at Aunt Jeanie's. Jackson kissed her goodbye and went to spend Christmas with his family in Royston. They'd intended to spend part of the next week together, but his father had gotten sick, and he'd not returned to Grambling until after she left for school.

They talked on the phone almost every night, and she expected to resume the every-other-weekend schedule they'd kept in the fall. But on the second weekend of January, his mother had mysteriously fallen ill, and he'd returned to Royston. And on the fourth weekend, he was detained by a work project.

Fighting a rising suspicion, Branigan drove home unannounced. It was her mother who broke the news: friends had seen Jackson out with Jimmie Jean. Grambling wasn't a small town any more, but it was small enough. Plus, as Jimmie Jean later told her, they went out as friends at first. That's why they weren't trying to sneak around.

By that point, Branigan was hardly listening to Jimmie Jean's explanations. Jackson's betrayal was bad enough. But to betray her with the cousin she considered so laughably melodramatic was a blow. It made her think she'd never known him.

When Jimmie Jean announced in early April that they were marrying and moving to Florida, Branigan, alone in Athens, crumpled, beyond the reach of her college friends, beyond the reach of her family. She wondered at the small civil ceremony to which neither she nor her parents nor even Gran and Pa were invited. After all, this was Jimmie Jean's chance to grab the spotlight. Only years later did Branigan realize that Aunt Jeanie had stepped in and refused to allow a flamboyant church wedding. By doing so, she had salvaged family relationships that might otherwise have frayed.

Now looking at Branigan's immobile face, Jackson tried again. "You had a newspaper career all mapped out, and I thought you might end up overseas or up North or on the West Coast, or who knew where? Jimmie Jean didn't have that kind of ambition. She'd dropped out of college and didn't want to go back, no matter what she told her parents. I felt like she needed me. I never felt that from you."

"That's pathetic," Branigan said.

"I know."

"My problem was not that you broke up with me," she said. "It was that you flat-out disappeared. I had to piece everything together from Jackson-and-Jimmie-Jean sightings. It was humiliating."

He hung his head and booted Cleo's tennis ball back into the yard. But Cleo, sensing tension, refused to leave Branigan's side. Now that she was alone with him for the first time in two decades, Branigan genuinely wanted an answer.

"Why didn't you just tell me? We talked on the phone for weeks when you were already with her. You could have told me so many times."

His eyes locked on the front yard, refusing to meet hers. "I knew how you felt about JJ. I guess I was embarrassed. And also a little giddy about having two beautiful women in love with me. I was immature, that's for sure." His eyes slid back to her face. "But believe me, I have paid for it. More than you know."

Branigan laughed, this time in amusement. "This is not the place you want to come for sympathy, bud."

He wiped a hand across his face. "I know." He pulled himself up. "I am truly sorry for the way I behaved. It was unforgiveable. But I am asking you to forgive me."

She shrugged, and realized that the words she had waited so long to hear had no power after all. Incongruously, she thought of the Annie Dillard quote about saving words for too long: "You open your safe and find ashes."

"No problem," she said with a sincerity that was freeing. "It was a long time ago."

He winced almost imperceptibly. "Okay, then. I'm headed over to the Rickmans'."

"Are you staying with them?"

"No, I've been with Mom in Royston. I don't know if you knew, but my dad died two years ago. So Mom's glad to have a Mr Fix-It around for a few days." He grimaced. "Wish me luck. Jimmie Jean is not happy with me these days."

"And she's got guns now."

"What?"

"Annie Get Your Gun. She's the lead."

"Ah, of course she is."

He climbed into his truck but didn't shut the door. "I know it doesn't matter now, but I realized within the first year I'd chosen the wrong cousin."

"You're right," she said, understanding it was true as she spoke the words. "It doesn't matter now."

After Jackson had left, Branigan went inside and traded her sundress for soft pajama pants and a sleeveless T-shirt. She came back to the den and fell full-length onto the sofa.

"Do you believe that, Cleo? I'm too driven? Is that a crock, or what?"

The dog whimpered agreement, Branigan could have sworn it.

"I think maybe we dodged a bullet, my friend. Those two deserve each other." Cleo laid her big head on Branigan's stomach. Branigan picked up the novel that lay open on the coffee table, but couldn't concentrate. She got up and paced the length of the house, from den to kitchen to office to bedroom and back again, Cleo remaining watchful but unwilling to leave the coolness of the den's tile floor. But to Branigan's surprise, it wasn't Jackson on her mind. It was Shack, holding up a biscuit and quoting the iconic line from *Hamlet*: "Alas, poor Yorick! I knew him, Horatio…."

She remembered Shack's handsome features and straight white teeth. What was he doing in a homeless encampment? He'd gone to prison for domestic violence, but lots of former prisoners overcame worse. Why'd he give up? She had a sudden thought. Or was he looking for a way out? Was the kidnapping somehow a way out of Tent City?

She turned on her laptop to check the *Rambler* website. Jody hadn't posted anything yet. She suddenly couldn't wait to get to the office tomorrow and see what the staff could unearth. She answered her emails, and spent some time checking what other newspapers had run about Grambling's kidnapping and murder. What would've been a local story got wide play because of the clown angle.

She glanced at the clock on her computer and saw with a start that it was nearly six o'clock. "I hope you got your exercise with that tennis ball," she called to Cleo, rushing to change into slacks to meet Isabella. By six-thirty, she was at Caprisano's, a glass of Prosecco in front of her.

"Ah, you read my mind," said Isabella, sliding into the booth across from her and accepting the second glass. "Busy day at the zoo."

"What's up?"

"Mostly a lot of bad information about Shack. He was a mobster. He was a drug runner. He was an arms dealer. He was a serial rapist. And my personal favorite, he was a Hollywood star hiding out."

"Oh, my. Liam and Malachi say there's a lot of false information on the street."

"I look forward to reading what you guys turn up on him. The real story."

"Did you ever meet him?"

"Not really. We passed at dinner one night. What was his real name again?"

"Brad Drucker. From south Florida."

"Speaking of which…" Isabella turned her glass in her hands. "I got a call from Mom."

"Let me guess. A brother-in-law from south Florida showed up at your house."

"How'd you know?"

"He came by the farmhouse."

"You're kidding!"

Branigan shook her head.

Isabella took a gulp of wine. "Does Jimmie Jean know?"

"She won't hear it from me. We stood in the driveway for the entire conversation – which was short."

"What'd he want?"

Branigan shrugged. "Nothing really. He sort of apologized. Do you realize that's the first real conversation we've had since he left town?"

"Well, you've done your best to stay away from him. I'll hand you that." Isabella hesitated for a moment. "Did you… feel anything? Was it upsetting?"

Branigan thought for a minute. "No, kind of jarring, but not upsetting. I think it was good, showed me how different we turned out to be." She blushed. "Of course, I think it helps that I'm pretty smitten with Detective Scovoy."

"I'm glad," said Isabella sincerely. "He's a good guy. So anyway, catch me up on the man with the snake tattoo. There's a title for your first novel, by the way."

Branigan laughed. "Malachi and I drove over to Tent City, but Randy was long gone. We saw Chester take his tent mate, Butch, to the station for questioning. Jody hasn't posted anything yet, but I'll keep looking tonight."

"So this Randy and Shack kidnapped Andre," Isabella mused,

"then had a falling out and Randy killed Shack? Is that what you're thinking?"

"Could be."

"To what end?"

"That, Izzy B, is the question. Did they have a problem with Oren, and try to hit him where it hurt? That seems more likely to me than Malachi's idea that Flora was involved. Or were they pedophiles? But you didn't get the sense that Andre had been molested, did you?"

"No, not molested," Isabella said slowly. "But he avoided our last questions. Maybe he was tired. Or maybe he was scared."

Branigan sat back, wondering at all the things that could scare a four-year-old who'd been snatched from his mother.

CHAPTER TWENTY-FIVE

The newsroom was as full as it ever got on a Monday morning. Whether the reporters were working the kidnapping/murder story or not, they wanted to hear about the local coverage that was getting national play.

"Everybody in the bullpen," Tan-4 shouted, pointing to the conference room.

"And here we go," Marjorie muttered.

"Jody, you're the lead-off batter," Bert started. "Catch everyone up."

Jody flipped open his notebook and carefully avoided Branigan's eyes. "The biggest break," he said, "is that yesterday the police got a clue from the kidnapped kid that the clown who took him had a snake tattoo on his neck."

The reporters stirred. "Wow," said Harley. "That guy we talked to in the camp?"

"Yeah," said Jody. "The police – and we, for that matter – remembered that this guy Randy who lived in the tent next to Shack had a snake tattoo. But when the police got to the camp, his buddy said he'd left on Friday. Police checked and he apparently caught a 6:15 bus for St Louis Friday evening. They've alerted the St Louis police. Plus, a city police officer and a county deputy are headed there as well."

"Jurisdictional issues?" asked Tan.

"Right. The kidnapping was in the city but the murder was in the county."

"The part about Randy, though," Harley pointed out. "That wasn't in your story this morning."

"The police asked us to hold off on his name and description until they can pick him up. If he doesn't know they've made the connection, he'll be easier to catch. Tan agreed to give them twenty-four hours."

"Back up a minute," Branigan said. "Do you know when Shack was killed?"

"Sometime Friday at the Satterfield place is all we know. Then apparently the killer took Andre to your property."

"Do we know why?" demanded Tan.

"Maybe so he could be found?" ventured Branigan. She thought for a moment. "So the timeline fits for Randy to have killed Shack and taken off. But I wonder why he would have."

"A falling out among thieves?" Harley guessed. "Or among kidnappers?"

They sat in silence, then Jody continued. "Here's what we've got on the victim. Some of this came from the police, and some from our phone calls. Part of it made this morning's paper, but a lot we couldn't use. For obvious reasons.

"Bradley Drucker, aka Shack, was born in 1990 in Jupiter, Florida. His father was a developer and the family was well off. Brad went to the University of Florida in Gainesville, and began smoking marijuana. Pretty heavily. His dad said he wasn't going to pay for that and he cut off his funding.

"Brad returned home, but he and his dad didn't get along. He drifted around doing odd jobs, and married a woman named Maria Quinoles. He seemed to straighten up for awhile, and got a construction job in West Palm Beach. With Solesbee Construction."

Branigan's head jerked up. "That's Jimmie Jean's husband," she said. "My cousin."

"Can you put us in touch with him?" asked Bert.

"Sure, I can give you Jimmie Jean's number. He's actually with her in Grambling right now."

"Annie Oakley?" Gerald said.

"Right."

When the other reporters looked puzzled, Gerald explained. "Branigan's cousin is the lead in *Annie Get Your Gun* at Theater on the Square."

Jody resumed his story. "Anyway, things fell apart in West

Palm Beach. Drucker left Solesbee Construction under a cloud. I couldn't get the full story, so I'd love to talk to your cousin-in-law or whatever he is, Brani G. Apparently things were crashing in on our guy, because around the same time, police answered several domestic calls at the Drucker apartment. Ultimately, he was arrested for CDV and sentenced to three years in prison. He got out after eighteen months.

"Then he went off the radar. He told Branigan he drifted from south Florida to Orlando to Valdosta to Macon, and there's no reason to doubt it. The folks in the homeless shelter in Macon did recognize his name, so we know he was living on the street by the time he got there."

"That happens a lot," said Marjorie. "Once someone has a felony, almost no one will hire them. Liam says that 'paying your debt to society' is a myth."

"Marjorie, you have anything else from Liam on this guy?" Bert asked. "Or from the Tent City folks?"

"Liam thinks Shack showed up in Grambling maybe three years ago." Marjorie took up the story. "But he never moved to Jericho Road. He lived for awhile by himself in the woods, but his shack or shed or whatever got destroyed in a storm. So he got hold of a tent and pitched it in Tent City 2. This was his third summer working on the stage and sets for Shakespeare in the Park."

"I see three places in that story to explore," said Bert. Everyone listened carefully, for they respected the city editor's incisiveness. "One, the intersection with the theater, since we think that's where he got the clown costume. Two, the intersection with Tent City, since that's where the kidnapping took place. And three, what happened at Solesbee Construction?" He looked at Branigan. "Sounds like we lucked out that the owner's in town. He may be able to give us some good color about what our guy was like."

She shrugged. "Go right ahead."

Bert paused and twirled his chair left and right in a motion the reporters recognized. "You know what else strikes me about this guy?" he asked rhetorically. "He reminds me of that girl who was killed last winter and had been living in the homeless camp. Turned out she was the daughter of that rich family in Gainesville, Georgia."

The reporters well remembered the story with ties to the local Rutherford Lee College.

He continued. "We think of homelessness as the end result of generational poverty, but that's not always the case."

"As Liam says, it's not either/or," agreed Marjorie in her raspy smoker's voice. "It's and/and/and/and."

When everyone looked confused, Branigan jumped in to explain. "There are all kinds of reasons someone loses a home. Some were always poor. Some were doing all right but got hit by a catastrophe – medical crisis, sudden disability, divorce. Some are mentally ill or disabled. Some are substance abusers. Some are sex offenders or former felons who can't get jobs. But hiding among them are criminals, and occasionally, people hiding out from something else – like our college girl last winter."

"So this Shack sounds like he's a mix of several categories," Bert said. "He had an upper middle class upbringing but a criminal background, too."

"And probably drug and alcohol use," Branigan said. "I kept wondering about his good teeth and his affinity for Shakespeare. His background explains that."

Bert slapped his hands on the conference table. "Okay, here's the line-up. Gerald, you help Branigan with anything she needs on the theater."

Gerald looked surprised. He rarely worked on stories outside previews and reviews and art features.

"Marjorie, you take the camp and see if there are any other details about Shack's time there that we've missed. Art's on vacation," he said, referring to the business writer, "so Harley, see what you can find out about Bradley Drucker's time with Solesbee Construction." He looked at the notes he'd scribbled. "And Jody, keep following law enforcement progress on Randy with the snake tattoo. That's definitely the most promising lead right now. All right? Let's knock it out of the park."

Branigan provided Harley with Jimmie Jean's cell phone number, then reluctantly pulled a chair up to Gerald Dubois' desk. He was a good-looking guy, around thirty-five, with an aristocratic nose and thick dark hair, but he was not among her favorite colleagues. She knew he'd changed his name from Jerry Dubert when he arrived from South Carolina – a fact that kept the other reporters doubled up in laughter during late-night sessions at Zorina's. Worse, he identified more with the arts community than with the newspaper. And that was dangerous. Tan-4 had clamped down on her the minute she started dating a police detective, but Gerald's socializing with painters and directors and musicians seem to go unchecked. Marjorie had once accused him of being "a handmaiden to the arts", and he'd looked pleased and said, "Yes, I suppose I am." The other reporters were dumbfounded that he hadn't recognized the remark as the insult she'd intended.

But the arts beat was Tan-4's call, Branigan acknowledged, not hers. She sighed, and plunged in.

"I've already talked to Reggie Fortenberry and Barbara Wickenstall about the clown costumes," she said. "But I guess I'll double back and talk to them about Shack. And see if they're acquainted with Randy. Any other ideas?"

"Yes, actually. The assistant director and facilities manager may have had more contact with this Shack than Reggie did. Sam Sebastian directs the Shakespeare, and Robert Mangione handles the stage and set building."

"Okay, good. Do you want to set up interviews and we'll talk to them together?"

He looked relieved. "Yes, let's do that. Do you want them together as well?"

Branigan thought for a minute. "No," she said. "Let's hit them individually. You never know – there might be something they're unwilling to say in front of each other."

He turned to pick up his desk phone. "I'll let you know when they can see us."

Branigan and Gerald met with Robert Mangione just before lunch. He came in earlier than his colleagues because he didn't need to stay for late rehearsals at this stage of production.

They followed the heavy-set construction boss into a high-ceilinged workshop that opened directly onto the main stage; the arrangement allowed sets to slide easily into place. A heavy velvet curtain in royal purple was closed, so they couldn't see the theater seats.

"We finished the outdoor stage on Friday," Robert called over his shoulder as he pointed them to paint-spattered chairs. "Today we started building sets. I've got one crew on *Annie Get Your Gun* and one on *Midsummer Night's Dream*." He looked from Gerald to Branigan. "But don't you need to speak to Reggie?"

"No, this isn't about the shows," Gerald said. "This is about the murder of your crew member, Brad Drucker. Or Shack."

"Oh, right," said the large man. "You said that on the phone. But I don't know anything except what I saw on TV."

"So was Shack at work on Friday?" asked Branigan.

"Oh, yeah, and he was a decent worker. When you could keep him from going off on monologues." He chuckled.

"Do you know what time he left?"

"We were pretty much finished by three o'clock."

"But are you sure he was here right up until three?"

"Yeah. I remember because I heard his buddy Slick ask if he wanted to get a beer. And he said maybe later, as he had somewhere to go."

"So he and Slick didn't leave together?"

"No, Slick was on foot. Shack had a bike."

"And the other nights. How late did he stay?"

"I'm sure he stayed until quitting time, which was anywhere from six to eight o'clock Tuesday through Thursday. I didn't notice him especially, but I woulda noticed if he'd been gone. The other workers woulda been squealing, believe me."

Branigan tapped the top of her pen against her teeth, thinking. "Mr Mangione, did you ever hire another worker named Randy, who lived with Shack and Slick in Tent City? I don't have a last name. He had a snake tattoo on his neck."

"No, that doesn't ring a bell. He didn't work here."

Branigan sat back in her chair, out of specific questions. "Did you notice anything at all throughout the week that could have a bearing on Shack's murder? Any argument he had? Anyone he didn't get along with? Any behavior that was off?"

He chuckled again. "Well, no one got after him except Barbara. She's a pistol."

"Barbara Wickenstall?" Branigan asked. "What was she after him about?"

"Apparently, she caught him in her costume room. You don't mess with Barbara's costumes."

"When was this?"

"Late in the week because I remember he was on the outdoor stage when she confronted him. There wouldn't have been a surface for them to stand on before Thursday evening."

"And do you remember what she said?"

"Not the exact words. But she was giving him hell, pardon my French, for messing around in her wardrobe."

"Is she coming in today?"

"Sure. She's always here by one. Every day, like clockwork."

As they stood to leave, Branigan saw a ripple in the heavy drape. Without thinking, she strode to the center opening and snatched one side of the curtain. No one was there.

"Something wrong?" asked Robert.

"I thought maybe…" she said, peering into the dark auditorium. "No, no, nothing's wrong."

Branigan and Gerald left their cars at the theater and walked through the park and over to Main Street, where they ordered sandwiches and iced teas from Bea's Bakery. They carried the food back to Reynolds Park, selecting a bench that gave them a good view of the stage and the theater as they awaited their interview time with assistant director Sam Sebastian.

"So what did you think of what Robert said?" Gerald asked her, unwrapping his lunch.

"Since Shack didn't leave here until three o'clock Friday, he narrowed the window for his murder," she said. "But more importantly, I want to talk to Barbara again. Did she learn by Thursday that Shack had taken the clown costume? And if so, why didn't she tell the police?"

They ate for awhile in silence.

"How well do you know Barbara?" Branigan asked.

"I'd say she's the glue that holds this place together," Gerald said. "She's super professional and capable and creative, but without the histrionics of some."

"Are you speaking of anyone in particular?"

Gerald smiled. "I respect Reggie, but he's kind of over the top, even for me."

Branigan raised an eyebrow. "Your reviews have had a lot to do with his success here," she said.

"Oh, yeah. His work is top notch, no question. He's a very talented man. But personally, he's quite the..." He appeared to search for a word.

"Divo?"

"Yeah, divo." Gerald laughed. "That'll do. And while you, being a normal person, read those reviews as positive, you should hear what he has to say when I criticize the least little thing."

"Like what?"

"Let's see. I said the sound system for *The Sound of Music* went in and out. You'd have thought I insulted his mother. I said the casting of actresses too close in age made the mother and daughter unbelievable in *The Glass Menagerie*. He went so ballistic over that with Tan and Bert that Tan threatened to end our theater reviews."

"I never knew that."

"And I wrote something about not being a Horton Foote fan – not even criticizing the production itself – and he completely flipped out. He's either your best friend or your biggest enemy. Depends on what day it is. Or what hour."

As if on cue, Reggie came flying around the newly erected stage, headed straight for the reporters. "I thought that was you!" he cried. "I saw you from my window! What in the world are you doing here?"

"One of your stage builders was murdered, and we're trying to trace his last hours," said Branigan.

"Yes, such a nasty business! I've been engrossed by your coverage. Simply engrossed! Makes me wonder if it's time to bring back Agatha Christie's *The Mousetrap*. Stuck in a snowy isolated mansion sounds delicious about now, doesn't it?" He looked delighted at the prospect. "So how can we help?"

"Did you have any contact with Brad Drucker? The one they called Shack?" Branigan asked.

"Not really. As I told your young reporter friend, I hardly know a hammer from a screwdriver. So I stay away from the construction site."

"Do you know if something happened between him and Barbara?"

He gestured at the outdoor stage. "Yes, she was stomping around and complaining of someone being in her wardrobe. But I wasn't really listening." He held a hand to his mouth and giggled. "Is that awful? Am I an awful boss? But that happened about the same time as I had an epiphany about letting Frank Butler and Annie Oakley use their rifles as fencing sabers. I've never seen that anywhere. Have you?" He looked from Branigan to Gerald, apparently expecting an answer.

"Can't say that I have," said Gerald. "And I've seen that show a dozen times."

If it was a slap, Reggie chose to let it pass. "I think the fencing's going to work," he said. "Both our Annie and our Frank are quite brilliant, willing to try anything."

Branigan struggled to keep a straight face. "We'll talk to Barbara ourselves," she said.

Sam Sebastian was a short, balding, rotund man in a profession that attracted whippet-thin, spiked-hair types. Gossip had it that Reggie, self-conscious about his five-foot-five height, had deliberately hired someone even shorter. For his part, Sam gave every appearance of not caring a whit for such things. He was affable and considerate. If some actors wanted to work with Reggie because of his reputation for high standards, others sought out Sam's productions for the assistant director's kindness.

"I understand you're directing the Shakespeare this summer," Branigan started off, having been briefed by Gerald.

"That's right," Sam said, ushering the reporters into his office adjacent to the workshop. It wasn't as cramped as Barbara's, but it was small. Someone had made an effort to make it cozy, painting it the palest blue, hanging colorful framed production posters, and placing an antique set of bound Shakespeare and family photos on a table beneath the single window. Branigan's eye took in a picture of a similarly rotund woman and two gawky teens and wondered if his wife had decorated the office. She and Gerald took seats in a pair of slim parson chairs covered in blue linen, while Sam settled behind his desk.

"Sometimes," he continued, "I work alongside Reggie, especially on a musical. It's hard for a single director to handle a musical. And sometimes I direct a separate fringe show, or in the summer, Shakespeare. That's my favorite."

"But Reggie is directing *Annie Get Your Gun* by himself this summer."

"Indeed, he is. Quite the undertaking. He's a gifted man, our Reggie."

Branigan smiled, looking for sarcasm, but not hearing it. "So, Sam, can you tell us anything about this man Brad Drucker, or Shack? We understand he worked on the stage and sets for three summers."

"Oh, yes, I knew Brad quite well," Sam said.

Branigan was surprised. "So he didn't just work with Robert?"

"Well, he *worked* with Robert. But he often stayed to watch our rehearsals. I'd hear him running the lines like the actors do. Last summer, I invited him to try out. But it just so happened that Reggie was directing the next Shakespeare production, and Brad declined. I believe he thought he wouldn't measure up."

"What about this summer?"

"He was coming around. He came into my office to talk, sat right where you're sitting."

"To talk about what?" Branigan asked.

"Just shooting the breeze, really. I got the impression he was trying to work up his nerve to try out. I brought it up, and he kind of backed off, so I let him ramble. For a little while, at least, until I had to get to work."

"Can you try to remember what he talked about?" Branigan pressed. "It might be important, because he was apparently planning the kidnapping around the same time."

"Oh, my, I suppose so. Let's see. He said he was living in that homeless encampment under the bridge but he planned to be out soon. I asked if he had a job lined up, because I figured that's the only way he'd manage it. And he said he was expecting a small inheritance from his family in Florida."

"An inheritance?" echoed Branigan. "That's the first we've heard of that."

"He said it wouldn't be much, maybe just one or two thousand dollars. But he indicated that once he had a permanent address, a shower, clean clothes, all that, he was confident he could find a real job."

She leaned back in her chair and looked at Gerald. "We can look into that," she said.

"So you think that wasn't true?" Sam asked. "He was expecting money from somewhere else? Like the kidnapping?"

"I really don't know," she said, "but that's a pretty small amount for an inheritance." She paused. "Sam, one thing occurs to me. Shack seemed awfully comfortable around this theater. He was at rehearsals and in your office. And we're on our way to see Barbara. Sounds like he was in her wardrobe."

"As you can see, we're not much on security," he said with a shrug. "Though now, we may have to institute further measures. That'd be a shame because it would change the culture of the theater."

"What do you mean?"

He toyed with a pen on his desk. "You may not realize it, but every theater has its own personality. I've worked in several, so I know. Some can be closed and paranoid and cut-throat. Some are light-hearted and creative and fun. This one is special. We have our share of melodrama – that's to be expected. But the range and diversity of shows, the elegant physical plant, the availability of terrific talent, the supportive community – all that is pretty special. It allows an openness to artistic risk and challenge. You might not think that goes along with an unsecured campus, but I think it does." He shrugged. "Anyway, that's my two cents' worth."

Branigan nodded, and thanked him. But her mind was on a theater where a calculating kidnapper felt free to roam.

Branigan and Gerald left Sam's office, traversing the workroom in time to hear the set-building hammers and drills start up after a lunch break.

"The offices around here aren't as lavish as I'd expect after seeing the lobby and theater," she commented.

"You haven't seen Reggie's," he said.

"Really?"

"Oh, yeah. His is huge, with high ceilings and expensive furniture and oil paintings and a private bath. Very posh."

"Hmm, so he doesn't share the wealth with the rest of his staff. What about the salaries?"

"The board sets those, so I'm not sure how much control he has," Gerald answered. "But he makes six figures. The next closest is Sam, who makes about half what he does. Then Robert and Barbara, a little behind Sam. Then the others way on down. And remember, they get a ton of volunteer labor on everything from playbills to fundraising to ushers."

They came to the anteroom that led to Barbara Wickenstall's office.

"She's expecting us," said Gerald. "This way."

As they entered Barbara's tiny office, she stood to welcome them. "Hello, you two. I'm going to give you my chair, Branigan," she said, indicating her rolling office chair and waving away Branigan's protest. She motioned Gerald into the ladderback, then moved into the office's only remaining space against the bookshelf.

"I'm sure you've read about the death of Brad Drucker, or Shack," Branigan started. "We are working on the assumption that he was one of the kidnappers. We heard that you had an altercation with him – last Thursday, maybe?"

"I hate to speak ill of the dead, but you better believe I did," she retorted. "When I passed by the park stage Thursday afternoon, I noticed that one of the workers – this Brad fellow – was wearing a distinctive pink and red kerchief around his head. We'd used one just like it in *Porgy and Bess* last season. I had seen this guy in the workshop and in Sam's office, and I got a bad feeling he may have taken that scarf."

Barbara's hands were in constant motion, accentuating her words. "I went back and checked my records and the rack where I keep belts and scarves. Sure enough, the *Porgy and Bess* scarf was missing. So I marched over there and demanded to know what he thought he was doing."

"What'd he say?" This from Gerald, who was leaning forward.

"He gave me this aw-shucks-ma'am kind of nonsense and handed it to me. Of course, it was nasty, all sweaty. I had to put it through the washing machine, and fortunately it held up. I wasn't sure it would."

"And this *was* on Thursday?" Branigan double-checked.

"Yes, that's right. Because it was two nights later that I read on your website that he was dead."

"So did you realize he'd taken your clown costumes?"

"Heck, no. Not until I read your story and put two and two together. If I'd known that on Thursday, I would've clocked him." She caught herself. "I'm sorry. I shouldn't have said that."

"Because somebody did clock him?"

"Well, yes." Barbara looked from one to the other apologetically.

"We spoke to Sam," Branigan said, "and he wonders if you guys are going to have to institute more security measures."

To Branigan's surprise, tears filled the woman's eyes. "I hope not," she said fervently. "This is such a magical place. I'd hate to see it ruined by something so minor." She checked herself again. "Not that the murder or kidnapping are minor. I don't mean that. But from our perspective, all that happened was some stolen costumes. I'd hate to see the culture changed because of that."

Branigan noted that she used the same phrase Sam had. She'd never considered a theater culture before, but she supposed it made as much sense as a college culture or a newsroom culture.

As Gerald stood to go, his lightweight chair scraped the floor. Immediately, Branigan heard a scrabble outside Barbara's open door. Holding a finger to her lips, she hurried into the hallway. A satin dress at the near end of the clothes rack fluttered.

"Who's there?" she called, plunging into the hanging garments.

A man stopped and turned, his shortly cropped blond hair all but hidden under a cowboy hat and his face flushed.

"Colin?" asked Barbara, coming up behind Branigan. "Can I help you?"

"Looking for those pants we talked about last night," he said, carefully looking past Branigan.

"I've already pulled them for you. They're in my office."

Branigan looked at him cooly. "You must be Colin Buckner."

He looked confused for a moment.

"Were you listening to our conversation?" she asked. "Here and in the workshop?"

"No. Yes." His face flushed a brighter red. "I wasn't trying to overhear you," he said. "It's just that I kept thinking I heard a voice I knew."

"Let me guess," she said. "Isabella Rickman?"

Now the blood rushed from Colin Buckner's face, and he turned nearly as pale as his white hat. He didn't respond.

She finally took pity on him. "I'm her cousin, Branigan Powers. People tell us we sound alike."

"Oh," he said. "Okay." Suddenly he couldn't get out of the wardrobe fast enough. "I'm so sorry to have disturbed you, Miss Powers. Miss Barbara." He tipped his hat and tried to push past them.

Branigan caught his arm. "Just a moment, Mr Buckner. Do you have a minute? In private?" She stared at him in a way that let him know that if he declined, she'd question him in front of Barbara and Gerald.

He met her gaze. "Sure."

"Gerald," Branigan said, her eyes never leaving Colin's face, "I'm going to step outside with Mr Buckner. I'll be right back."

They brushed past a bewildered Gerald and Barbara and stepped onto the sidewalk outside the theater. By the time Branigan turned to face him, she could tell he had regained his composure. His face was set politely; Branigan registered an aquiline nose, blue eyes and a square jaw that undoubtedly had landed him the Frank Butler role. She saw what Jimmie Jean meant. *So... normal.*

She didn't waste any time. "I know what you did to my cousin in Atlanta," she said. "As, of course, do the Atlanta and Grambling police. What I don't understand is why you're here."

"I'm doing community theater, as I do every summer after the school year," he said, smiling. "Valdosta, Macon, Atlanta, even Dillard and Helen occasionally."

"And you just happened to come to the hometown of someone whose condo you broke into and whose tires you slashed?"

He threw back his head and laughed. "Miss Powers, I assure you I did none of those things. Your cousin and I went on one date and I sent her flowers. She didn't like them, or didn't like me, I should say, so I stopped. End of story."

"And your school principals? They were mistaken?"

"I'm not acquainted with her principal. As for mine, we didn't see eye to eye on a classroom matter. So I resigned."

He had an answer for everything, Branigan realized. A well-rehearsed answer. "So why Grambling?" she asked.

"I ran across the audition notice on Theater on the Square's website. I'd heard of Reggie Fortenberry and wanted to work with him. Believe me, I had no idea that my leading lady would be Izzy B's sister."

He'd had all the right answers – right up until his use of Isabella's nickname.

"Izzy B?" she said softly.

Instantly, he realized his blunder and remained silent.

"After one date, you called her Izzy B? I don't think so."

Colin Buckner's eyes hardened, and his smile faltered. But he fought to keep his affable mask intact. "I didn't call her that," he attempted to backtrack. "I heard Jamie say it."

She didn't speak, which made him more nervous, as she knew it would.

"Anyway, as I told Jamie, I've moved on. I'm dating one of our ensemble players and any interest I had in Isabella is long past. Quite frankly, between your over-reactive police department and your murderous clowns, I can't wait to get out of this town. So if you'll excuse me, Miss Powers, I have a wardrobe fitting."

Instead of heading back to Barbara's office, however, he strode toward the park. Branigan returned to find Barbara and Gerald chatting. Barbara broke off in mid-sentence. "What was that about?"

Branigan figured the more people who knew, the safer Isabella would be. So she gave Barbara the shorthand version of Colin Buckner's stalking.

"Since Jimmie Jean and I and the Grambling PD and the Atlanta PD have confronted him," she concluded, "we don't *think* he'll try anything else. But who'd do that stuff to begin with? Who knows how people like that think?"

Barbara looked aghast and again her eyes filled with tears. "I'm sorry," she said, embarrassed. "It's just that this theater has always been such a wonderful place. And all of a sudden there's this darkness creeping in." She slashed angrily at her eyes. "I'm furious that people have brought this darkness in."

Branigan nodded at Barbara's point. She looked around at the theatrical clothes, the furs, the satins, the accoutrements of this make-believe world. Like clowns turned creepy, a visitor to this place had turned lethal. A thief and a kidnapper and a stalker had roamed this theater. The question was, was that one person? Or two? Or three?

And the murderer? Was it the thief, the kidnapper or the stalker? Or was it yet someone else who had seized an unexpected opportunity among the chaos the others had created?

CHAPTER TWENTY-SIX

It was early May, but northeast Georgia was already spiking temperatures in the high 80s. Trudging through the heat waves rolling off the asphalt of Main Street, Malachi thought about going to the library, popular for its bathrooms, air conditioning and Internet connection. But he could get cool in Jericho Road's art room, too. Plus, he figured Miz Flora might be there, working with Miz Isabella on finding a new place. He wanted to hear how that turned out. He wanted to see if the family got a place or got their hands on the money and took off from Grambling as fast as they could get.

He set out for the grocery-store-turned-church. The automatic door slid open, and Dontegan, manning the desk, looked up and waved. Malachi threw up a hand in response and headed down the hall for the art room. He could hear the commotion in Miz Isabella's office before he got there. Javion and Andre were whining to go swimming, and their mama was hushing them as she tried to talk on the phone. From what he could tell, she was on hold.

He stuck his head into the office, and Miz Isabella looked up sharply. Her nerves looked near shot. "Mr Malachi," she said, standing up and coming around her desk. "By any chance, could you take Javion and Andre to the art room? Is that all right, Mrs Arneson?"

When Miz Arneson hesitated, Miz Isabella jumped right back in. She wasn't giving up on getting those boys out of her office. "Liam and my cousin and I will all vouch for Mr Malachi."

"All right," their mama whispered, covering up the phone with one hand. "You boys do what Miz Isabella and Mr Malachi say."

Isabella showed Malachi and the boys to the eye-popping art room lined with shelves of paint, brushes, canvases, clay, fabric, wood scraps, knitting needles, yarn, pattern books, faux jewels, sequins, glue and magazines. Scuffed wooden tables were covered with paint-spattered cloths and the lime-green walls were hung with the work of dozens of Jericho artists.

"There's no volunteer today, but Mr Malachi knows where everything is – don't you, Mr Malachi?" She looked at him with pleading eyes.

"I do," he said with exaggerated politeness. "No problem at all, Miz Isabella. I take good care of them."

Malachi set Javion and Andre up with paper, colored pencils, felt-tip pens and crayons. "If you decide you rather paint," he told them, "let me know." He made his way to the snack table, filled the electric kettle with water from the sink, and located a box of instant hot chocolate packets.

"You boys want hot chocolate?" he asked, now that the air conditioning made it possible. "We got that and oatmeal cookies."

"Yes!" shouted the boys, their heads already bent over their artwork.

Malachi fixed three cups of steaming chocolate and placed cookies on a paper plate, then carried the snack to the boys' table. He pulled out a chair next to Andre, but began talking to Javion.

"Tell me 'bout your swimming pool," he started.

"It's cool!" Javion said with enthusiasm. "But Mama says our new place might not have one. That's why we wanna go swimming today."

"Yeah," said Andre.

"Is that what you drawing?" Malachi asked. "The pool?"

Andre's paper showed blue scribbles at the bottom. He nodded solemnly.

"Is there a pool where Cleo lives?" Malachi asked.

Andre shook his head, but smiled broadly. "She has a lake. She likes to swim in her lake."

"Did you get to swim with her?"

The boy shook his head, but he continued to smile.

Malachi leaned back on two legs of his chair. "Yeah, that Cleo, she a good dog," he said, hoping to open the door with his chatter. "One time, I spent the night in her barn, and that Cleo, she brought a ball for me to throw." Malachi's version wasn't far from the truth.

"Why'd you spend the night in her barn?" Andre asked. "Did a clown get you, too?"

"No, no, nothing like that. I was worried about Miz Branigan and Miz Cleo and wanted to watch after them good. Like your mama wants to watch after you real good." He needed to get the conversation back to Cleo and the barn, but wasn't sure how. Then Javion did it for him.

"That clown didn't take you to Cleo's barn, Andre. It was the farm next door."

"Oh, yeah."

"Tell me about that barn," Malachi invited. "The one where you spent the night."

"It had sleeping bags and brown grass under them," the boy said. "It had a cool ladder going up to another floor where there was lots more brown grass. It had boxes along the walls for horses or cows, but there weren't any there."

"Were there other animals, like mice or snakes?"

Andre shook his head. "Just Cleo," he said, his voice rising in childish excitement. "She came to visit. She wouldna let any snakes in there. She woulda chomped their heads off!"

Malachi smiled in agreement. "But you saw a snake on the clown's neck, didn't you?"

Andre continued to scribble, but nodded.

Malachi tried to make his next question casual, pulling from something Miz Branigan had told him. "When one clown hit the other clown with a funny hammer, did he have a snake on his neck?"

Andre stopped coloring and looked up. "No," he said seriously. "That was a little clown."

"A little clown?" Malachi was puzzled. "Little like you?"

"No, but littler than the others." He returned his attention to his drawing.

Malachi let his chair settle onto four legs, but made sure they didn't slam onto the floor. He didn't want to startle the boy.

"Can you tell me more about this little clown? How little was he?"

Andre shrugged and didn't answer.

"As little as Javion?" Malachi asked.

Andre glanced at his brother and shook his head.

"As little as Stacy?"

He shook his head again.

"As little as Miz Isabella?"

Andre kept his eyes on his paper, sticking his tongue between his lips in concentration, but he nodded.

Malachi added softly, "As little as your mama?"

The boy nodded again. "I'm going to draw a diving board next," he said.

"That's good," said Malachi, giving him some space. Then after a moment: "Andre, do you remember how many clowns were in your barn?"

Andre put down his crayon. He held up one finger, then two, and hesitated. Then he held up a third finger.

"I believe you told Miz Isabella there was two clowns, didn't you?"

"I forgot the little clown."

Malachi nodded. "Okay."

Javion looked up from his drawing. "Can I have another cookie?"

As Malachi rose to get more cookies, Miz Flora burst into the room, followed by Miz Isabella.

"Boys, Miz Isabella's going to take us to look at an apartment," she said. It was the first time Malachi had seen her smile. "And guess what? It has a pool!"

Javion and Andre jumped up, cookies and artwork forgotten, and ran to their mama, hopping up and down and pulling excitedly on her arms.

Miz Isabella smiled at Malachi and mouthed a "thank you" before escorting the family from the room.

CHAPTER TWENTY-SEVEN

Branigan and Gerald ran into Marjorie as they pulled into *The Rambler*'s basement parking garage.

"Got anything?" Branigan asked.

"A little, but let's wait so we just go through everything once," she said, pushing the elevator button.

When they reached the newsroom, they found Jody and Harley already at Bert's desk. They rolled their chairs over.

"The officers found Randy," Jody started. "They're on their way back, but it'll be around midnight before they land. He's been charged with kidnapping, but not murder yet. We posted that much."

Bert ran a hand over his shaved head. "So what's everyone else got?"

Harley started. "I got hold of Jackson Solesbee and he gave me quite a bit. Said Brad Drucker came to work for him seven years ago. He was eager, newlywed, in his early twenties. Really knew his stuff, especially as far as being a finishing carpenter. That meant that he and one other guy would spend weeks alone at the end of a residential project, installing crown molding, mantels, doorjambs and so forth." He looked around to make sure everyone understood. "But then his houses started having break-ins. Appliances stolen. Lighting fixtures. Even an HVAC unit. Mr Solesbee said it took him forever to figure it out because he trusted his team. But other workers started noticing Drucker's drug use. Then they got word about him beating his wife.

"The police down there hadn't arrested anyone on the thefts, so finally Solesbee confronted Drucker. Drucker denied everything, tried to blame it on the other carpenter. But that guy had worked for Solesbee for years before the thefts with no problem.

"Long story short, Solesbee gave Drucker's name to the police, and the police found some of the stolen items in a storage unit in his back yard. But it turned out the day before they found them, he was arrested for beating the crap out of his wife. He was going to prison, and Solesbee said he didn't want to pile on. He told the police that as long as Drucker was going to prison on CDV, that was enough for him."

"Your cousin's husband sounds like a decent guy," said Bert. Branigan shrugged.

"Wait, that's not all," Harley said. "I called the West Palm Beach police to fact check. The detective there backed up the entire story. But then he kind of laughed and said, 'Did Mr Solesbee mention his relationship with the wife?' Like a moron, I said, 'The wife from Grambling, Georgia?' And he said, 'No, the Cuban wife from Miami. Solesbee was having an affair with Drucker's wife.'"

Branigan froze. As one, Bert, Jody, Harley, Gerald and Marjorie swiveled to look at her. "I ... I ..." She stopped, steeling herself against the sudden thundering in her ears. "I didn't know that," she said. "He'd better hope my Uncle Bobby doesn't either."

"So Brad Drucker moved to Grambling three summers ago," said Bert, "but he wasn't killed until his old buddy Solesbee arrived on the scene. Interesting. Sorry, Branigan."

She was unable to speak, and gave a shrug as if it didn't matter.

"What do you and Gerald have from the theater?"

Branigan wanted nothing more than to go to the privacy of a conference room, shut the door and think, but she shoved Harley's revelation aside for the moment.

"We nailed down that Shack left the theater about three o'clock Friday. He was on a bike, so he could have made it to the Satterfield farm by 3:40 or so. That's well before Randy left the bus station, so it fits that Randy could have killed him.

"Mostly we got color to flesh out our portrait of Shack. The assistant director thinks he was going to try out for Shakespeare in the Park. He roamed freely around the theater, and ran afoul of the wardrobe mistress for taking a scarf used in *Porgy and Bess*. Nothing earth-shattering, but nice details." She paused, her mind whirring. "Anything else, Gerald?"

"Shack told the assistant director, Sam Sebastian, that he was expecting a small inheritance to get him out from under the bridge," he said. "We'll call the family to check that."

"Oh, right," said Branigan.

Bert raised an eyebrow at her. "And Marjorie?" he said. "Anything new from Tent City or Liam?"

Marjorie yanked her wavy hair off her neck, and fanned herself furiously. "Hot flash," she barked as her colleagues laughed.

"Don't hold back out of delicacy," Jody told her.

She shot him a withering look. "Butch was back at the camp," she said. "That's Randy's tent mate. Mr Sensitivity here," she said, indicating Jody, "and I compared notes, and it sounds like Butch told me exactly the same thing he told police. Which is that he had no idea what Randy was planning. But as I kept circling back, asking about earlier in the evening, he said something interesting.

"All the men in the camp were around the fire as usual, drinking beer and passing around bottles of whiskey. If I were betting, I'd say a crack pipe, too. It was Wild Man, Butch, Randy, Shack, and Slick from the other side of the hill, and Oren and Jaquan Arneson. Butch said they were talking about the clown sightings because there'd been three in a row. As the evening wore on, Shack got really drunk and pointed to Wild Man and shouted, 'You're a clown!' and then to Randy, 'You're a clown!' then to Butch, 'You're a clown!' And he fell down laughing. But then he looked at Oren Arneson and said, 'But not you. You can't be a clown.'"

"How did the others respond?" Bert asked.

"Don't know." Marjorie extended her palms to signal indecision. "I tried to follow up, but he said nobody said much after that, and they started talking about something else."

"All right." Bert rubbed his head again. "It doesn't sound like there's anything usable there. Harley, why don't you take the lead on who Brad Drucker was, with Branigan and Gerald feeding you.

We'll lead with a couple of sentences from Jody on Randy being arrested and facing questioning in the morning."

He spun around to face his computer, effectively dismissing them.

Branigan walked slowly back to her desk, and saw her message light flashing. She punched into her voicemail and was delighted to hear Chester's voice asking if he could bring dinner to the farmhouse.

She dialed back and got his voicemail. "It's me," she said. "Yes, yes and yes. I should be home by six o'clock, so come whenever you like."

She hung up, smiling to herself.

Branigan was able to get away even earlier than she'd planned, pulling up to the farmhouse in late afternoon, with the sun still hours from setting. She'd make it a point to show Chester the fiery view from the back porch. She called for Cleo, who came bounding from the direction of the empty chicken houses.

"At least you stayed out of the lake today," she said, patting the dog's regal head.

Branigan changed into running shorts, and led Cleo back outside. After shimmying under the barbed wire, Branigan turned left and began to jog. She passed the first lake and Pa's fishing shack where they'd found Andre – was it just two days ago? She was sure she could see another six inches of growth on the vine that crept over the porch rail.

She kept going. Pa's pasture spread out in shades of deepest jade, since Uncle Bobby's cows hadn't grazed this far in a week or more. She passed the second lake and came to a barbed-wire fence that usually marked the end of her run. But today, she parted the wires and crouched to pass, standing on the bottom one to let Cleo through.

She could see the Satterfield barn in the distance, and headed for it. Her neighbors' property lay still in the somnolent heat; any wildlife was resting in the cooler woods that surrounded it.

Like Pa's, the next-door barn had, for decades, sheltered cattle and the hay that fed them. Its wooden walls were cracked and aged, with gaps ranging from pencil thin to an inch wide. The barn door was closed, but there was no lock; it screeched a complaint as Branigan, breathing hard, pulled it open.

Cleo entered happily, nosing the hay that lay on the floor, Andre's "brown grass". The police had taken the sleeping bags and Shack's bicycle as evidence. Cleo didn't move, instead keeping her nose melded to one spot. Branigan shoved the door open wider to allow more light into the gloomy interior. She stooped to see what held Cleo's interest, and was able to make out differences in the color of the hay. She grabbed a handful and carried it into the bright daylight. Here the differences were marked, with some of the stalks showing dark, rust-colored stains against their natural light brown.

Sweating, Branigan sat down on the bare dirt to catch her breath – and to consider what were undoubtedly bloodstains. Of course, it made sense that Shack's murder would have left bloodstains. She stared into the barn's dimness, trying to picture the unlikely scene of two manically posturing clowns, one killing the other in such a way as to disguise it as play in the mind of a small boy. A sudden gust of wind whistled through the uneven boards, and Branigan jumped. This was such a lonely place. A good place for secrets. No wonder someone chose it.

So what did Andre see? She looked around at the isolated barn in its verdant field rimmed by a semi-circle of woods. He claimed to have seen one clown hit another with a "funny hammer" so that he "went to sleep". Jody had mentioned that police had visited toy stores borrowing hammers to show Andre. But did he see bloodshed as well? And if so, why didn't he tell?

Troubled, she stuffed the hay into her shorts pocket, shut the squealing barn door, and took off across the Satterfield pasture before she'd had a chance to catch her breath properly.

Branigan showered and dressed in clean shorts and a flowing top before Chester arrived with paper cartons of shrimp lo mein, vegetable fried rice and cashew chicken.

"Couldn't decide on one, so I got everything," he said, unloading the food onto the kitchen island. "But before we eat, can I get a giant glass of your iced tea?"

"Done," she said, filling a glass with crushed ice and tea. "I even have sliced lemon if you want it."

"Bring it on," he said, gratefully finishing the tea in three gulps.

"You must have spent the day outside," she said refilling his glass, then turning to pull plates from a cabinet.

"In and out," he said. "This case is breaking fast, but I fear we may be back to square one on the murder."

She whirled from the cabinet. "*What?* It wasn't Randy?" When he hesitated, she added, "Obviously you're off the record."

"It's not that. I'm just thinking where to start. Can we talk while we eat? I'm starving."

She put a plate in front of him and slipped onto a stool across the island. She stared at him expectantly.

"I won't get to question Randy until tomorrow morning," he began, "so this isn't written in stone. But we sent Jim Rogerson and one of the county boys to St Louis to find Randy. He didn't realize anyone was looking for him, so they found him in the second shelter they came to, sitting there eating lunch."

He scooped a big helping of lo mein onto his plate, and when she nodded, spooned some onto hers. "While the deputy was making arrangements for them to fly back, Jim questioned him. He's a heck of an investigator, which is why I'm confident he got the story right." He took a big bite.

"The upshot is that when Jim told Randy that Andre had identified him as the kidnapper by his neck tattoo, Randy was scared to death. I think this all started as sort of a lark and went south quickly."

"A lark?"

"Yeah. Randy was working with Oren Arneson."

Branigan sat up straighter. "So it *was* a scam." She shook her head. "But not Flora?"

"No, the distress we saw in her was real, though I almost wonder if she suspected her husband. Randy said that Oren recruited him and Shack to pretend to kidnap the boy and take him to a safe place he'd identified. The plan was to hold him a few days, figuring that the folks of Grambling would rush to get the family out from under the bridge."

"Which they did," said Branigan.

"Oren got the idea from those clown sightings in the news awhile back. It never happened here, but it popped up all over the country and in Canada. South Carolina had so many, they made *The New York Times*.

"Anyway, to set the stage, Shack stole the clown costumes from Theater on the Square, and he and Randy went into the woods behind those apartments and the elementary school. Randy planned to snatch Andre the night Stacy took him to the bathroom, but Shack called him off. He was afraid Stacy would raise an alarm."

"So a night or two later, when Jaquan fell asleep, Randy did take Andre?" Branigan asked. "And rode him to the Satterfield farm on his bike?"

"Right. Then Shack dressed as a clown and came to relieve him. Oren couldn't go at all, because even with a costume, they figured Andre would recognize his dad. So Shack and Randy took turns babysitting Andre."

"But we saw Randy *and* Shack in the camp the morning after the kidnapping."

"I know. Apparently they left Andre alone sometimes."

"Oh my gosh! There were two lakes out there. Anything could've happened to him."

"I guess that's where Cleo came in," Chester said, bending to pat the dog. "She apparently spent some time in your neighbor's barn."

"I'm so glad," Branigan said. "But you're saying Randy didn't kill Shack?"

Chester shook his head. "He admitted to everything else. Apparently he was sobbing in front of our detective. But he didn't admit to that. With all the publicity from the kidnapping heating up, Randy got scared and decided to leave town. When Shack took over for the Friday night babysitting shift, Randy rode his bike to Oren's motel and demanded his share of the money. But Oren told him that he hadn't been able to get his hands on the money. He promised to mail it if Randy would send him an address. Randy doubted he'd ever see it, but he hightailed it out of town anyway."

"So he didn't even know about the murder?"

"He heard it on the news in St Louis," Chester said. "*And* heard about us finding Andre. Detective Rogerson asked him if he thought Oren killed Shack. Randy said it was possible they got into some sort of fight, but Oren had been dead set against going to the barn where Andre was. He said Flora and the kids were taking the kidnapping much harder than he thought, and he couldn't risk Andre recognizing him."

Branigan laughed in disbelief. "They were taking it 'harder than he thought'? Who *is* this guy?"

Chester continued, "Even when Randy told Oren he was leaving town, Oren didn't indicate he planned to go to the barn. He was going to catch Shack back at camp."

"While his four-year-old stayed alone," Branigan mused. "Stand-up dad."

They were silent for a moment, contemplating the casual evil behind the ruse.

"So I take it you've arrested Oren Arneson?"

"Oh, yeah. And we'll keep hammering at him and Randy." Chester helped himself to the cashew chicken. "But at this point I think someone else figured out their plot and came out of left field to kill Shack."

"Wow," said Branigan. "And then moved Andre to a place where he would be found." She ate in silence for a moment. "It makes me wonder if the killer was angry about the kidnapping."

"It makes me wonder something else," Chester said, putting both elbows on the island and leaning forward. "Whether you are in danger."

Branigan looked up, a question in her eyes.

"As long as we thought it was Randy and he was in St Louis, I wasn't worried," he continued. "But the situation has changed. We don't know who the murderer is. And he deliberately moved Andre onto your farm. I don't want to scare you, but it may be someone who knows your land, knows your routine. Someone who knows you."

"I guess I assumed Andre was simply left on the next inhabited farm."

"And he could've been. But it could've been more personal." He looked directly at her. "I'd rather you not be out here alone."

"You're welcome to stay," she smiled.

"And I will. But I'll be working long hours. Can you and Cleo stay at your folks' place for a few nights?"

"Let me think about it."

Her mind returned to Harley's disclosures about Jackson Solesbee's history with Shack. She knew she couldn't cover the Grambling PD for *The Rambler.* But could she share *Rambler* investigations with the Grambling PD? And should she when her own family was involved?

She silently refilled their iced tea glasses, lost in thought.

"Branigan, is something wrong?"

"I'm just thinking through the ethics of telling you things I learn in the newsroom."

He nodded seriously. "Our situation is tricky," he acknowledged. "I don't want to tread on your space any more than you tread on mine. But maybe I can help. Harley and Jody have both called me about following leads on Jimmie Jean's husband."

Branigan let out a sigh. "Oh, good. Then you know all about Shack working for Solesbee Construction."

"Yep. And the thefts and the Solesbee guy having an affair with Mrs Shack." He smiled. "Too many names in this case." He took another bite. "But I don't know if Jimmie Jean knows about her husband's affair."

"Neither do I. You haven't even met Jimmie Jean yet, have you?"

"Nope." He cocked his head. "Anything else bothering you?"

Branigan wondered how much to tell him about Jackson and Jimmie Jean. But she shook her head and changed the subject. "I went to the Satterfield barn on my run this afternoon," she said. "And something occurred to me."

Chester's fork stopped in mid-air.

"Andre said another clown hit Shack with a 'funny hammer' and he 'went to sleep'," she said. "But there was blood on the hay in the barn."

"Yeah, Shack was killed by a blow to the head. Lots of bleeding."

"So why did Andre say he fell asleep? Did he not see the blood?"

"You think he's repressing what he saw?"

"I'm not sure. We can ask Izzy B." Branigan shook her head slowly. "But I don't know how much we should pry into that boy's psyche. Maybe a pediatric psychiatrist could do it safely?"

"The department could arrange that."

They sat for a moment, their empty plates in front of them.

"Can I get you anything else?" Branigan asked. "Your dinner was delicious."

"No, let's just find the fortune cookies," he said, rooting in one of the paper bags.

He pulled out a cookie, unwrapped it and pretended to read. "You will fall in love with a mysterious blonde farm girl masquerading as a reporter."

She laughed. "Oh, yeah? Let's see what mine says: 'You will have dinner with a goober of the first order.'"

He laughed and came around the island to encircle her from behind. "Let's clean up later," he said, nuzzling her neck.

At sunset they sat in the Adirondack chairs on Branigan's back porch so Chester could see the flaming pink and red and indigo of the rural sky. They could smell newly ripening cantaloupes in a sunny patch under the kitchen window. Though Branigan still hadn't gotten around to adding annuals, she was glad to see some salvia and vincas peeping up from last season.

But Chester couldn't take his eyes off the riot of colors that hovered above the pasture and lake. "Man oh man, you get this every day?" he asked. "This is as good as Mallory Square in Key West."

"I've been there," she said. "The sun's there one second and gone the next."

"But even those colors aren't as vivid as these," he said with an expansive wave at the sky, which was fading to a soft purple at the horizon's edge. "This is incredible." A moment later he said, "Maybe we could go sometime. To Key West." He took her hand and kissed it.

"That would be heavenly."

Mention of Florida brought Jackson to mind once more, and Branigan considered saying something to Chester. But the moment passed.

CHAPTER TWENTY-EIGHT

Malachi stood before another Georgia sunset – this one painted on a scrap of age-darkened wood that was once part of a barn wall. The fields in the picture were shorn and dotted with baled hay, all dreary gray and brown and mottled black. Above, streaks of red and yellow and orange blazed in contrast.

Malachi felt someone move up beside him, and out of the corner of his eye saw a slim man, shorter than himself, with coppery skin and coal-black freckles.

"You done this?" Malachi asked.

"Yeah."

"It's good. Remind me of Miz Tiffany's." Malachi motioned toward the three panels of Tiffany Lynn's Good Samaritan mural that illustrated the gospel parable in shades that moved from gray and brown in the first scene to tans and golds in the second to vibrant reds and oranges as the Samaritan paid for the beaten man's care. His granny would've approved of its Bible lesson.

The man studied the mural. "You mean in the way the colors change," he said finally.

"Yeah."

"You're Malachi, aren't you?" asked the man, turning to face him.

"And you Alphonse Jasper," Malachi said, having asked around about the new artist. Malachi appreciated the painters who worked in Jericho Road's art room. Tiffany Lynn. His buddy Vesuvius, who'd died last summer. This Alphonse was right up there with them in the talent department. "Yeah, you a good artist," he said again. "You sold any yet?"

"A woman ax me about buying one of these, but I don't know if she was serious."

"What she look like?"

"Long blonde hair. Axed a lot of questions."

Malachi smiled. "That's Miz Branigan. If she say she want to buy it, she'll buy it."

"Good. I can sure use the money."

"Dontegan say you work at the chicken plant."

"That's right, but don't know how long I can take it. It's freezing in there, and chemicals been dripping on my neck." He pulled his shirt collar away to reveal an open sore. "I'm headed to the clinic today."

"Yeah, I worked there, too. Didn't last but two months." He noticed that Alphonse was leaning slightly crooked, favoring one leg. "What kinda work you like to do?" he asked idly.

"My favorite ever?" Alphonse said. "Rodeo clowning."

Now he had Malachi's attention. The church worker in charge of breakfast called out an invitation, so Alphonse headed for the serving window. Malachi followed, joining dozens of people he recognized from Tent City and the street. After accepting plates of eggs, grits, bacon and toast, the two found a table.

"So you a rodeo clown?" Malachi repeated, as if there'd been no interruption. "Where'd you do that?"

"All over. But last week in Hartwell."

Malachi took a bite of toast and leaned back in his chair. "That's where I'm from." He paused and drank some coffee, watching the smaller man eat. "What's a rodeo clown do, exactly?"

"You keep bulls away from the riders any way you can."

"I seen them clowns going head first into barrels. On TV anyway."

"Sure. You dive into barrels. You dive over fences. Sometimes you do it so good, the bull completely forgets about the rider and gores you instead." Alphonse laughed and pulled up his pants leg to show Malachi his scar. "I'm living proof."

Malachi thought about that. Thought about a bull getting distracted from the rider he'd thrown off and going after a clown instead.

Thought about somebody getting distracted by a kidnapping and losing focus on a murder.

CHAPTER TWENTY-NINE

Branigan pulled her Civic into the Jericho Road parking lot and stopped to admire the flowers. Liam and his volunteers and shelter residents couldn't do much with the parking lot in front of the former grocery store, but they had transformed land on both sides into fertile beds. Dogwood trees provided dappled shade; while lilies, gerbera daisies, zinnias and marigolds provided a bank of blooms from palest cream to deepest gold. Even the nay-sayers admitted the abandoned store had been successfully reclaimed. Developers were turning fresh eyes onto similarly deserted stores all over the county.

Bert wanted yet another follow-up on the Arnesons and the money trail in reaction to Oren's arrest. Did the citizens of Grambling want their money back, or were they content to let Flora and the children keep it?

The automatic door slid open. Branigan helped herself to coffee from an urn near the door, and noticed that the dining hall was half filled with people eating breakfast, including Malachi and a slim black man sitting off to themselves. She craned her neck and recognized Alphonse Jasper.

Dontegan stood at the serving window and asked if she wanted eggs or toast; that was all that was left. She declined, and asked where Liam was.

"In his office or the prayin' room," came the familiar answer.

She walked down the hall, passing Isabella's closed office and the conference room. Liam's door was open, so she knocked on the doorjamb. He swiveled from his computer and stood.

"Come in," he invited. "What brings you out so early?"

"We're still following this Arneson money saga," she said, plopping into her favorite chair. "I guess you heard Oren Arneson was arrested."

"Yeah, Izzy B called me while she was apartment hunting with Flora," he said, taking the other rocker and crossing his long legs. "Oren was picked up at the motel."

"Are you getting complaints from donors wanting their money back?"

"They wouldn't dare!" He wagged his head and laughed. "As much as I've preached *against* rushing in with cash, that would take some nerve. I *have* heard from the other pastors and the TV station. They have no problem with housing Flora and the kids, so we're going ahead with that. But it's sticky. People gave that money as a direct result of a crime."

"How much is the final tally?"

"Eleven thousand, give or take."

"Maybe the arrest will turn off the tap."

"You'd hope so, wouldn't you? We'll see."

"And where is Flora? I need to talk to her for an update."

"As far as I know, still at the motel. It's paid through Friday. I think they did find a place, so you can ask Flora or Izzy B how soon they'll move in."

She leaned into the comfortable rocker. "What'd you think of this whole thing?" she asked. "Did you suspect Oren?"

Liam sighed. "Did it cross my mind? Yes. But I really didn't think a father would do that to his own child." He looked down at his hands. "I guess I couldn't stay in this job if I thought like that."

Branigan smiled sadly. "We need people like you, you know. Who see the best in us."

"Naïve people, you mean," he said ruefully.

"No, I don't think it's that, Liam. You tell people all the time that money and 'things' are not the answer. You're pretty clear about that. This was a whole new level of crazy. Or evil."

"We'll tell ourselves that anyway." He smiled at his old friend.

"How well did you know Shack and Randy?" she asked.

"Randy I'm not sure I ever laid eyes on. But Shack ate here a good bit, came to worship sometimes, and was very handy. He helped us renovate a bathroom last fall." His feet hit the floor with a thump. "Oh, I meant to ask you!"

"What?"

"This morning's paper. It said Shack stole from a Jackson Solesbee in south Florida. That's our Jackson?"

"Yeah, Solesbee Construction in West Palm Beach. That's him."

Liam eyed her closely. He and Liz had watched first-hand as Branigan fell in love with Jackson after their freshman year in college. She met his gaze.

"Coincidence that he's back," he remarked.

"Not really. Jimmie Jean's here because of her mother, and he's here because of Jimmie Jean. He rode in on a white horse to save his marriage."

"Oh. Okay." Only a single line between his eyebrows betrayed his concern for his friend.

"So anyway, back to Shack," she said briskly. "Could you see him taking part in this kidnapping?"

"That's hard to say, Brani G. The side of people I see here is different than what they show on the street."

"What do you mean?"

"Especially here in the South, most of the people we run into have had church somewhere in their background. A grandmother took them, or an aunt, or somebody. And when they're at Jericho Road, they're very aware they're in a church."

"Like you're always Pastor Liam, never just Liam."

"Exactly. So the Shack I knew, no, I could never imagine him kidnapping a child. Not in a million years. But you have to remember, it was the dad's idea. So I guess in Shack's mind – and I guess in Randy's – this wasn't really a kidnapping. As in a federal offense, prison sentence, all the rest of it. It was more of a scam." Liam held up his hands. "But I'm speculating."

"Is there anything you can think of that might have got Shack killed, if it turns out to be unrelated to the kidnapping?"

Liam rocked for a moment. "The thing he talked about most was his wife. How he'd messed up his marriage."

"Yeah, he told me about his domestic violence conviction. He said his wife wanted to recant and the judge wouldn't let her. I got the impression he was saying it hadn't happened."

"No, it happened," Liam said. "He owned up to it when he talked to me. He said he'd caught her in an affair and lost it."

Branigan stopped rocking. Liam would probably read about Jackson's affair with Shack's wife soon enough, but it hadn't made this morning's paper.

She spoke slowly, thinking out loud. "So the affair led to the domestic violence charge, which led to prison, which led to homelessness. Was he bitter?"

"You better believe it," said Liam. "He blamed a former boss for ruining his life." Liam's rocker slowed again. "Wait a minute. Was that the same boss he stole from? Was he talking about *Jackson*?"

"I didn't think that was my news to tell," she said. "But yeah, same boss."

"Do the police know this, Brani G?"

She sighed. "They do. But I'm not sure they know the affair led directly to the CDV charge. I hate to say it, but it ties Shack and Jackson together even more closely."

Branigan ran into Malachi, quite literally, as he swept the hallway outside Liam's office.

"Can you sit for a minute?" she asked him.

He agreed, and propped his broom against the wall. Isabella was in her office when they passed, so Branigan looked in.

"Hey, Cuz! Can you give me the address, price and specifics on the apartment for the Arnesons?"

"Sure," Isabella said. "The people paying for it deserve to know. I'll write it down and bring it to you. Where are you headed?"

Branigan looked at Malachi.

"Art room," he said.

They reversed course and walked to the vacant art room, pulling out chairs at one of the tables.

"So what are you thinking?" she asked.

"I was in here yesterday with Andre," he said without preamble. "He told me about a 'little clown' who hit Shack with a 'funny hammer'."

"A little clown? What does that mean?"

"Hard to say," Malachi said with a shake of his head that swung his dreadlocks. "He quieted way down when I asked. Got mighty interested in his coloring and wouldn't hardly answer."

She tilted her chair back and stared at the visual cacophony on the opposite wall. "How tall was Shack?" she asked abruptly.

"Six foot, maybe taller. Why?"

"Because someone might look 'little' compared to him, right?"

Malachi considered that for a moment. "I asked him if he meant as little as Miz Isabella or Miz Flora, and he said yeah."

"Well, Izzy B is five foot six, and his mama is – what? – about five foot four?" *And Jackson, about five foot nine. Would that look little next to a man over six feet tall?* "Interesting," she said.

"And one more thing, Miz Branigan."

She gave him her full attention.

"You know how you talk sometime about what's not there rather than what is?"

"Sure," she smiled. "That's your specialty."

"I been thinking on that. We been looking at this like a crazy clown kidnapping. Hard not to because that's the whole idea of a clown. 'Hey! Look at me! Look at me!' But in the end…" He trailed off.

"In the end, no one was kidnapped," she finished for him. "Someone was murdered."

Isabella walked into the art room brandishing a piece of notepaper, and Malachi slipped out to finish his sweeping.

"Here's your information," she said. "Flora and the children are renting a three-bedroom, one-bath apartment for $795 a month. Not the nicest place in Grambling but it's got a washer and dryer and a pool. The donations will cover a year's rent, plus deposits for water and power. The complex waived the security deposit since we were paying so far ahead."

"And the Arnesons are happy with it?"

"Over the moon is more like it. St James AME can give them vouchers for thrift store furniture and dishes and bedding. Liam's hope is that with rent taken care of for a year, Flora and Jaquan will be freed up to find part-time jobs."

"Is there anything to prevent her from bailing Oren out of jail?" Branigan asked.

"Bite your tongue!" said Isabella, perching on a table. "I suppose if they find jobs, they can use their money for whatever they want. Let's hope the judge sets bail really high or considers him a flight risk. Which he is."

"All right then," said Branigan, gathering her notes and purse. "I'll make one more call to Flora, and this story is done. The *Style* editor has something else she wants, so I'd better get going."

"One more thing," said Isabella, walking her out. "Do you want to come with me to a rehearsal tonight? Jimmie Jean asked if we could come and give her some feedback. Privately."

"Really? Is she second-guessing Sir Reggie?"

"Maybe. She says he's gotten kind of erratic lately, and when she's in the middle of a show, it's hard to tell what will work and what will be incredibly corny."

"You're not worried about Colin Buckner being there?" Branigan asked.

"Not with all those people around. And I can't let him dictate where I go and what I do."

"Good for you. What time?"

"Meet me there at seven."

Branigan drove to the Heart of Grambling and found Jaquan and Javion at the pool. Their mom, they told her, was leaving for the thrift store with Stacy and Andre. Jaquan gave Branigan the room number, and she walked across the parking lot, catching Flora as she was locking the door.

"Mrs Arneson, may I speak to you for one quick minute?" she said after reintroducing herself. "My editor wants an update on the money that has come in and what it's being used for."

Flora gave her a wide smile. "It's going for an apartment, praise the Lord!"

"With a pool!" yelled Andre. "We saw it, didn't we, Mama?"

"I heard about the apartment from the folks at Jericho Road," Branigan said. "I just need to get a comment from you."

"Tell the people of Grambling we can never thank them enough," said Flora. "They are giving us a second chance. When school starts, I can look for a job during school hours. And Jaquan's gonna look for a job after school. It's a dream come true for us."

Branigan wasn't sure how to ask the next part. "And your husband?" she broached. "Did you suspect what he'd done?"

Flora squared her shoulders and pulled Andre protectively toward her. "No, ma'am," she said emphatically. "I can't sanction what Oren done. And I don't know how long he'll be locked up. So all's I can do is take care of these children."

Branigan waited, but the woman didn't say anything more. She smiled. "All right then. Thank you. Happy shopping."

She watched as Flora, Stacy and Andre walked away, Andre skipping excitedly at the thought of a Sponge Bob comforter or whatever his mom had promised. Funny how things worked out, Branigan thought. A mother's most frightening nightmare had turned into a financial windfall and extrication from a bad marriage, at least temporarily. Was she lucky? Or had something more orchestrated occurred? And if so, how much had the newspaper abetted it?

Branigan arrived in the parking lot of Theater on the Square a few minutes early, having written her story on the Arnesons and churned out a quick piece on a popular local chef who was opening a barbecue restaurant. She leaned against the Civic, feeling the day's heat give way to evening cool. She hadn't eaten and thought she wasn't going to be able to stay long at this rehearsal without dinner.

She glanced idly up at the back of the mansion, its original windows bricked over to eliminate natural light from the stage. She walked around to the front lawn, where Sam Sebastian was overseeing his Shakespeare troupe on their newly constructed stage. As she watched, she was surprised to see a familiar figure duck out from under the X-shaped stage supports. He wore a dirty orange bandana around his forehead and a long gray ponytail down his back. Malachi's neighbor under the bridge. Slick, wasn't it? The man glimpsed Branigan and hurried off.

At that moment, Isabella came up behind her. Quietly, so as not to disturb Sam's actors, they walked up the steps and into the lobby.

"Remind me why we're here," Branigan said softly.

"Jimmie Jean is getting nervous about some of the blocking and choreography and staging," Isabella said. "Reggie wants Annie Oakley and Frank Butler to use their rifles as swords, which she claims is almost impossible to do one-handed. And something about not letting Annie mature through the production. JJ said he wants to keep her 'cornpone', whatever that means."

"And she wants our take on it?"

"Right."

The pair slipped into the darkened theater, taking seats near the rear. Without house lights they stood a good chance of going undetected.

An accompanist was working with Jimmie Jean and Colin Buckner, and Barbara Wickenstall was conferring with a large group of ensemble players. She began arranging them for a musical number, calling Jimmie Jean forward. Reggie was nowhere around.

"Is she like a stage manager in addition to costumer?" Branigan whispered.

"Yeah, JJ says she works with them a lot. Apparently she was quite a character actress at one time. JJ looked up her reviews from LA."

"I had no idea."

There was a rustle to Isabella's right, and a man dropped into the seat next to her. Branigan peered around her and stiffened. It was Jackson.

"I wanted to see what's got JJ in such a snit," he whispered to Isabella. "Why are we sitting so far back?"

"She didn't want Reggie to know she'd asked for a critique."

He leaned across Isabella. "Hey, Brani G."

She nodded mutely.

Suddenly Barbara Wickenstall called out, "From the top," and the pianist broke into "I've Got the Sun in the Mornin' (and the Moon at Night)". Branigan recognized that the song from the second act would be performed when Annie Oakley had acquired a veneer of sophistication, so she was surprised when Jimmie Jean leapt onto a ballroom table and swung from a rope into splits on the floor. Barbara signaled the pianist to stop.

"Jamie," she said, "this isn't what we rehearsed. You're going to be wearing an evening gown in this number."

"This is the way Reggie re-choreographed it last night," she answered, hands on her hips, breathing hard.

Barbara looked around. "Does anyone know where Reggie is? Maybe he's forgotten the costuming." She turned to gaze into the darkened theater, and a spotlight on her face showed her confusion. "Reggie? Are you out there?"

"Indeed, I am!" came a shout from midway back. Branigan, Isabella and Jackson instinctively slumped in their seats, but all eyes were on the director as he bounced up the aisle to the stage. "Just wanted to see if everyone was paying attention," he crowed.

Barbara started to explain about the rather confining dress that Jamie would wear for this number, but Reggie cut her off. "Since when is the show in service to the costumes?" he demanded. "Or maybe you don't like my idea for Annie to keep romping and stomping through the second act? And here I was thinking *I* was the director. Silly me!"

The cast froze. Jimmie Jean cleared her throat. "Actually, Reggie, I like the idea of Annie growing and changing a little in the second act. I think the 'gee-shucks-Colonel-Bill' stuff can get a little old."

"Do you, *Jamie*? Or is it *Jimmie Jamie Jean*?" He didn't wait for an answer. "Well, my dear, that may be the way you do it in south Florida, but up here in Georgia," – he drew it out mockingly as *Jaw-ja* – "we like our Annie down home. We'll just slit that evening gown so you can carouse and cavort and spin and split. We may even accessorize it with a cowboy hat."

Jimmie Jean pressed her lips together, and Barbara's face went blank. Reggie pirouetted to face the ensemble. "Anybody else have director's notes? Anybody else think it's their job to direct this old war horse?" Again, he didn't allow time for a response. "All right then! From the top!"

Branigan and Isabella looked at each other. Jackson leaned across the armrest he shared with Isabella and spoke loudly enough to be heard over the piano. "Is that guy high?" he asked.

"All you gotta do is look at his pupils."

Branigan and Isabella jumped as the voice came from behind them. "Mr Buckner," said Branigan icily. "Shouldn't you be on stage?"

"I don't come in until the end of this number," he said. "Hello, Isabella."

Branigan could feel Isabella's body go rigid next to her, and she saw her cousin reach for Jackson's arm.

Jackson turned in his seat. "Is this him?"

Isabella nodded mutely. In one fluid motion, Jackson turned and grabbed Colin Buckner by the collar. With one hand holding him, he drew back his other fist and punched his face as hard as he could. Branigan heard a crack, and Colin Buckner dropped to the floor.

On stage, Jimmie Jean hopped onto a table, flinging her arms wide as she sang. She caught a rope that would be a ballroom chandelier by opening night, and swung to the floor, gracefully sliding into a split.

Wide-eyed, Branigan and Isabella stared at Jackson in horror. Colin Buckner didn't move.

"Run tell your boyfriend, Brani G," Jackson said, before walking up the aisle and out of the theater.

Oblivious to what was going on in the darkened theater, one of the men from the ensemble swooped in to lift Jimmie Jean to her feet, and they performed a Texas Two-Step.

Barbara Wickenstall walked silently off stage.

Branigan dialed 911.

CHAPTER THIRTY

Malachi sat on a bench in Reynolds Park, enjoying the evening. To one side he could see a rehearsal on the Shakespeare stage, starting and stopping as the fat little director called out lines and suggestions.

On the other side of the park, people pushed strollers, ate ice cream, rollerbladed. Malachi saw two familiar figures with backpacks. He watched idly as Wild Man and Butch split up, Wild Man approaching people for money, but getting too close and scaring them. Butch spied Malachi and walked over, tossing his pack on the bench with a tired sigh.

Up close, Malachi could see that Butch's eyes were blackened and one cheek was swollen and purpling.

"What happen to you?" he asked.

"That damn Slick. Jumped me and took my money."

Nothing that happened on the street surprised Malachi. He knew Butch wouldn't report it. But the fact that Butch *had* money – that was a surprise. "Where you get money?"

"Shack."

"Why Shack give you money?"

"He didn't *give* it to me," Butch said, morosely kicking at the grass. "He asked me to hold it, then he got killed and never came back. I was going to use it to go to Florida and find work. But now it's gone." He kicked again in disgust.

"There Slick now." Malachi pointed to the side of the stage, where a bent-over Slick was crab-walking from underneath. Butch clearly had no stomach to tangle with him again, but Malachi wondered what he was up to. Maybe he'd follow him back to Tent City and ask him. Maybe they'd have a beer.

Malachi left Butch sitting on the bench and dodged park-goers to catch his neighbor. But something in Slick's manner made him hold back. What would you call it? *Furtive*, came the answer from his granny's vocabulary quizzes.

From Main Street, Malachi expected that Slick would turn westward to head for the bridge, but he continued north instead. Malachi hung back, keeping people between them, but Slick never looked behind him.

As he neared the Heart of Grambling, the motel where the Arnesons still stayed, as far as Malachi knew, Slick turned into a liquor store. He came out, balancing a case of beer under one arm and holding a bottle of whiskey in the other hand.

He continued on to the motel, heading straight for a room. The door opened and Malachi saw Slick's old lady, Elise, inside. Slick kicked the door shut behind him.

How much money you take off Butch? Malachi marveled. Enough to buy beer, whiskey, a motel room *and* bail Elise out of jail.

He walked to the motel's small office, where a young man sat watching TV. "Help you?" he said.

"I'd like to know how many nights one of your guests paid for."

"Sorry, we can't give out that information."

Malachi thought fast. "I work with Pastor Liam, Miz Isabella and Dontegan over at Jericho Road," he said. "Pastor Liam ax me to check on the man and woman in Room 42, make sure they got settled okay. He the one give them the money for a room." He doubted Pastor Liam would mind the white lie.

The young man visibly relaxed. "Oh, yeah, we work with Pastor Liam," he said. "He usually pays us directly." He peered at Malachi, then shrugged. "Room 42 has paid up for a week."

"Thank you," Malachi said. "I'll let him know."

Malachi did the math in his head. Slick had spent around $560 on a room, $50 on alcohol, plus whatever it'd cost to spring Elise. He knew he'd made some from his job building the Shakespeare stage, but not that much. So how much did he take off Butch? And more importantly, where'd Shack get the money that Butch was holding? He was pretty sure Pastor Liam hadn't released a penny of the donated money for Oren Arneson to share with Shack or Randy.

So where did Shack get money beyond his piddly theater pay?

Follow the money, he'd advised Miz Branigan. But wait a minute. He had only Butch's word that Shack asked him to hold the money. What if Butch had stolen the money from Shack?

Did that make Butch the killer? As Randy's tent mate, could he have watched the whole kidnapping unfold, then stepped in? He was – what? – five foot seven. Maybe he could be the "little clown" next to the well-built Shack.

But there was no payoff from the kidnapping. That's what Malachi kept coming back to. No one but Flora and her kids benefitted.

He asked himself the question again: Where did Shack get money?

CHAPTER THIRTY-ONE

The *Rambler* staff had gone as far as they could go with the murder story on Brad Drucker, at least until the police turned up something new. They'd run an in-depth profile on Brad/Shack, including interviews with his parents, his former wife, Jackson Solesbee, residents of Tent City, and the officers and attorneys in West Palm Beach who'd put him away for domestic violence. In checking with his family, the reporters learned he wasn't getting an inheritance; it sounded as though he'd told Theater on the Square's Sam Sebastian that to cover any sudden infusion of cash he might get – presumably from the kidnapping.

Jody was keeping one ear out for developments, but the others turned their attention to new stories. Branigan spent Wednesday on a piece about summer farmers' markets – both the stationary one near downtown and seasonal stands all over the county. As she wrapped up, she received a text from Chester Scovoy: *Call me when you can talk.*

Only Bert and Julie were in the newsroom, and their desks were far from hers, so Branigan dialed Chester on her desk phone.

"Jackson Solesbee is out on bail," he said as soon as he picked up. "What got into him?"

"You didn't handle it, I take it?"

"No, it was assault. Our uniformed guys caught it."

Branigan sighed. "You know how we all love Izzy B. I guess Jackson couldn't stand the thought of that guy tormenting her."

"Well, I don't think he's going to be tormenting anybody for awhile. He was treated for a broken nose, and that's the least battered part of his face."

"You don't sound too upset over it," she ventured.

"Nah. Couldn't have happened to a nicer guy. But that's not why I called. Can you get away this weekend?"

"Yes, but I doubt you can," she laughed.

"You're not going to believe this, but since the chief is convinced that Brad Drucker's murder was not committed by the kidnappers, it's now officially in the county's jurisdiction. I'm off the case, and the sheriff's office is on it."

"You're kidding!"

"And that's not even the best part. He wants me to take comp time because of all the overtime I worked the week of the kidnapping. So I have a long weekend. It's not enough time to go to Key West, but is there anywhere you'd like to go?"

She thought for a minute. "How about Isle of Palms, near your own stomping ground?"

"That'd be great. Want me to call about a rental?"

"My parents have a place. Let me see if it's available."

"Better and better. Call me when you know something."

Branigan's mother told her that Liam and Liz were borrowing the house for the weekend, but she was sure they'd welcome Branigan and Chester as well. "In fact, Liz even mentioned she'd like to get you and Izzy B to come, but she wasn't sure how tied up you were with that murder story."

"If you really think it's okay, I'll call her."

"I'm not charging them, so I can't imagine it will be a problem," said her mom. "And I know they're not expecting Charlie or Chan."

Branigan dialed Liz's cell next. "How would you like some intruders on your beach weekend?" she asked.

Liz squealed. "Yes! I should probably tell you that when you've been married as long as we have, you welcome intruders. Who are you bringing?"

"Let me get back to you. But possibly Chester and Izzy B."

"That's fine. Is Jimmie Jean tied up with the play?"

"Yes, and it's changing by the minute, so I know she can't get away."

"Fantastic! It'll be like old times."

"Except we can cook if you want to. Mom has done up the kitchen."

"Surely you jest. We're going out for seafood, girl."

Branigan called Chester back. "I know it's not the getaway you had in mind," she said. "If we want the beach house, it comes with Liz and Liam. Is that all right, or would you rather get a rental?"

He laughed. "I want to get to know your friends anyway. That sounds good."

With the weekend squared away, Branigan sat back in her chair with satisfaction. Except that here came Julie Ames, and it was too late to look busy.

When she finished work, it was nearly six. Branigan knew she could catch her mom and dad at Wednesday night supper at First Baptist, so she drove to the sprawling campus and entered the fellowship hall. She greeted family friends who were lined up to pay two women with a metal cash box at the entrance. Realizing she had no cash, she went in search of her dad.

"Hey, moneybags," she said when she saw him and her mom at a table in the middle of the dining room. "Got enough spare change for my dinner?"

Her father laughed. "When am I going to get you off the dole?"

"I imagine the day I die," she said cheerfully. He pulled a five-dollar bill from his pocket and Branigan went to pay. "Save me a seat," she called over her shoulder. A few minutes later, she set her grilled chicken, baked potato and broccoli beside her mom's plate, and spoke to people at surrounding tables.

"How nice to see you," said her mother, squeezing her shoulders in a sideways hug. "What brings you out?"

"Well, besides seeing you guys, I thought I might run into one of the sheriff's deputies," she answered. "Does Cornel still help with boys' basketball?"

"Yes," said her mother. "And Mark Wiseman teaches Bible study to middle schoolers."

"Ah, he's bucking for his own little corner of heaven."

"Yes, he is. Your dad taught that age group for years. Pushed him to the edge. Now he'll only teach the eighties and above."

"We don't hear well enough to know if he's being heretical," said a senior adult at their table.

Branigan laughed. "Well, I can assure you he is," she said.

She enjoyed the easy camaraderie of her longtime church, staying to chat with her parents as most of the crowd left for choir practice or Bible classes. They wanted to hear first hand her account of finding Andre.

"That old fishing shack," her mother mused. "Pa must be rolling over in his grave."

"I lost many a hand of Texas Hold 'Em in that shed," said her dad. "Those old farmers had the best poker faces I ever saw."

"Really?" asked Branigan. "They could beat the banker?"

"They could stomp the banker, loan him money and stomp him again."

Watching the clock, Branigan said goodnight to her mom and dad a few minutes before the classes ended, and walked to the hallway she remembered from her own middle school days. She peered inside each glass door, located Mark Wiseman and then leaned against the wall outside his classroom. Minutes later, the door swung open and sixth-graders noisily erupted.

Branigan stuck her head inside and spoke to the young man she used to babysit. Though he was more than a decade younger than Chester Scovoy, he had the same close-cropped hair and bodybuilder's physique common to the city's law officers. "I saw Caroline and the boys at supper," she said. "Police officers in training?"

"I sure hope not!" he said, grinning widely. "I'm trying to raise computer programmers." He walked over and hugged her. "How are you, Brani G? If you're still in the nanny business, I can get you a job."

"Nah," she laughed, "one Wiseman was enough."

"Unfortunately, that's pretty much the reaction of all our babysitters." He finished stacking Bibles and quarterlies. "So what's up at *The Rambler*?"

"Well, since you asked…" she said.

"Uh-oh."

"I'm interested to know if the sheriff's office was able get Andre Arneson in front of a psychiatrist."

"Sorry, but I'm not working that case."

"We wouldn't be able to print it anyway," she said. "I'm wondering if – off the record – you could say what came of it."

"Off the record and also realizing I don't have first-hand knowledge?"

"Absolutely. I'm looking for background, nothing more."

"Yeah, we brought in Dr Harold Totten. He's supposed to be real good with kids."

"And?"

"And I heard from some investigators that he thought the kid was holding back on something."

"Any idea what?"

"According to what I heard – and remember, this is second-hand – the kid talked pretty openly about the two clowns he spent time with. Talked about what they wore, jokes they told, what they fed him – which was all junk, by the way. He even talked about the third clown wearing something different, but he was vague on details. Maybe different colored pants. Maybe a different print shirt. But same bushy orange hair, red nose, white face, red shoes.

"But when Dr Totten tried to get specific about the third clown's voice and size, any antics or jokes, that's when the kid shut down."

"Did he talk about the clown being little?"

"Not that I heard."

"Did Dr Totten ask anything about the weapon, the 'funny hammer'?" Branigan asked.

"Yeah, the kid said something like it was a big red hammer that could bonk people. But then he refused to talk about it any more. The psychiatrist didn't want to push too hard. Our investigators told him there was lots of blood and there was no way the kid didn't see it."

"Could Andre have repressed that part? Maybe even repressed the real murder weapon?"

Mark shrugged. "I have no idea. I'm the last person you'd want rooting around in a child's brain."

Branigan paused, lost in thought. "You guys got on this fast," she said. "Didn't you just catch the case today?"

"Early this morning. But our investigators were so behind on it, they took a shotgun approach. Visited the crime scene, interviewed the kid, talked to the dad and his accomplice in the LEC. They hit the ground running."

"Sounds like it."

"They also heard a lot about your Cleo," Mark added. "From what I heard, if this kid survives intact, it'll be because of her."

Branigan was surprised to feel tears stinging her eyes. She blinked as she turned away. "Cleo has saved my sanity on more than one occasion, too."

It was still light when Branigan left First Baptist; on a whim she turned back toward town instead of the farm. There had been a third clown in the Satterfield barn and so far the investigation had accounted for only two costumes missing from Theater on the Square. She wanted to talk to Barbara Wickenstall.

She stopped for a moment on the theater lawn to watch the rehearsal for *A Midsummer Night's Dream*. The scene was the intentionally terrible play within a play for the wedding of Theseus and Hippolyta – so bad that the guests think it's a comedy. Branigan noted Sam's gentle pauses and suggestions, so different from Reggie's diatribes and sarcasm of the night before.

Not seeing Barbara, she continued inside, sliding into the back row of the theater. To her surprise Colin Buckner was on stage, his face bruised and puffy, his nose bandaged. She had to hand it to him: he was a trouper.

He and Jimmie Jean were rehearsing the crowd-pleasing "Anything You Can Do, I Can Do Better". Jimmie Jean was going full volume, but Colin was hardly audible, no doubt nursing a tender jaw and teeth. She could see Reggie on the front row, his head unmoving. She watched until the end of the number. Jimmie Jean stood, beautiful in a ball gown that Barbara had readied early, her brown hair swept into an elegant knot. Colin gently massaged his face; Branigan assumed Jackson had altered his signature jawline.

Reggie didn't move from his seat, only raised his voice. "Well," he drawled, directing his comments to the accompanist, "it's hard to tell what's going on with Annie Oakley getting louder and more aggressive, and Frank cringing like she's going to hit him. But no, that's her husband who hits people, isn't it?"

"Very funny," said Jimmie Jean coldly. "I've apologized. I don't know what else you want me to do."

Reggie ignored her. "Colin, what does the doctor say? How long until you can sing semi-normally?"

"The soreness should be gone in a week," Colin murmured.

"Then let's work on the ensemble scenes, and we'll bear down on your pieces starting Monday." He clapped his hands. "Places, everyone, for the final shooting match. Maybe someone will shoot me and put me out of my misery."

Still not seeing Barbara as the ensemble scattered across the stage, Branigan slipped out through the foyer and walked around to the side entrance. The wooden block still held the side door open; so far, she noted, the theater hadn't imposed further security measures.

She wasn't sure how sound carried to the nearby stage, so she didn't shout for the wardrobe mistress, and instead walked to Barbara's office. She raised her hand to knock on her doorjamb, but was arrested by the sight of the costumer, seated in her ladderback chair, sewing an Indian headdress. But it was Barbara's face, blotchy and red, that caught Branigan's attention. Branigan finally did knock, and Barbara's head jerked up. She swiped a palm across both cheeks and pasted a smile on her face.

"I hope I'm not interrupting," said Branigan.

"Are you kidding me? I love company while I'm sewing. It's solitary, boring work."

"So how's it going?"

"Fine. Except, of course, that our leading man is mumbling like Moses."

Branigan laughed. "I heard him tell Reggie that he should be able to sing by next week."

Barbara shrugged. "Let's hope so." Seeing Branigan lean against the door, she motioned her inside. "Please take my desk chair."

As Branigan picked her way over stacks of buckskin and beads and feathers, she asked, "Are you all right?"

Barbara didn't answer. Branigan sat down without speaking.

"It seems we're snake-bit," Barbara finally responded. "Someone steals our costumes for a kidnapping and murder. Our leading man turns out to be a stalker. Then he's assaulted." She stopped and Branigan got the distinct impression she cut herself off.

Branigan pressed gently. "And Reggie? Is something wrong with him?"

Barbara kept her head bent over her work. "What do you mean?"

"I don't know what he's usually like as a director, but he's being pretty caustic with his actors."

Barbara nodded. "He's always flamboyant," she said in a neutral tone.

"*That* I've seen," said Branigan. "This feels like something else." She gathered her courage, remembering what Colin Buckner said right before Jackson hit him. "Could he be on drugs?"

She imagined that Barbara would react with horror, if not outrage. But she didn't. She kept her eyes firmly on the headdress in her lap, and carefully pulled a needle through the heavy fabric. "I don't know," she said.

Which told Branigan all she needed to know. She waited a moment. "What I came for," she continued as if nothing had been revealed, "is to ask about a third clown costume."

Now Barbara did look up. "A third?"

"Yeah. As you've probably read, Andre Arneson was kidnapped by two men his father recruited from the homeless camp. Shack, who worked around here sometimes, and Randy. Apparently they wore the costumes described by witnesses from the very beginning: ballooning white pants with red stripes, orange wigs, red noses, shoes, et cetera. The costumes you were missing."

Barbara paused from her sewing to listen.

"Then there was another clown who killed Shack," Branigan continued. "Randy was long gone to St Louis. So where did Clown No. 3 get his outfit?"

"He didn't use the costume from – who did you say? – Randy?"

Branigan tried to remember what Jody and Chester had said about locating Randy in St Louis. Did he have the costume with him? She made a note to ask.

Barbara spoke again. "Do you want me to look through our inventory?"

"If you could."

"Sure. Come on." Barbara carefully placed the headdress and needle on her chair seat, stretched her back, then led Branigan down the familiar gauntlet of silk, satin and fur. They entered the room of specialty items, devoid now of cowboy, Indian or horse gear appropriated for the Wild West Show.

Barbara reached for the clown pants, counted to eight, then did the same with the shirts. "Eight of each," she said. "We're good. No more missing than those original two costumes."

"Thanks for looking," Branigan said. Standing in the middle of the crowded room she turned slowly in a circle to take in the riot of color and texture, the Easter bunnies and cats and cows, the tambourines and swords and capes. She made another circle and saw Winnie the Pooh and Eeyore and Piglet. She was beginning to get dizzy when she spotted a flash of red.

She stood still for a moment to regain her balance, then walked to a rack of what appeared to be unicorn horns tied to individual clothes hangers. She scooted the horns aside to see the floor underneath and gasped.

A giant plastic red hammer leaned against the wall.

"Oh, my gosh!" exclaimed Branigan, pulling out her cell phone.

"What?" Barbara asked in alarm. "What is it?"

"That hammer!" Branigan pointed. "That's what Andre described."

Barbara looked mystified. "Described when?"

Branigan remembered that the newspaper had withheld the detail about "a funny hammer" that put the clown to sleep. "I've got to call the sheriff's office."

Barbara was staring at her. "We have more than one of those."

Branigan whirled on her. "You're missing a plastic hammer? Why didn't you tell us that?"

Barbara sputtered, as though she hardly knew where to begin. "You never asked me about plastic hammers!" she said, raising her voice. She threw up her hands. "They weren't even from a clown show. They came from a children's production about building things."

Branigan tried to calm down. "I'm sorry. I didn't mean to yell at you. But when Andre described Shack getting killed, he said one clown bonked the other one on the head with a funny hammer and the clown went to sleep."

Barbara sank to the floor, sitting cross-legged. "Ohhh," she said. "I didn't know." She thought for a minute. "But Branigan, that hammer couldn't hurt a fly. Look at it."

"I'd better not touch it," Branigan said. "Is it hollow? Could you put a metal rod or something inside?"

Barbara looked blank. "I honestly have no idea."

Two deputies from the Criminal Investigations Division of the Cannon County Sheriff's Office arrived at the theater within fifteen minutes, bagged the plastic hammer and interviewed Barbara about her inventory system.

"We've read the Grambling PD file on your missing clown costumes," one said. "But it didn't mention a toy hammer."

Branigan kept quiet, embarrassed that neither she nor Chester nor Jim Rogerson had thought to ask if the hammer could have been a theater prop. Their minds had been on toys. Branigan knew that Chester had assigned officers to scour local toy stores and discount stores for the red hammer Andre described.

"I am so sorry," Barbara told them. "This is the first I've heard of a toy hammer. We have two, but I haven't noticed whether they were here or not for more than two years. That's when we used them in a children's show."

When the investigators had finished, they turned to Branigan.

"You're one of the *Rambler* reporters, aren't you?" asked the one who had introduced himself as Dan Stonebrenner. "And the kid was found on your property?"

"Yes."

"Thanks for calling this in, Miss Powers," he said. "It's never good playing catch-up when you didn't start on the case."

"I can imagine," she agreed. "You just got it today?"

He nodded. His partner walked on out of the crowded room, but he lingered. "We spent time at the murder site today," he said. "The Satterfield barn. But I'd like to come out to your place in the morning and see where you found the boy. That might help me get a clearer picture of this whole thing."

"Sure," Branigan said. "That will be fine."

Casually, he continued. "I'm having a hard time understanding why people who lived in the core of the city went all the way out to the middle of nowhere for this murder." He fixed Branigan with a stare.

She frowned. "I'd hardly call it the middle of nowhere. Grambling is surrounded by farms."

"Yeah, but how would the kidnappers know the Satterfield property was vacant? And for that matter, how would they know about an outbuilding on your property?"

"I guess you'll have to ask the kidnappers," she said. "I have no idea."

"Oh, I will," he said. He looked at her for a long moment. "But don't you find it strange that the reporter who breaks the story just happens to live on the property where the boy was found? I know how important it is for you reporters to be first at everything, to beat the competition. So it was rather convenient, don't you think?"

Branigan could hardly believe what she was hearing. "There are things more important than breaking a story," she snapped. "And the welfare of a child is one of them."

"Is that right?" he mused, then turned to go. "Well, thanks again for the tip on the hammer."

"I'm beginning to regret it," she muttered under her breath.

Branigan left the theater disconcerted, partly over her failure to recognize the murder weapon as a theater prop, and partly because Investigator Stonebrenner seemed to suspect her of something. She wasn't too worried; Police Chief Warren and Chester and deputies Mark Wiseman and Cornel Arnett would vouch for her. But still.

Night had fallen by the time she left the theater, and Reynolds Park was emptying rapidly. But Stonebrenner had gotten under her skin. How *did* Oren Arneson find the vacant Satterfield barn? And how did the murderer find her fishing shack? That put the murderer way too close to her, which was exactly why Chester wanted to be at the farm when she was. But he was working late.

She shivered, though the evening was still warm. She got into her Honda, locked the door and sat for awhile, thinking. She hoped she'd set the alarm at the house this morning. She thought she had.

Since she'd already lost the opportunity to arrive home before dark, she decided to make one more stop. She crossed Main Street to Grambling's west side, passing Jericho Road. Heading further west still, she pulled into the weak light of Ricky's Quick Mart, eyeing three young men who stood under a broken streetlight. She parked in the spot closest to the door, and hesitated. Was this a bad idea?

She got out, and remembering what a Rape Crisis counselor had once told her about assertiveness, gripped her keys firmly, sliding one between her fingers like a weapon. She clicked her door lock, then walked straight for the three men, who fell silent. She made eye contact with each as she passed, saying, "Good evening."

To her surprise, each responded. She passed them, not looking back, headed for the familiar Garner Bridge. Sporadic streetlights illuminated small pools along the potholed road. When she reached the path that led to Tent City, she released a tremulous breath she scarcely knew she'd been holding. The streetlights ended because this area was never meant for human habitation. She pulled out her cell phone for its glow and tiptoed past the discarded bottles and mattresses and weeds that lined the dirt trail.

When she reached the edge of the encampment, she was met with a wall of blackest night, and she was reluctant to go further, even with the light of her phone spearing the way. But then she heard the squeak of a rusty lawn chair, and a welcome voice.

"Miz Branigan? That you?"

She turned to the sound, so relieved she wanted to laugh. "Malachi?" she whispered into the void.

He suddenly appeared at her side. "What you doing out here after dark?" he asked. "Ain't no place for you."

Now she did laugh as her anxiety gave way and her legs all but buckled. "I really needed to talk to you," she said. "You got another chair?"

"Stay here." He left her for a moment, and then returned dragging two lawn chairs into a weedy patch outside the bridge's protection. "Moon be up in a little bit and give us some light."

She sat, feeling the straps sag. "You sure this will hold me?" she asked. "I don't want to tear up your furniture."

Malachi laughed softly. "I imagine there more rusty chairs we can pull out the dump." He waited for her to explain what was so important that she would venture into Tent City at night.

"Let me think where to start," she said. "First, the sheriff's office took over Shack's murder investigation from the Grambling PD. Once they figured out neither Oren nor Randy killed him, it became a murder, not a kidnapping. And the murder took place in the county."

"Okay."

"So I had my first conversation with a sheriff's investigator tonight. He was curious about how Oren Arneson and Randy and Shack decided on the Satterfield property for the kidnapping. How they knew it was vacant. And then how the murderer knew about my grandfather's fishing shack."

"I been thinking on that some myself."

"What'd you come up with?"

"I never talked to Oren Arneson. But Shack was living up in here last summer, when I spent some nights in your barn."

"And you told him?"

"Didn't have to, Miz Branigan. It was all over your newspaper."

Branigan nodded, though Malachi couldn't see her. He was right. His nights in her barn had culminated in an explosive story about a string of murders.

"So he saw the coverage?"

"Even if he didn't, that's all anybody talked about rest of the summer."

"So when Oren came up with his kidnapping idea, Shack knew of an isolated place," she surmised.

"Him and Randy had bikes," Malachi added. "I betcha they come out your way and looked round till they seen that barn next door with nobody living there. That's my guess anyway. Those detectives find out for sure when they talk to 'em."

Branigan sighed. At least she had a reasonable explanation for Investigator Stonebrenner. She then filled Malachi in on the plastic hammer found at Theater on the Square. "It probably wasn't the one Andre saw," she said, "even though the deputies took it for testing. But one like it is missing."

Malachi mulled that development over until Branigan spoke again. "Anything else in that steel-trap mind of yours?" she asked.

He snorted. "I run into Butch, Randy's old buddy. He says Shack gave him a bunch of money to hold. So I been trying to figure where Shack got money."

"He told me he worked. And we know he helped build the Shakespeare stage."

"Still seem like more money than he shoulda had. And Shack was one to burn up money on crack. You go through a lot on crack. Fast."

"He told the assistant director at Theater on the Square that he was coming into an inheritance," Branigan said. "But when our reporters checked, his family said he wasn't. We figure he told Sam that because he thought he'd be getting kidnap money."

"But he never got no kidnap money. Pastor Liam seen to that."

"And you're saying he got money from somewhere else? And then he turns up dead. Interesting."

They sat in companionable silence until Branigan spoke again. "Malachi, do you think Shack was blackmailing someone?" she asked.

"I dunno." His mind went to a paid-up motel room with a bailed-out girlfriend and plenty of alcohol.

Her mind went to a husband's infidelity. What might he do to keep his wife from finding out he'd cheated?

CHAPTER THIRTY-TWO

The ringing of Branigan's seldom used front doorbell Thursday morning sent Cleo into a barking frenzy.

"Settle down," Branigan told her. "Deputy Dawg doesn't know any better."

She opened the door to Investigator Stonebrenner and offered him coffee. To her surprise he accepted, but then stood in her kitchen and sipped it without speaking, openly eyeing his surroundings. He was younger than she, maybe mid-thirties, and heavyset. He might be a top-flight investigator, she thought, but he had none of the courtliness of Chester and older detectives of her acquaintance.

"Shall I walk with you to the fishing shack?" she asked.

"If you don't mind." He placed his cup in the sink and followed her to the door. Cleo galloped ahead of them.

Branigan led him single file on the path through the cotton patch, past the barn and chicken houses, then held the barbed-wire fence for him to duck under. It wasn't easy, given his bulk, and he'd broken a sweat by the time they entered the pasture. They turned left and walked toward the lake.

"Those chicken houses are vacant," she said, pointing to where they'd come from, "but the barn is used by my Uncle Bobby next door. The fishing shack" – she pointed ahead to the mound of green at the lake's shoreline – "is vacant, too."

Stonebrenner returned to his question of the previous evening. "So why do you think three homeless guys decided to come way out here?"

"Were you in Grambling last summer?" she asked.

He nodded. "I know all about what happened here. But why would that attract them?"

238

"Well, the newspaper stories mentioned how isolated my barn is, how far apart the houses are. We know that Shack was in Grambling last summer *and* that he and Randy had bikes. I would guess that when Oren Arneson came up with his plan, they rode out this way looking for a place. When they found the Satterfield farm was deserted, bingo."

"I guess it could've happened like that," he conceded. "And that dog of yours runs loose all day?"

Sheesh. "She's a farm dog. She grew up having the run of the place."

Stonebrenner looked around. "Pretty property," he said.

"Thank you. It belonged to my grandparents."

They reached the fishing shed. "The Grambling PD's theory was that someone killed Bradley Drucker but didn't have a reason to hurt the kid," he said. "So he brought the kid here knowing, or at least hoping, that someone would find him."

Branigan shrugged. "I guess so."

"Or was it more pointed?" he asked. "Did he know that *you* would find the kid? You personally?"

Her sense of dread returned – the idea that a murderer had stalked her property, had known her routine well enough to know that she passed this shack often. "I can't imagine that it'd be personal," she said, "but I suppose it's possible."

"It makes me wonder if someone's been watching you, Miss Powers," the investigator said, turning his gaze once more to the Satterfield land, then following a slow arc all the way to her Uncle Bobby's. "It makes me think the murderer knows you."

A cloud slid over the sun, and this landscape that Branigan knew as intimately as her own bedroom looked suddenly gray with unknowing.

Stonebrenner spoke again. "Any idea who that might be?"

She shook her head mutely.

Branigan had trouble sleeping Thursday night, and not only at the thought that someone had been studying her routine as she obliviously jogged, played with Cleo, watered flowers. She had resisted Chester's suggestion that she spend the night at her parents' house, because she needed to pack. Now her overnight bag was filled with swimsuits, sunscreen, beach towels, cards, and a novel. Her cooler awaited frozen pina colada mix along with soft drinks, orange juice and milk. She was excited about the first beach trip of the season, but a question hung over her, and she knew it would worry her like a ragged splinter until it was answered.

So when Chester pulled up early Friday morning, Branigan made a decision. She swung a beach bag into the back and casually asked, "Is it okay if we stop to see my Aunt Jeanie on our way out?"

"Sure," said Chester. "How's she doing?"

"That's what I want to check on," Branigan responded, not entirely truthfully.

With Cleo wedged happily between them, they drove the short distance to her Uncle Bobby's house. He answered the kitchen door, grabbing her in a hug. "Is this your young man I've heard so much about?"

"Yes, Uncle Bobby, and we're headed to the prom," Branigan said with a grin.

Chester raised an eyebrow at her, and held out his hand. "Chester Scovoy, sir. It's a pleasure to meet you."

"I'm used to my niece's smart mouth," her uncle assured him. "Please come in and have coffee." He raised his voice. "Jeanie! Company!"

"Has Izzy B already left?" Branigan asked. She knew Isabella intended to ride down with the Delaneys.

"No, she's packing. And Jimmie Jean's around somewhere. She's taking her mother to chemo this morning."

Jeanie bustled in through the living room, buckling the belt on her jeans. "I thought I heard someone out here. How are you, Branigan? And this must be Chester! What a pleasure to finally meet you."

"We just wanted to check in before we left town," Branigan said, hugging her aunt. "How is everything going with the chemo?"

Jeanie filled her in with a breezy abbreviation of her sessions while pouring coffee and placing an uncut coffee cake on the table. "The church is sending over more food than we can eat, so Chester, please help us with this."

"Gladly," he said, accepting a piece.

Branigan kept a nervous eye on the hallway across the living room. Finally, she stood. "I'm going to speak to Izzy B for a minute. I'll be right back."

Leaving Chester chatting easily with her aunt and uncle, Branigan made her way to the bedroom she knew as well as her own. Isabella was making her bed, a small suitcase packed and waiting by the door.

"Brani G! You didn't come to pick me up, did you? I told Liz I'd ride with them."

"I know. Just wanted to see your mama before I left town."

Isabella looked at her closely, suddenly understanding. "Is Chester with you?"

Branigan nodded without speaking, a sudden lump in her throat.

"Oh, honey," said her cousin. "Just because one man doesn't know a good thing when he's got it doesn't mean every man is like that."

"I know. But it'll always be there, hanging over me."

"Well, then, I'll get her."

Isabella squeezed Branigan's arm as she passed, heading to her sister's room. "JJ, we have company. You want to say hi?"

"Not if it's more of those church people."

"It's Brani G and Chester."

"Oh, okay. I'll be right out."

Branigan and Isabella walked arm in arm down the hall and into the house's spacious living areas. Branigan took a chair next to Chester and sipped her coffee while Uncle Bobby and Aunt Jeanie questioned him about finding Andre and Shack. In a moment, Jimmie Jean came in, dressed in tight-fitting jeans and an indigo blouse, her hair newly brushed and shining.

Chester stood.

"Chester," said Isabella, "this is my sister Jimmie Jean. JJ, Chester Scovoy, Brani G's friend."

She held out her hand. "It's such a pleasure, Detective. Any friend of Cuz is a friend of ours."

Branigan couldn't help it. Her eyes darted from one to the other.

"I've met your husband," Chester said politely. "He's been helping us with a case."

"Was that before or after he was charged with assault?"

"Jimmie Jean!" said her mother warningly.

"What?" She turned to her mother. "It's the first thing he's done right in quite some time, standing up for Izzy B like that." She poured herself coffee and flounced into a chair. "I suppose he's been telling you about that dreadful Brad Drucker. I guess I shouldn't say it now that he's dead, but he was a thief. And a liar. And a wife-beater."

Chester smiled perfunctorily and turned his attention back to Bobby and Jeanie, and resumed their conversation.

Jimmie Jean's eyes flitted from Branigan to Isabella. "So you three are going to the beach? What I wouldn't give to go with you!"

"We figured you couldn't get away from rehearsals for a whole weekend," Branigan said.

"You got that right. Colin sings like he's got a mouthful of marbles, and Reggie's taking it out on me."

"Are ya'll going to be able to pull it off?" Branigan asked.

"Oh sure. 'The show must go on' and all that. One way or another, we'll throw something up there." She focused on her cousin. "Oh, I meant to ask you, what did you think of Tuesday's rehearsal? *Before* the action in the seats, I mean."

"Reggie did seem a little… out there," Branigan said slowly. "Like making you wear a cowboy hat in the ballroom scene."

"Maybe he'll back off," Jimmie Jean said, sounding doubtful. "But you know…" She paused, sounding wistful.

Branigan and Isabella waited.

"What?" her sister finally asked.

"Something's changed," Jimmie Jean said, darting a look at Chester. "Even before Jackson took out my leading man."

Isabella and Branigan looked at each other, and Isabella raised her coffee cup to her lips. Branigan knew she was trying to hide a smile. Was JJ going to make Jackson's assault on Colin Buckner about her?

"For the first week of rehearsals, I could do no wrong with Reggie," she continued. "Now I can't do anything right. I even wonder…" She lowered her voice to a whisper, glancing at Chester again as he talked to her parents. "I wonder if he's high a lot of the time."

"Colin Buckner hinted at the same thing," Isabella said.

Branigan didn't tell them that Barbara Wickenstall had virtually confirmed the same suspicion. She didn't want her professional life and her personal one overlapping any more than necessary.

"Well, whatever it is," Jimmie Jean said, "he's way more irritable and snarky than he was at first."

She sat back and sipped her coffee, shooting another glance at Chester. There was a pause in her parents' conversation. "So, Detective," she said, "did Jackson tell you *all* about his relationship with Bradley Drucker. *Everything*?"

"I don't know," Chester said blandly. "What are you referring to?"

"Did he tell you, for instance, about his affair with Maria Drucker?"

"*What?*" Uncle Bobby's face darkened. "Jimmie Jean Rickman, is that the truth?" Aunt Jeanie bowed her head in such a way that Branigan thought she might already know.

Jimmie Jean tossed her hair over one shoulder. "It is, Daddy," she said, though her eyes remained on Chester. "It's been years. We're past it. My point is that Brad Drucker might've had a reason to kill Jackson, but Jackson had no reason to kill him."

"As you said, we have to look at everything," Chester said. "Or rather the Cannon County Sheriff's Office does. They've taken over jurisdiction."

"So you're not working it any more? But why?"

"The murder happened two farms over. That's in the county."

Jimmie Jean sat back.

Her dad looked at her. "Let's take a walk, JJ," he said abruptly, standing and motioning his daughter toward the kitchen door.

"Oh, Daddy, it's ancient history," she protested, getting up nonetheless and staring straight at Branigan. "Jackson knows better than to *ever* do something like that again."

Chester looked at Branigan thoughtfully, then began chatting with her aunt once more. Despite her cousin's theatrics, Branigan felt her lungs expand and her muscles loosen. Five minutes later, she and Chester told her Aunt Jeanie goodbye and followed Isabella out of the door.

They'd been driving for a few miles before Chester looked over Cleo's head at Branigan. "Do you want to tell me what that was all about?" he asked.

"What? Meeting my aunt and uncle?"

"Is that what it was?"

"That's what it was."

He looked at her face, more relaxed than it had been all morning. "All right then. Let's go to the beach."

After that they talked non-stop on the way down. Branigan had briefed Chester two days before about finding the plastic hammer at Theater on the Square. Both were chagrined that they had been thinking "toy" rather than "theater prop" from Andre's description, and hadn't pursued any missing props.

"But honestly, the sheriff's investigators don't seem terribly concerned about it," Chester said as he drove. "After looking at the hammer you did find, they said it couldn't possibly be a murder weapon. Something much heavier, something with a sharper edge, killed Shack."

"Yeah, but I bet they're going to find that a plastic hammer was somewhere in that barn," Branigan persisted. "Too coincidental to be in the costume room *and* to be so close to what Andre described."

"I think you're right. They've still got the psychiatrist working with Andre, so they're listening to what he says. And they're interviewing folks at the theater."

"Well, if anything breaks, Jody's got it for the next few days," Branigan said, willing herself to drop the shop talk. "Nothing we can do from the Isle of Palms."

"Thank goodness!" Chester then went on to tell her about the three houses and condo he'd toured the day before.

"Any possibilities?" she asked.

"Yeah, I really liked this renovated mill house," he said. "Near the old Brookmont Mill."

"That area's coming back," she said. "My dad has talked about financing houses in that inner circle around the mill."

"This house has two bedrooms, one bath, but a good-sized front porch and an extended deck out back. A wall has been torn out so the living room and kitchen are wide open. I'd have more yard work than with the condo, but I think I'd like that. You seem to manage all right with cutting grass and planting flowers."

"And you can always buy a goat."

He laughed. "Yep, there's that."

"I have to admit I love the idea of you settling into Grambling to stay," she said.

"Me too." He reached past Cleo to caress the back of Branigan's neck. "It's past time."

They stopped at a rest area as they crossed the Georgia–South Carolina border and bought snacks and soft drinks, and let Cleo run. As they traveled the flat interstate that traversed the Lowcountry, Chester said, "So tell me about this beach house. When your folks got it, how often you came, all that stuff."

"How much time you got?"

"All the way to the island."

So Branigan told him about the 1960s house on stilts that, alone among its neighbors, had survived Hurricane Hugo in 1989. In the aftermath, surrounding properties had been sold and razed, so it now stood as a lonely reminder of the island's earlier days.

"There are mansions on either side, and we suspect they've been adding more trees to block us from view," she said. "Inside, it's got that paneling thing going on, like virtually every beach house built mid-century. It's just four bedrooms and a living room and kitchen, not huge. But Mom and Dad have added lots of decking and a gazebo and updated the kitchen."

"Does it have one of those cutesy beach names? Like Powers Aid? Or Branigan's Barefoot Beachfront Hideaway?"

"It does," she laughed. "Twin Palms."

"Ah, for you and your brother. Clever."

"Originally there were real twin palms too, by the front door. Hugo blew them down, but Dad planted two more. They're big now."

"And did you always vacation there?"

"As far back as I can remember. When we were kids, we'd come down with these two other families, the Harrisons and the Barnhills. All the parents had bedrooms, of course, so that left only one, plus a maid's room downstairs, for eight kids. In the beginning, the older kids went downstairs, and the little ones upstairs. As we got older, it was one for boys and one for girls, and we fought over who got the downstairs room."

"Sounds like fun."

"It was. And we did the normal beach stuff. Crabbing. Fishing. Bingo. Ghost stories."

"Ghost stories are 'normal beach stuff'?"

"Absolutely. I thought you grew up in Charleston, young man."

"I did."

"And you never heard of Alice's grave in Pawley's Island? Or the Gray Man warning of hurricanes?"

"Yeah, but we didn't link those stories with beach trips. Our beach trips were more like day excursions."

"Well, if you grew up in northeast Georgia, you did link those stories to the beach, because that's where they were set."

"Makes sense, I guess. For you hillbillies."

Branigan hooted. "I'll tell my dad you said that. Ought to win him over."

He reached past Cleo to rub her shoulder. "No, don't do that. I've been making good progress asking his advice on my house hunting."

When they came to the bridge leading over the inland waterway to the island, Branigan lowered her window and gripped Cleo firmly in case the dog got the urge to jump. "That's got to smell like home for you," she said, the wind whipping her hair.

"It sure does," he said. "I haven't been back in awhile."

"I forgot to ask you. Are you going to see your folks while you're here?"

"They're not in town," he said. "They're at my mom's sister's in Phoenix. I'll have to bring you to meet them later this summer."

She sat back, her stomach somersaulting with pleasure.

Once they came to the two or three blocks that made up the Isle of Palms' downtown, Branigan instructed Chester to turn right. Quickly passing condos, ice cream parlors and bars, they drove along the oceanfront road until they turned onto the crushed oyster shells of the Twin Palms driveway. The house was flanked by palmettos, palm trees and the wind-bent post oaks that protected the house from storms.

Cleo jumped out of the truck and ran around the yard, sniffing excitedly, as Branigan and Chester unloaded luggage and groceries. Branigan gave him a quick tour of the house, then pulled a blender from underneath a kitchen cabinet. "First order of business," she said, "is a pina colada and a beach walk. Are you game?"

"Count me in," he said, rummaging in the cooler for the drink mix. "I'm up for a girlie drink. I bet you've got paper umbrellas."

"Of course I do. And straws."

Minutes later, they opened the sliding glass door onto the oceanfront deck. "This is a good place to see up and down the island." Branigan pointed left. "That way is Wild Dunes, golf courses, a hotel, lots of houses and condos." Then right. "And that way is the inlet and Sullivan's Island. But you probably know all that."

"Not really. We always went to Folly." They took a few moments to take in the view of the low-tide beach and blue-green water with occasional gray stripes where the waves churned the sand to the surface. Few people were visible. With no hotels or condos on this section, it was seldom crowded in May, even with locals coming in on weekends.

"Man, this is the life, Brani G. Good call."

"Before the others get here," she said, turning to him, "there was something I wanted to ask you. About Shack's murder."

"The one I'm no longer on?" he said with a smile. "The one that was taken over by the county so *I'm getting a vacation*?"

"That's the one." She paused. "*Is* the sheriff's office really investigating Jimmie Jean's husband?"

Chester's smile faded. "They are."

"Is there any indication he even knew Shack was in Grambling?"

"He claimed he didn't," Chester said. "But Shack stole from him, and he stole Shack's wife. So bad blood between them. And then he shows up in Grambling, and within days Shack is dead? Pretty suspicious, don't you think?" Chester watched her closely.

The strong wind off the ocean blew her hair into her eyes, and she grabbed it to keep it off her face. "I see how it'd look that way. But Jimmie Jean really did come up to help with Aunt Jeanie, and Jackson really did come after her."

"Are you sure about that?"

"Pretty sure."

Chester gazed out toward the sea. "Well, since he's your family, it's probably a good thing I did get taken off the case. Saved by the location of the crime."

"About that," she said, almost reluctantly. "I've been thinking."

Chester waited.

"If Shack was killed in the Satterfield barn and Randy was already gone," she said, "that means the murderer carried Andre to the fishing shack on my property."

"That's right."

Chester almost couldn't make out her next words over the roar of the ocean. But he was pretty sure he heard her say, "Jackson knew where that shack was."

CHAPTER THIRTY-THREE

Malachi hadn't seen Slick in four days. He kept thinking he might come by his tent to pick up some clothes, but he never did. So on Saturday evening, frustrated, he walked to the Heart of Grambling motel.

Another family, not the Arnesons, were in the pool: a mama, daddy and two little blonde girls. There was no sign of Flora and her kids; Malachi figured they'd moved to their new place.

He looked around at the twelve or so cars in the parking lot and guessed that travelers stayed here during weekends. He saw a couple at the ice machine, a pre-teen at the vending machine, and several families entering and leaving the attached restaurant. Nobody took any notice of the slim black man in a dark do-rag and dreadlocks. Malachi was used to that.

He walked to Room 42, and saw that the door wasn't closed all the way. He waited for a moment and heard snoring inside. He pushed the door open with his boot. Elise lay on her back in the rumpled bed, snoring loudly. Malachi's eyes darted to the empty bottle of Jim Beam by her side, the crumpled beer cans in the trash, the full ashtrays on the dresser and night stand. Slick was nowhere in sight.

"Elise," he said in a normal tone of voice. "Elise." She didn't stir. Malachi carefully shut the door behind him and tiptoed to the bathroom to make sure Slick wasn't in the shower. The bathroom was empty.

He stood indecisively at the foot of the bed, every part of his street identity screaming that he shouldn't be here. Then he pictured Andre in the art room, head down, some unknown fear keeping him from answering Malachi's questions. He pictured Shack, killed in his prime. Malachi made a decision.

He opened each drawer as quickly and quietly as possible, not sure what he was looking for. He found new women's clothes and underwear, still bearing their Walmart tags. A duffle bag sat on the floor, and he nudged it with his foot until he could see that Slick too had bought new underwear and socks and khakis.

There weren't a lot more spaces to search. He went through the closet, flapping open an extra blanket to make sure nothing was hidden within its folds. He opened the refrigerator, and saw only beer, beer and more beer. He stood, hands on his hips, staring around the room. He went into the bathroom and opened a shallow medicine cabinet, but it was empty. He returned and looked at Elise, still out of it. He scanned the edge of the mattress where she'd kicked off the covers. A tiny piece of yellow-brown paper was visible between the mattress and box springs. He gently eased it from its hiding place, keeping his eyes on Elise's slack face.

The envelope was the size of a letter folded in half. He unbent the clasp and slid out two pictures – the kind you got developed at a drugstore. The subject was something Malachi had seen before, many times in fact. Something he could have photographed, had he any desire to do so.

Two men stood in the glow of a car's headlights, one with money in his hand, one with something that looked like a sandwich bag of sugar. Which, of course, it wasn't. One of the men was Slick. The other, his face glistening with sweat, was Reggie Fortenberry.

Suddenly, a hand ripped the pictures from Malachi. He'd not heard anyone slip into the room, and when the voice came, it was quiet, too, and menacing.

"What you doing here, Malachi? Nothing here concern you."

He looked up to see Slick brandishing a box cutter in one hand, the pictures in the other.

"I don't unnerstand," Malachi said. "It don't make no sense for you to blackmail your own customer."

Slick waved the box cutter in Malachi's face. "Like I said, it don't concern you."

"Why you beat up Butch? Take his money?" Malachi was half talking out loud, half talking to his old drinking buddy. "What got into you?"

"I ain't telling you again, Malachi. You best leave."

"But why you turn on your own customer?" Malachi asked again. "Why you got a picture of the theater director?"

Elise began to wake up, her face showing surprise at seeing her old Tent City neighbor. "Mal-chi," she said, still groggy. "You wanna drink?"

Slick tossed the box cutter on the dresser, where it landed with an angry clatter. "Ah, long's you here, man, go ahead and have a drink."

Malachi figured he'd have a better chance of learning something if he could get Slick drinking and talking. So he helped himself to a beer from the fridge and took a seat.

CHAPTER THIRTY-FOUR

Branigan, Chester, Liam, Liz and Isabella gathered on the back deck, freshly showered and aloe-d after a day on the beach. Branigan brought out a bowl of mixed nuts and a plate of hummus and baby carrots.

"Who's up for Coconut Joe's tonight?" suggested Liz.

"Do we have to dance?" asked her husband.

"You better believe it. They have a reggae band."

After a day and a half with Branigan's friends, Chester felt at ease. "Whenever I hear the first reggae song," he said lazily, "I'm like, 'Wow, that's good.' The second, 'Wow, that's good.' The third, 'Wow, that sounds exactly like the other two.'"

Liam laughed. "I'm with you."

"In that case," Isabella said, "don't get mad if Liz and Brani G find someone else to dance with."

"I can't believe she's threatening us," Liam protested.

"So how long have you guys been going there?" Chester asked.

"From the minute it opened in 1997," Branigan answered.

"Branigan is the keeper of our history," Liam told him. "She has a memory like an elephant."

"And how long have you been friends?"

They looked at each other. "Well, Brani G and me since we were born," said Isabella.

"And Liz and Brani G and I were in high school together," Liam said. "Mr and Mrs Powers brought us here when we were teens. We met Izzy B at some point in there, too, at their house."

"That's really cool," said Chester. "A definite benefit to staying in your hometown." He grabbed a handful of nuts.

"I'm fascinated by what you do, Liam," he continued. "Chief

Warren and I talk a lot about street policing and whether we ought to be more proactive in reaching out to the homeless rather than simply reacting to citizen complaints."

"I'm all for that," Liam said. "If you guys could arrest less and do more placements in shelters or the mental health clinic, it could only help."

"You knew this Shack, right? What causes someone to choose being homeless over getting a job? Someone able-bodied and mentally healthy, I mean."

Liam shrugged. "There are as many reasons as there are people. The only thing I'm pretty sure of is it's never a conscious 'choice' per se. It's more a result of many, many bad decisions."

"But this guy Shack," Chester pressed. "My understanding is he had every opportunity. Parents with money. College. A decent job and marriage. He turned his back on all of it."

"Yeah, but he probably got addicted to alcohol or drugs somewhere in there. At Jericho Road, whenever we can't figure out why someone is making the decisions they are, whenever everything ought to be working but it's not, we'll find out it's addiction. And I mean every single time."

Chester sat back in his porch rocker, thinking. "How about trauma? Does that send somebody spiraling into homelessness?"

"Oh, yeah. You've met Malachi, right? I don't know if he's ever been officially diagnosed, but I'm pretty sure it's post-traumatic stress disorder. From the Gulf War. He self-medicates. We see that in almost every veteran who's on the street."

Branigan listened closely. "Have you noticed that he's gotten worse lately?" she asked.

Liam nodded. "Yeah, worse, then a little better recently. I don't know what the trigger was."

"Veterans, I can sure understand," Chester said. "But what about the others?"

Liam was warming to his subject. "Sometimes, it's a big medical bill or a divorce. A household is barely hanging on and something happens to tip them over. And one thing I wasn't expecting: we see middle-age men become homeless when their mothers die. Turns out Mom was renting all those years, and when she died, the house went away."

"So is it ever simply generational poverty?"

"Sure. And a lifetime of low-paying jobs. There's a man with us right now who was a rodeo rider and clown, of all things. You can imagine the sporadic pay and the potential for injury."

Branigan looked at Liam. "Yeah, I met him. The artist. Alphonse Jasper." She turned to Chester. "I sent word about him through my colleague, Jody."

"Yeah, my guys looked into him but found no connection between him and Randy and Shack. Or the Arnesons for that matter. Their paths never crossed."

"He has his rodeo clown costume hanging in his room," offered Liam, dipping a carrot in the hummus.

Branigan stopped with her hand halfway to the vegetable plate. "What's it look like?"

"Oh, Brani G, you're taxing my memory." Liam closed his eyes. "A loud floral shirt. Shiny purple pants. Red tennis shoes – I guess because rodeo clowns have to run."

"Why didn't you say something when we were looking into all those clown sightings?"

"Because your stories talked about white pants with red stripes."

Chester looked at Branigan. "What are you thinking?"

"I'm thinking the theater was missing two costumes, but there were three people dressed as clowns. Randy. Shack. And the little clown Andre told Malachi about. The murderer."

"And the third costume wouldn't necessarily fit the description we had of clowns in the woods," Chester mused, "because no one saw him but Andre." He turned to Isabella. "Did Jackson ever visit you at Jericho Road?"

Isabella looked surprised. "Yes."

"When?" Branigan and Chester leaned forward.

"I think the day after he showed up at your house," she said to Branigan. "That was Sunday, right? So this past Monday."

Chester flicked a glance at Branigan. She couldn't tell what he was thinking. "Shack was already dead by then," she said.

Liam looked confused. "What are you getting at?" he asked. "If you're asking when Jackson came to Jericho Road, he was in much earlier than that. He came in the week before."

Chester and Branigan whirled on Liam. "Before Friday?" Branigan asked. "That's when Shack was killed."

"Yeah, I'm pretty sure," Liam said. "He was looking for Izzy B and she was helping the Arnesons find a motel room."

"You never told me Jackson came by," Isabella said.

"He asked me not to. When he couldn't find you, he said he hadn't got in touch with Jimmie Jean yet and would try to see her first. Then you started talking about him after the weekend, so I figured he'd contacted all of you and everything was fine."

Everyone was silent.

Liam looked around. "Did I screw up?"

Branigan tried to meet Chester's eyes, but he was studying the floor. Isabella and Liz looked baffled.

Finally Branigan spoke. "Why don't you guys head over to Coconut Joe's, and Chester and I will meet you there?"

When the others had gone, Branigan and Chester remained on the oceanfront deck. She scarcely knew where to begin, but she wasn't surprised at the point Chester chose.

"So Jackson came to your house?" he said.

"Yeah."

"What'd he want?"

"To apologize."

"For the way he left you?"

Branigan's head snapped up. "You knew?"

Chester looked at her. "Of course I knew, Brani G. What I didn't know is that you'd been alone with him last week."

She waved a hand dismissively. "I didn't even let him in. We stood in the driveway for all of ten minutes."

Chester tilted his head. "But you still have feelings for him. You obviously don't want to consider that he might have murdered Shack. Even after he showed his violent streak with Colin Buckner."

Branigan shook her head. "Oh, Chester, no. You've got it all wrong." She gathered her thoughts. "Jackson was my first real boyfriend. When I was nineteen. When I went back to UGA, he and Jimmie Jean started dating and very quickly got married. Was I hurt? Oh yeah. But it's been twenty-three years. I got over it a long time ago."

"So why did he come to the farm?"

"He was on his way to Uncle Bobby's to try to work things out with Jimmie Jean, I guess. We didn't really talk about it. But he said he wanted to apologize for the way he broke up with me. We literally had not been alone to have a conversation since he and JJ got married. As I told Cleo," she smiled, "I think I dodged a bullet. The Jackson who had an affair with Brad Drucker's wife, or for that matter the Jackson who dated Jimmie Jean behind my back – he obviously was not who I thought he was."

Chester's shoulders relaxed. "That's what I wanted to believe, but I got shaken when Isabella said he'd been to your house."

"To my driveway."

Chester laughed. "Okay. But Jimmie Jean is worried. She was shooting fire at you this morning when she said he would never have an affair again."

"Yeah, I caught that." Branigan thought for a minute. "You know, she shouldn't worry about Jackson and *me*, but I suppose she should worry in general. What is it people say? If someone cheated to be *with* you, sooner or later they'll cheat *on* you."

"But you don't think Jackson is capable of murder?"

She blew out an extended breath. "I hope not. But that doesn't have anything to do with my feelings for him." Her eyes locked on to Chester's. "It's about my feelings for my family. After last summer, and what they went through with my brother, I don't want them ever going through that again." She thought for a moment about the murders that had rocked Grambling – and the Powers clan – then shoved the memory aside.

They sat in silence, the tension between them draining away as they stared at the ocean.

"But more importantly," she said, sitting up in her rocker, "how did you know everything already? That I'd even dated Jackson?"

"Well, first off, I'm a detective. You knew that, right?"

She laughed. "But I didn't know you were detecting me."

"Goes with the territory."

"Seriously. Who'd you talk to? Izzy B?"

"I didn't even know Izzy B back then. Remember when I said Grambling could be a very small town? I didn't even have to ask. Some of your townspeople opened right up – even asked my intentions, really – as soon as they started seeing us out together."

"Please tell me it wasn't my dad."

"Nope."

"Then let me guess. Bea Boswell."

"You got it. Not only did I hear about the scoundrel Jackson Solesbee, but lesser offenders. Hank Monarch. The improbably named Tank Dubreski. And more recently, Jason Hornay."

Branigan clapped a hand over her mouth to keep from shrieking. Then she shrieked anyway. "Oh my gosh! She did not bring up all those people!"

"She did. She admitted she didn't know about the boyfriends in Detroit, but she was pretty forthcoming about the ones in Grambling."

Branigan collapsed in helpless laughter. "What's even more unnerving is to think of you actually listening to all that," she said when she could catch her breath.

"It was not my proudest moment," he said wryly. "But I was already falling hard and I thought I'd be wise to hear her out." He stood and pulled Branigan to her feet, then placed his hands on both sides of her face. He bent down and kissed her. "I was just glad to hear you were free at the time," he murmured. "That's all I really wanted to know."

"Well, I'm glad it's out in the open," she replied, wrapping her arms around his neck. "About Jackson, I mean. I started to tell you several times."

He pulled away. "That reminds me. This morning? At your aunt and uncle's? You wanted to see me with Jimmie Jean, didn't you?"

She looked sheepish. "I admit it."

"Brani G, you're breaking my heart." He pulled her against his chest. "Don't you know by now that I'm in love with you? Not some crazy cousin of yours?"

She settled her head comfortably on his shoulder. "I do now."

When Branigan and Chester walked solemnly up the steep outdoor steps to the rooftop deck of Coconut Joe's, Liam and Isabella looked up anxiously. Liz stood by the table, dancing to the reggae band.

"Did we put our foot in it?" Isabella asked. "We've been going over and over what we said."

Liam's eyes shot between Chester and Branigan. "We didn't mean to…" he began.

"I know it wasn't me," Liz said. "All I said was, 'Let's go to Coconut Joe's.'"

Branigan took pity on her friends and broke into laughter.

"It's fine," Chester told them. "We needed some air-clearing anyway."

Isabella looked as though she might have another question, but she let it go. "In that case, here's our biggest decision," she said. "Have a drink up here or go on down to the restaurant below?"

Branigan gazed out at the Atlantic pounding far below on one side, the band on the other, and the large tiki-style bar in between. "Can't come up here without getting a banana daiquiri," she said. "Then we'll get Liz her seafood."

"Sounds like a plan," Liam said, the relief apparent in his voice.

Hours later, Isabella finally asked the question that was on her mind. "I'm still curious about the costume in that rodeo clown's room at Jericho Road," she said to Branigan and Chester. "Do you think Jackson could have taken it?"

"I don't know," Chester told her honestly. "But I made a call to the investigators in the sheriff's office. They'll check it out."

Chapter Thirty-five

Malachi warily took the only chair in the motel room. It allowed him to sit with his back against the plate glass window, his eyes on Elise, still rousing herself from sleep, and Slick, flopped on the bed beside her. He popped the top on his beer can, savored the cool stream running down his throat.

"You lookin' to spend the night?" Slick asked him. Whenever someone on the street scored a motel room, his friends were likely to appear, looking for a roof or a bed or a shower. Folks tended to share when they had it; it wouldn't be long till they didn't, and they'd be the ones asking. The practice had gotten Malachi kicked out of more rooms than he could count – until he'd learned to say no.

"Nah," Malachi said. "Looking for somethin' else."

Slick sighed. "What?"

Malachi took another long pull on his beer and felt the release of it. He leaned his chair back on two legs. His demands to know why Slick had a photograph of a drug exchange between him and Reggie Fortenberry had gone nowhere. He'd need to come at it from another angle. *Slant*, he'd read somewhere in phrasing he liked. *Come at it slant.*

"Been thinking why anybody'd want to kill Shack," he mused, his eyes on the popcorn-textured ceiling. "What Shack done to anybody?"

Elise looked confused, but Slick was listening.

"Now I know he could be annoying, going round quoting Shakespeare all the time: 'Alas poor Yorick!' Like he some English lord wannabe. But that ain't really no reason to kill somebody. Maybe just slap 'em round a little."

Elise laughed. "Wanted to do that myself," she said.

Malachi went on as if she hadn't spoken. "Or then, somebody

mighta got really mad about him kidnapping that boy. Though seems to me they woulda killed the daddy, not Shack."

"We heard about that in the jail," Elise said. "Everybody talking about a clown done got that boy. But he all right, ain't he? That boy all right?"

Malachi nodded at her. "As far as I know. Him and his mama and brothers and sister was staying right here at this motel. Now they got them a place."

Elise sank back on the bed. "That's good. Don't like seeing no chirren out here in this mess."

Slick was still watching Malachi. "So you think somebody killed Shack because they was mad about him grabbing that kid?"

"Maybe somebody want to be a hero, rescue the boy," Malachi said as if he were thinking out loud. "But when he got to the barn, Shack was there and they got into it. After he killed Shack, he couldn't reveal hisself." Malachi fixed Slick with a stare. "Coulda been a accident even. What you think, Slick?"

"I think you got a wild 'magination."

Malachi's eyes flicked to the box cutter still lying on the dresser. He wasn't sure he could get to it before Slick could. He continued in the same conversational tone. "But the thing I can't figure is why you got a picture of you and your best customer. So here's what I'm thinking. You didn't use it. Somebody else did."

Slick sighed. "I always said you a smart one, Malachi."

"Shack was blackmailing the theater director, warn't he? That's where his money coming from."

Slick nodded wearily, his dirty ponytail bobbing.

"Shack gave the money to Butch to hold while he biked out to the barn," Malachi said. "But you jumped Butch and took the money. Which is how you got this motel and sprung Elise on bail."

Slick shrugged. "So what? He had no business threatening my customer."

"But things got messy. You was afraid Shack's blackmail gonna roll back on you. So you followed him to the barn and kilt him."

Elise bolted upright and stared at Slick. "You kill Shack?" she yelled.

Slick's head snapped up, all weariness gone. "No! No! That's not what happen! Malachi, you crazy!" He made a move to roll off the bed, but Malachi leaped first and palmed the box cutter.

Slick groaned. "I ain't gonna cut you, man. Just trying to show you something."

He retrieved the photo of himself and Reggie Fortenberry in the headlight beams. "Who in this picture got the most to lose?" he demanded. "Ain't me. I'm already living under a damn bridge, in case you hadn't noticed."

Malachi raised his eyes to Slick's as everything clicked into place. Who had the most to lose? Who had access to clown costumes?

He stood abruptly. "Thanks for the beer," he said.

He went out into the night to make a phone call.

CHAPTER THIRTY-SIX

"That's funny," said Branigan, checking her phone as she poured coffee Sunday morning. "A missed call from Malachi. I put his number in my phone last summer, but I don't think he's ever called me."

Liam looked up from the newspaper he'd bought during a jog to the sleepy island's downtown. He walked to his bedroom and found his phone on the dresser. "I missed one from him too. No wonder. It came in at two this morning."

They looked at each other. "Something's up," she said, punching redial. A recording told her the user's voicemail hadn't been set up.

She looked at Liam. "What do you think that's about?"

"No idea." He turned to Chester reading the sports page on the living room couch. "Do you want to call your department to see if anything's changed?"

Chester called Jim Rogerson, who told him nothing had occurred on the murder investigation. "The county hasn't made an arrest," he said. "I can call you if something breaks."

"Yeah, do that," Chester said. "I'll be back in Grambling tonight." He turned to Branigan and Liam. "Nothing on our end."

"That's good," said Liam. "I don't want to rush back on the one Sunday I've got somebody covering worship." He stood and walked over to the sliding glass door, enjoying the ocean view.

Isabella and Liz joined them a few minutes later, and they shared coffee, cinnamon rolls and the paper. The women were applying sunscreen for a few extra hours on the beach when Branigan's phone rang. The caller was barely discernible, so she went into her bedroom and shut the door.

"I'm sorry," she said, "who is this?"

"Branigan, it's Barbara. Barbara Wickenstall." Her voice was hushed. Branigan placed a hand over her other ear in an attempt to make out her words. "Maybe I should be calling the deputies. But I didn't know what to do." Her voice sounded as if it was about to break.

"What is it, Barbara? What's wrong?"

"I came in this morning to do some mending. Colin ripped his trousers during rehearsal yesterday."

Branigan waited for Barbara to get to the point.

"And I saw…." Her voice faded out.

"Barbara, can you get closer to the phone?"

"Okay." Her voice still sounded tremulous, but it was a little clearer.

"And you saw what?"

"I saw the other plastic hammer. The one we were missing."

Branigan's heart beat faster. "Where?" she asked. "Where'd you see it?"

"It doesn't make sense," Barbara said. "It makes no sense."

"But where, Barbara? Where did you see it?"

"In the dressing room we reserve for our stars."

"Where's that?"

"Backstage. We have a separate dressing room for our lead actors because they usually have more costume changes than anyone else. I went in to leave the mended trousers for Colin. That's when I saw it."

"So it was in Colin Buckner's dressing room? In plain sight?"

"No, it was under a cot we have in there for the actors to rest. It was all wrapped up in some fabric from my sewing closet. I'd been looking for that fabric, and that's why I pulled it out. And found the hammer."

"You need to call Dan Stonebrenner at the sheriff's office right away," Branigan said. "Tell him about Colin Buckner."

"But Branigan, it wasn't under Colin's cot."

Branigan was getting confused. And exasperated. "You said it was in the dressing room for the lead actor."

"Lead actors. Plural. The hammer was under Jamie's cot."

Branigan felt light-headed, and abruptly sat on her bed as the room started spinning.

"We don't have a lot of space," Barbara said, "so the leads share a room, even if it's a man and woman. There's a screen down the middle and a cot on each side."

The murder weapon that killed Shack was under Jimmie Jean's cot? No way. Branigan remembered her cousin's parting words two days earlier: "Jackson knows better than to *ever* do something like that again." Chester had seen the comment as a veiled threat directed at Branigan. Branigan had dismissed it as more of Jimmie Jean's theatrics. But now her mind danced around a question, retreated, approached it again: Had Jimmie Jean somehow seen Shack as a threat to be removed?

"Was the hammer..." Branigan trailed off, started again. "Did the hammer... did it have blood on it?"

"I don't know!" Barbara whispered. "As soon as I saw the handle, I called you."

"So you're in the dressing room now?"

"Yes." The costumer's voice sounded strangled.

"Barbara, get out of there and go to your office and lock the door. Don't touch anything else. When you get there, call Investigator Stonebrenner."

"Can you come too?"

"I'm five hours away. But Stonebrenner and his men will know what to do." She thought she heard Barbara's shallow breathing. "And Barbara, one more thing."

"What?"

"Could you tell if there was anything heavy inside the hammer?"

There was a moment's silence. "I think so," she said shakily. "When I unfolded the cloth, it did feel like something heavy in it. But when I saw the red handle, I dropped the cloth and didn't touch it again."

"Good job. Get out of there now, okay?"

"I'm going. Bye, Branigan. And thank you."

Branigan flung open the bedroom door and tossed her suitcase onto the bed, almost in a single motion. "We need to get on the road," she called to Chester as she threw shorts and T-shirts haphazardly into the suitcase. "I'll explain while we drive."

After instructing the Delaneys and Isabella to stay as long as they liked then lock up the house, Branigan and Chester loaded Cleo into the truck and roared out of the Isle of Palms. Chester immediately contacted Stonebrenner's partner, Austin Pillsner, who was in his phone directory. Investigator Pillsner assured him they had received a call from Barbara Wickenstall and were on their way to Theater on the Square.

"Nothing more we can do," Chester said, pitching his phone onto the truck dashboard. "They've got it covered." He glanced at Branigan, sitting rigidly against the door. "Tell me what you're worried about," he said.

"I'm worried that Jimmie Jean or Jackson may be tied up in this," she said unsteadily. "They knew about the Satterfield farm, and they knew I run by Pa's fishing shack. Jimmie Jean had access to clown costumes at the theater. Jackson had access to Alphonse Jasper's costume at Jericho Road. And getting mixed up with Shack had threatened their marriage, had threatened Jimmie Jean's version of herself, if you know what I mean. Who knows if one of them had a run-in with Shack when they saw him in Grambling?"

Chester was quiet for a few miles, running over various scenarios in his head. "I see what you're saying," he said finally. "And I can see Jackson and Shack coming to blows. But as for Jimmie Jean, I'm not sure. Number one, Barbara told you she was never missing a third clown costume. So Jimmie Jean would have had to sneak it out *and* return it. Number two, even if Jimmie Jean knew about Jackson and Maria Drucker, why harm Shack? He got cheated on just like she did. And number three, is she stupid enough to put the murder weapon in her own dressing room?"

Branigan smiled faintly. "Let's hope she's not." She looked out of the window at the landscape rushing by. "The thing is, Chester, I don't think my family could take it if it's one of them. We'd all have to leave Grambling." She felt a lump rising in her throat and tears pricking her eyes as the emotions from last summer came rushing back.

Chester knew better than to try to downplay what she and her family had experienced. "I know, Brani G," he said, reaching over to rub her neck.

As they approached Augusta, Chester pulled over for gas. "We can grab something to eat while we drive," he offered.

"That'd be great," she said, opening the door to let Cleo run. "I'm anxious to get home."

Back on the road once more, Branigan tried Malachi's number again. This time he answered.

"Did you try to call me last night?" she asked. "I've been out of town."

"Yeah, Miz Branigan. I might know why Shack got killed."

Her body tensed, and she placed a palm over her other ear to hear more clearly. "Why?"

"I think he blackmailed that theater director 'bout buying drugs."

"Reggie Fortenberry? So he was on drugs?"

"Oh, yeah. Slick been selling to him long's I remember. But don't no dealer blackmail you. Shack took pictures of Reggie Fortenberry buying from Slick. I'm pretty sure that's where Shack got his money."

Reggie Fortenberry. His life was wrapped up in Theater on the Square. But he was not universally popular. If his board members learned of illegal drug use, they'd fire him in a heartbeat.

"It fits," she said aloud, as Chester struggled to hear both sides of the conversation. "He could get the clown costume. And the plastic hammer. And he's – what? – five foot five or so. He could definitely be the 'little clown' Andre described."

She breathed unevenly, relief flooding her even as adrenaline kicked in. She heard Chester's cell phone go off, and pressed her hand tighter against her ear to block the sound. "We're still an hour and a half away," she told Malachi. "Do you want Detective Scovoy to call this in and put the sheriff's investigators on to Reggie?"

"That'd be fine," he said.

"Where are you?" she asked.

"Sittin' on a bench in Reynolds Park."

"Is Reggie in the theater?"

"Yeah, he in there. I saw him go in this morning. But Miz Branigan, deputies already been in and outta there today."

"That was about the murder weapon. We called that in from the beach. Long story. I'll fill you in when we get home." She heard sirens faintly pierce the background, even as she became aware of Chester trying to get her attention. "What is that?" she asked Malachi, as the sirens grew louder. Chester and Malachi were talking at once, and she couldn't make out what either was saying. Malachi hung up, so she turned to Chester.

His face was set, and he pressed his foot to the gas pedal. The truck shot forward. "If we get stopped, I'll get professional courtesy," he said through clenched teeth.

"What's going on?" she cried, as they swerved into the left lane, blowing past cars.

"I'm trying to get you to *The Rambler*," he said. "Reggie Fortenberry confessed. And committed suicide."

Chester filled her in on his phone call from Investigator Austin Pillsner as they rocketed down the highway. "They took the plastic hammer in for testing. It had a lead pipe inside it – a pipe that looked like it could've come from the outdoor stage construction. They left a deputy at the theater and told Reggie and Barbara to gather staff, cast and crew for interviews this afternoon. Before they could get back to conduct them, they got a call from Sam Sebastian. He'd found Reggie in his office, overdosed, a confession on his laptop."

Branigan stared at Chester in disbelief. "Overdosed on what?"

"Heroin. Needle in his arm."

She sat back. "Boy, we picked a bad time to leave town, didn't we?" She stared out of her window. "Reggie Fortenberry. I've known him since high school. This is hard to believe."

"We've both heard Liam say that all bets are off when drugs are involved," said Chester.

"Yeah. But Reggie. Wow." Her mind leaped ahead to the newsroom. She knew that all available reporters would be gathering there or at the theater. "So you can drop me off downtown?"

"Sure. Want me to take Cleo home with me?"

"That'd be great. When we finish, I'll get one of the reporters to drive me to your apartment."

When Branigan entered the newsroom, Bert waved her over. "Everybody's at the theater," he said. "Jody's with the investigators, and Harley and Gerald are trying to get what they can from board members, staff, volunteers, whoever they can snag. I've put two sentences online. Can you take it from here?"

"You got it."

Branigan called Jody for the official version of Reggie's confession and suicide to flesh out Bert's online post. She added Jody's information about the discovery of the murder weapon earlier in the day – a finding that investigators surmised had spooked the director into thinking his arrest was imminent. Then she began gathering material from Harley and Gerald before making her own calls to prominent theater supporters for comments.

The Rambler posted its story online before Channel 5 went live at the theater with Investigator Stonebrenner – a coup that made Tan-4 happy when he called in from his own beach weekend. Once the story was up, Branigan began a more detailed rewrite for the next morning's print edition, incorporating a recap of Andre's kidnapping, a sidebar on Reggie's career that she and Gerald cobbled together, and quotes from the *Annie Get Your Gun* cast and crew about Reggie's recent erratic behavior. She held back the one fact she had that investigators didn't: the identity of Reggie's dealer,

Slick, and the incriminating photo of them together. Malachi, she knew, wouldn't want to burn his friend.

She pieced together more of the story when Jody wrangled Reggie's confession from investigators and emailed it to her. Though self-serving and flamboyantly Reggie-esque, it provided some motivation for his actions.

My dear citizens of Grambling and supporters of Theater on the Square,

I must ask your forgiveness. My drug use, which started as a harmless prop during the crushing pressure of opening nights, was discovered by a most unscrupulous man. At first, I met his demands for money, wishing above all else to keep the good name of Theater on the Square above reproach.

But alas, his demands grew more insistent. Then I learned that he was involved in the vile kidnapping of the child Andre Arneson. I followed this man, Bradley "Shack" Drucker, to the rural site where he held the boy captive, hoping to rescue the child and return him to his family. However, Mr Drucker grew violent, and we struggled. I killed him in self-defense. Though I sincerely believe I would have been acquitted by any fair-minded jury, I panicked at the threat to the theater's reputation which I have held aloft, torch-like, for all these years. I carried the boy to a neighboring farm where I knew he would be found quickly and returned to safety.

With the authorities closing in, I do the honorable thing to save this theater from further embarrassment. I hope the end will not obscure what we have accomplished in the grand experiment known as Theater on the Square.

I bid you adieu.

Reginald S. Fortenberry

Branigan gave the confession to Bert to run in a box as a sidebar. It didn't answer why Reggie dressed as a clown to confront Shack, nor how a blow to the back of Shack's head could be construed as self-defense, but she wasn't surprised that Reggie would spin even a murder confession as a tragedy starring himself.

CHAPTER THIRTY-SEVEN

I t was June 8, the final dress rehearsal for *Annie Get Your Gun*. A festive crowd of women in sundresses and heels, along with men in summer-weight blazers, filled the theater, which was electric with buzz on the late Reggie Fortenberry. The curtain was open to reveal a red-and-white striped Big Top for Buffalo Bill's Wild West Show. The orchestra was warming up in the pit, so strains of "There's No Business Like Show Business" were interspersed with painful squeaks of violin bows and the deep rumble of kettle drums.

Theater on the Square wasn't going to let a little thing like the death of its director stop the show. The very theme of the musical dictated the board's decision, and as a practical matter, Reggie had the production well underway before his suicide. Sam Sebastian and Barbara Wickenstall had stepped in to tweak the show during its remaining rehearsals, working especially hard with Jimmie Jean and a healing Colin to rein in Reggie's more flagrant eccentricities.

A half-page picture of the stars, back to back, rifles ready, had run on *The Rambler*'s *Style* front the previous Sunday, along with a feature by Gerald Dubois lamenting that it would be the last production with Reggie Fortenberry's stamp. As a result, two weeks of performances were sold out, and Sam and Barbara were contemplating adding more.

Corporate sponsors generally bought out dress rehearsals, and the theater offered ten free tickets to Jericho Road. Liam gave half of them to Flora and her children, half to his shelter residents. Jimmie Jean snagged another three tickets for Isabella, Branigan and Chester, even though her sister and cousin planned to return for opening night with the rest of the family. Jackson had returned to West Palm Beach, citing work. Branigan didn't know, or care, what was going on with her cousin's marriage.

Chester's arm rested along her seat back; on her other side was Andre, then Flora, then Isabella and the other three Arnesons. Andre was excited about his first-ever live show, especially one that promised cowboys and Indians. Before the lights went down, Barbara Wickenstall took the stage to address the audience. Dressed in a severe black pantsuit, her black and gray hair swept back, she commanded the stage with a presence that belied her stature. Branigan remembered she'd once worked as an actress and could see it in her carriage.

"For the past six years," she began, "our director, Reggie Fortenberry, stood on this stage before every production of Theater on the Square. And he always said the same thing: 'There is no higher art than theater of the people, by the people, for the people.'"

The audience murmured appreciatively and applauded.

"As you know, we have endured unspeakable tragedy this spring. But the board of directors, along with the good people of Grambling, have determined that the show must go on. And just as the show must go on, the theater must go on."

The audience erupted into applause once more.

An unpleasant smell wafted in Branigan's direction. Almost immediately one part of her brain identified it and dismissed it. That smell had no place in this elegant theater. She tried to concentrate on Barbara, who was waiting for the applause to die down.

"After all," she continued, "when the night's opening number is 'There's No Business Like Show Business', how could it be otherwise?" She threw out her arms and mugged for the audience, who responded with laughter.

There was the smell again – a smell, oddly, that Branigan had encountered at Jericho Road. She couldn't deny it, even in this fancy place: it was urine.

She glanced to her right to see both Isabella and Flora staring at Andre, who sat wide-eyed, pressed as far back in his seat as he could get. Flora was already half standing, pulling on the boy's arm, undoubtedly to take him to the restroom.

Something was wrong. Branigan nudged Chester, but he had already seen Flora stirring as well.

"Andre, what is it?" Isabella whispered, as Barbara resumed her remarks on stage.

The boy pressed his feet against the chair in front of him, physically pushing himself into his own seat back. A whimper rose in his throat. The woman in the seat in front of him turned, irritated. The whimper turned into a wail. And then people in two rows were turning, shifting, murmuring at the disturbance. On stage, even Barbara could hear it, and shading her eyes with a hand, she glanced toward the commotion. And in that glance, Branigan saw her become rigid, her practiced speech falter.

Flora lifted Andre and he wrapped his wet legs around her waist and buried his face in her neck. Isabella, Branigan and Chester rose with her, and followed her to the foyer.

Branigan spun to face Chester. "Were we wrong?" she whispered.

"I think so," he said.

He knelt in front of Andre, who stood shivering, hanging on to his baffled mother's knees. "Andre, did you see somebody you knew?" Chester asked. "Or did you hear somebody you knew?"

Branigan scarcely breathed, awaiting his answer.

Andre stuck his thumb in his mouth, the first time she'd seen him do so. He nodded solemnly, then pulled his thumb out long enough to say, "She hit the clown with the funny hammer and made him go to sleep."

Chester was on his phone almost before Andre finished speaking, barking commands for back-up. He told the dispatcher to alert Austin Pillsner and Dan Stonebrenner at the sheriff's office, but added that he was going in for the arrest without them.

"You know the quickest way backstage?" he asked Branigan. When she nodded, he grabbed her arm. "Show me."

Branigan led him out of the front door and around to the side entrance. The wooden block wasn't there, but the door was unlocked. The two tore through the hallway to Barbara's office. Chester slammed open her office door in case she'd returned, but the room was empty. They raced through the labyrinthine hallway to where it opened into the edge of the stage, and there Branigan collided with Barbara Wickenstall. They fell into a heap on the floor as cowboys and Indians and Western townspeople stood gaping.

Chester hauled Barbara to her feet. "Can someone direct me to Reggie Fortenberry's office?" he asked.

Sam Sebastian stepped forward and asked a script girl to do so. "Detective," he said tentatively, "can we go on with the show?"

The overture was playing insistently. Chester's eyes swept over the little director, Jimmie Jean and Colin and another several dozen actors dressed and ready to step on stage. "Sure," he told them. "Why not?"

He turned to Sam. "When the other officers get here, send them to Reggie's office." Pushing Barbara ahead of him, he and Branigan followed the script girl to a stairway nearly hidden at the rear of the workroom. As they climbed the stairs, they heard Colin's voice ring out in the slow cadence of the opening line: "There's no business like show business like no business I know..."

"Good," Barbara said, her eyes glistening. "That's good."

Branigan and Barbara sat in Reggie's opulent high-ceilinged office as Chester briefed Investigators Stonebrenner and Pillsner in the hallway outside. Branigan knew the deputies would evict her when they came in, so she was eager to get a few answers from Barbara first.

Barbara was sitting in Reggie's office chair, looking out of his window, a half-smile on her lips. Branigan cleared her throat, and the wardrobe mistress turned to her.

"I don't understand," Branigan said. "Why would you kill Shack?"

"Don't you, Branigan? Don't you understand that he was prepared to bring this theater crashing down?"

"He was prepared to bring Reggie down," Branigan said. "But not the theater."

"Oh, but Reggie *was* the theater. And that man, Shack, that talent-less, no-account *blackmailer*, had the power to destroy him. To destroy us."

"So you *did* know who had taken your clown costumes?"

"Not at first. But I overheard Reggie accusing Shack. Instead of taking action, which the *real* Reggie would have done, he did nothing. So I knew Shack had something on him. Simultaneously, Reggie's drug use was becoming glaringly apparent. I put two and two together."

"So you took a third clown costume and followed Shack to the barn where he was keeping Andre?"

"Yes."

"And you got rid of the threat."

Barbara raised her chin and met Branigan's eyes. "I did. But instead of being grateful, instead of accepting his second chance as the miracle it was, Reggie kept right on using."

"And worse," Branigan said, catching on, "his drug use was affecting the production."

"You *do* understand," Barbara said gratefully. "He was close to wrecking *Annie Get Your Gun*. Everybody could see that." She pulled herself erect in Reggie's chair, and tapped the armrests. "He was sitting right here. Right here." Her eyes took in the high ceiling, the abstract oil painting above the fireplace. "He brought heroin into *this room*, this magnificent office. It was like he didn't know what he had."

Branigan scarcely breathed. Would Barbara admit it all?

The costumer swiveled her chair, and her eyes bore into Branigan's. "So of course I had to take care of him, too, didn't I?"

Branigan sat back, stunned in spite of herself. "I didn't think Reggie would kill himself."

"No, I suppose not." Barbara shot her a pleading look. "But it was all for the theater. Don't you see? The theater is bigger than any individual."

Stonebrenner opened the office door, followed by Pillsner and Chester.

"Miss Powers, we need for you to leave, please," Stonebrenner said. "We'll have a statement for you shortly."

She was disappointed but not surprised. "I'll be waiting in the hall," she said. She glanced for a final time at Barbara, composed and competent to the end.

The door was hardly closed behind her before Branigan was calling the *Rambler* office.

CHAPTER THIRTY-EIGHT

Branigan stood at the doorway to Jericho Road, enjoying its artistic welcome: "Where the elite eat – with Jesus." She never tired of Tiffany Lynn's depiction of diverse diners around a table. That reminded her: she wanted to buy an Alphonse Jasper painting while she was here.

She stepped close enough to trigger the automatic door, accepted coffee from a bright-eyed volunteer and looked around for Dontegan.

"I'd like to buy the Jasper landscape," she told him. "The one with hay rounds in the field."

"I wrap it up in newsprint for you," he said.

"How fitting." She wrote out a check for the price she'd seen on the corner of the piece, then looked around for Malachi. He was finishing his breakfast, *The Rambler* spread in front of him. She slid into an adjacent chair.

"What do you think?" she asked.

He tapped the front page, where a flash-illumined Barbara Wickenstall was being led in handcuffs out of the theater. She looked tiny between the bulky figures of Stonebrenner and Pillsner. "I think she fooled us all. Big time."

"That she did. Want to walk over to Reynolds Park?"

"Sure," he said. He threw his paper plate into the trash and told Dontegan he'd return to get a chore assignment later in the day. Malachi liked to "pay" for his meals.

They walked the few blocks to the park, and settled onto the bench closest to Theater on the Square. The Shakespeare stage was empty this early in the morning, and no activity was visible anywhere on the theater grounds.

Malachi stretched his legs, enjoying the early morning coolness that would be gone within an hour. "So that Miz Barbara was the 'little clown'," he said. "Not the theater director."

Branigan nodded. "You were on the right track. It was Reggie Fortenberry's drug use that triggered everything. Shack was blackmailing him. Reggie had given him money *and* figured out that he had stolen the clown costumes. Barbara wanted to eradicate the most immediate threat, which was Shack. With him gone, she thought Reggie would get back to normal and continue to lead the theater."

"So she dress like a clown from her own costume room and went to the Satterfield barn," Malachi mused.

"Right. She already knew she was going to kill Shack, so she needed the disguise to keep Andre from recognizing her."

"But why she willing to kill for Reggie? She in love with him?"

"No, it wasn't that," Branigan answered. "But she loved this theater." She gazed over at the magnificent edifice, the old stones that had overlooked this little section of Grambling for a century. "It was her life. She told me that Theater on the Square was the best theater she'd ever worked in, and she honestly thought its success depended on Reggie. She saw Shack as a threat to it. He was willing to destroy everything for a few dollars."

"So she put a pipe inside a giant plastic hammer and went after him?"

"She did. We think Andre saw all the blood and was traumatized enough that he didn't want to talk about the little clown. She told him that Shack had gone to sleep, so he latched on to that."

"Whooee," he whistled. "But then she was stuck out there with Andre. How'd she know about that shed in your pasture?"

"She didn't. But Cleo was there with Andre, and she figured the dog had to live somewhere nearby. So she started walking with Andre and Cleo, and ran right into the shed. She could see Uncle Bobby's cattle and knew that people must live around there. So she left Andre, hoping for the best. She told investigators she would've gone back in a day or two if no one had found him. But who knows?"

Malachi thought for a moment. "So did Reggie find out what she done?"

"I don't think so, but his drug use didn't let up after Shack's death. She had given him a second chance and he was blowing it. She began to believe that she could lead the theater as well as he could. She planted the murder weapon in Colin and Jimmie Jean's dressing room to begin the set-up. When she had investigators sniffing around, she took a cup of tea with a sedative to Reggie's office. He dozed off, and she overdosed him with his own heroin and left him for Sam Sebastian to discover. She removed the tea cup so no one would ever know it was there. The state lab told the deputies there were sedatives in Reggie's bloodstream, as well as cocaine and heroin, but that's often the case in an overdose."

"And she wrote that note supposed to be from Reggie?"

"Yes," said Branigan. "She didn't dare try to forge his handwriting. But his laptop was sitting right there."

The friends leaned back on the bench, looking out over the peaceful park and contemplating the machinations that had gone on at its edge.

"Theater gonna stay open?" Malachi asked.

"Looks like it. *Annie Get Your Gun* opens tonight and Sam Sebastian's taken charge. For the summer, at least."

Malachi nodded toward a man striding toward them. "We got company."

"I got a call about a couple of ne'er-do-wells causing trouble in the park," Chester said.

"Everybody's a clown," Branigan said, smiling at him.

"So, Malachi," said Chester, shaking his hand, "I wanted to thank you for pointing us toward the theater crowd. You caught on to that before we did."

"Didn't never think it was that costume lady though."

"Still, you had the right idea with Reggie Fortenberry's drug use."

"Well, Mr Chester, you got informants," Malachi said. "But you don't live out here, hearing things every day."

"That's the truth. We ought to make you an undercover cop."

Malachi looked alarmed.

"Don't worry," Branigan assured him. "He's kidding."

"The heck I am," Chester said. "I can talk to Chief Warren. Think about it."

"No, I 'preciate it, but I'm not interested," Malachi said hastily. "In fact, I better be getting back to Jericho Road. I promised I'd help Dontegan."

"You don't have to run off," Chester said. "I'm going to get coffee." He pointed at a mobile cart set up on the park's perimeter. "Anybody want one?"

"I'm good," said Branigan, placing a hand on Malachi's arm to keep him from leaving. When Chester had walked away, she lowered her voice. "I wanted to ask how you are. You seem more like your old self."

Malachi looked at the ground. "I think I'm better."

Branigan waited. When he didn't speak again, she asked, "Did something happen?"

He raised his head and met her eyes. "Yeah, but it was a long time ago. A little boy I knew died, and I got messed up. I started remembering him, dreaming about him, even before Andre showed up. Then it got worser. You saw it."

"And now?"

"And now I have a few drinks instead of a lot of drinks." He shrugged.

"You know, Liam says an alcoholic can't have a few drinks."

"Yeah, I know."

She clapped her hand on his knee. "Well, I'm here if you need to talk, or think about rehab, or anything else."

He got up. "I know," he repeated, and walked away.

Chester returned, placing two coffees on the bench. "I brought one for Malachi. Where'd he go?"

"He thought you were going to make him an undercover cop, so he fled."

"Oh, well," he said, pulling her up from the bench. "How are you doing for time?"

"I'm good. After last night's marathon, Tan said to stay out of the office."

"Then how about coming over to measure my new place for furniture?"

Her face broke into a delighted smile. "They accepted your offer? On the mill house?"

"They did."

"Chester, that's fantastic! Congratulations."

"Yep, I may stay in this town for awhile. I'm kinda sweet on a gal who lives here."

"How very lucky," she said, stretching to kiss him. "For her and for Grambling."

DISCUSSION QUESTIONS

1. In this third book in the series, we finally glimpse the reason for Malachi's homelessness. Why do you think he blames himself for the Bedouin boy's death?

2. What did you think of the townspeople's insistence on giving money to the Arnesons despite Liam's misgivings? Does that occur in your town? Why do we want to address the symptoms rather than dig deeper into the causes of homelessness?

3. Have you given much thought to the difference between empowering and enabling? How does that play out in the case of an unscrupulous character such as Oren Arneson?

4. Why do you think Flora stayed with her husband?

5. Branigan sees a different side to Malachi in this book. How do you think he was able to hide his excessive drinking from her for so long?

6. "Creepy clown" sightings have popped up all over America and other places. What do you think is behind them?

7. Branigan's cousin Jimmie Jean behaved badly in the past, and hurt Branigan deeply. Do you think either woman changed? Who has the more promising future?

8. Why did the staff and board of Theater on the Square put up with Reggie's behavior?

DISCUSSION QUESTIONS

9. At the book's end, Malachi shows no inclination to stop drinking or end his homelessness. Were you rooting for him to do so? Why do you suppose the author chooses not to have him change?

10. The authorities and reporters nearly got the murder wrong. What would've happened if the Arneson family had not attended preview night of *Annie Get Your Gun*?